SISTERS OF ELEMENT

THE LUNA FAMILY CHRONICLES

BOOK ONE

O. SALAZAR DE BREAUX

Cover design by Robin Vuchnich
Dragonfly design by PinkPolish Design
Edited by M. Brianna Stallings

Printed in the United States of America

First Printing, August 2019

ISBN 978-1-7338937-0-1

O. Salazar de Breaux
Post Office Box 331
East Olympia, WA 98540-0331
hola@osalazardebreaux.com

www.osalazardebreaux.com

ACKNOWLEDGEMENTS

I would like to thank the following people for their individual roles in getting *Sisters of Element* published.

My greatest love and soulmate Andy, for always believing in me. No matter how crazy my ideas have been, you cheered me on and made me feel like I could achieve the impossible. When I've fallen, you've lifted me up. Thank you for supporting me and our family in every way possible. There is no me without you.

My sons Alejandro and Julian, for constantly inspiring me to be a greater person with your exceptional brilliance, your kind hearts, and your big dreams. Thanks for being so patient when I've been working; then making our moments together epic and fun. I hope that the sacrifice paid off and that you are proud of your mama.

Sage Adderley-Knox, my mentor, coach, and friend. Without you, this book would not have happened. Thank you for being with me every step of this journey. You guided me with solid tools and advice, helping me make this dream come true between herding all of the kittens.

My sisters Diana, Esther, Rita, Andrea, and Mercedes, for your support and for inspiring me with your spirit, your stories, and your beautiful hearts. I love, love, love you forever.

My Mom Sandra, my father Bernardino, and my step parents David and Alberta for your love and for telling me that I could.

Shelby and Iana for allowing me to tap into your expertise and industry knowledge for important plot points.

M. Brianna Stallings for your insight and editing skills.

Amanda, Hayley, and Sarah for providing valuable time and feedback as beta readers.

Robin Vuchnich for bringing my vision of the Luna sisters to life with your book cover artwork.

Kate Harmon of PinkPolish Design for the beautiful dragonfly design, for your support and friendship, and for always being game to take on a new collaboration with yours truly.

To my indiegogo campaign backers for believing in my project and for making the first print run possible.

DEDICATION

For Esther and Bella, for teaching me to breathe when the wind was knocked out of me, to move forward when I didn't think I could take the next step, to find joy even in the darkest times, and for showing me that love never dies... it only evolves.

PROLOGUE

H OT TEARS STREAM DOWN MY face as I try to catch my breath, my chest heaving with each painful inhale. She watches me, triumphant and menacing. I search her face for signs of hope or recognition. Nothing. All I see is hatred and disgust in her black eyes, seeping back liquid from the corners. A thought crosses my mind. Could they be tears?

Her hand is strong and unyielding, grabbing the razor sharp black dagger that has pushed its way past my heart and lungs. She forcefully pulls it out and blood spurts from the wound, trickling down the front of my blouse onto my feet. With my legs weakened and suddenly unable to carry me, I drop to my knees on the ground below. Each intake of breath feels like I'm drowning. I can't get enough oxygen no matter how much I try.

Crawling weakly over to the creek, I hold my hand over my heart in a futile attempt to keep the wound closed. My inner voice tells me to get to the water so I can use my healing abilities from its energy. I inch my way toward it slowly until my body gives way, not allowing me to move anymore. So close, but not close enough.

I lay down on my side, just steps from the embankment. My mouth tastes metallic from the blood, salty gurgles rising from inside my throat. I know I don't have very long before my breath stops along with my heart. I keep telling myself to hold on, just hold on a little longer.

"Val...please..." I try to beg, but the sound just comes out like a hollow whisper. With her eyebrow lifted, she bends down so that her face is inches from mine. Her skin radiates with unnatural heat, almost like the scorching sun.

"I told you. Val is gone." Her voice is so cold and unfeeling that it chills me to the bone. "You should hope that your other sisters make the right choice so they don't end up like this. Pathetic."

Standing up and looking down at me, she cocks her head to the side. Bringing the dagger in front of her with both hands, she squeezes it and it bursts into dark purple flames. She sprinkles the ashes into the ground next to me, casually cleaning her hands on her clothes.

With the finality of her words sinking in, I say an internal prayer and focus my thoughts on my family. I failed them, including Val. I hope they find it in their hearts to forgive me.

My body and brain are both so tired. Rest is beckoning to me, seducing me. All I want is to close my eyes. My head turns toward my outstretched arm next to me, and to my engagement ring. The diamond shimmers despite the late evening sunset, casting little rainbow reflections into my eyes. A promise of the most beautiful life I will never get to have with a man who I just can't bear to leave.

I hear my heartbeat pounding in my ears, slower and slower. She kneels down and turns her ear toward my mouth, listening to my breathing.

"Goodbye, Lina," she whispers, then stands, kicking a rock out of the way into the creek. I watch my sister walk away, her image fading with each step...

CHAPTER ONE

TEN DAYS EARLIER

"A HHHH! SOMETHING SMELLS AMAZING!" I say as I walk into our family home, a one storey moss-green craftsman in Percival Falls, Washington. It's the house where we all grew up, and where my three younger sisters still live. Wafting from the kitchen to the front door is a tantalizing mixture of savory spices: garlic, onion, *chile de árbol*, and oregano. It has been simmering all day in one of our family's favorite comfort food dishes and the smell only gets stronger as we follow our noses. Even though it's been a few years since I've moved out of my childhood home, I never miss our weekly family dinners.

"Because IT IS AMAZING!" Val shouts back from the kitchen. Gabriel and I grin at each other and bring the flowers and wine into the kitchen. Though there have been some upgrades to the house to modernize it, the walls are still the canary yellow color our mother painted them when our parents first moved here in the early 80's. My sisters and I discussed painting the kitchen a different color until Val reminded us that mom said she always wanted the kitchen to feel happy. We had to agree: yellow is a happy color.

My sister Val is standing over the stove, dancing and singing to *reggaetón* with gusto as she stirs the pot of *pozole*, a spicy pork and hominy soup that isn't just a meal — it's an event. We've learned the hard way that when word gets out that *pozole* is on the menu, people tend to show up unexpectedly at your house. To prevent having a house full of uninvited guests, we only tell the people we really want to come and swear them to secrecy.

Tonight it was supposed to be just family, but Val invited the mystery boyfriend she has been gushing about for the past several months. Val has invited him to family dinner a few times but he cancelled, citing his work commitments. Tonight seems to be the night that the stars align and we'll finally get to meet him. She's in an especially good mood. Bringing the soup spoon out of the pot, she blows on it gently, then bring it to her lips for a taste.

"Whoo! That's what I'm talking about. Damn, I'm good!" Val exclaims with fake bravado, laughing at herself. Setting the spoon down, she points her fingers in the direction of the fire underneath the pot, concentrating on the blue flames and shrinking them until they extinguish. Val has the ability to control fire, which comes in handy with her cooking talent. Out of all of our sisters' powers, hers has been the most challenging to master because of its destructive nature. As a child, I used my ability to control water to put out a lot of her fires.

She eventually learned to hone her gift. She works as a cook at a local pub, but I know that one day she wants to own her own restaurant. She has talked about it for years.

Gabriel steps up to kiss her on the cheek, "Hey, sis. Are you going to let me try some?" He tries to grab the spoon but she pushes him back playfully.

"Just because you are practically my bro doesn't mean you get special privileges! You need to wait." She waves the spoon at him.

I love watching him interact with my family. Gabriel and I have been inseparable since our first date almost two years ago. I honestly couldn't imagine my life without him. From the moment we met, I felt whole. Seeing him integrate into our family as if he has always belonged is just one of the million things I adore about him. He loves my sisters like his own, and to them, he is the brother they never had.

He is also one of the only people that knows about our abilities. Our parents discovered what we could do when each of us were babies. We didn't know how or why we could do what we could do, only that we were special. Or cursed. They had us tested by doctors to see if anything was wrong with us but we were perfectly healthy. My parents decided to teach us how to control our gifts, while stressing the importance of keeping our powers hidden. My mom especially was terrified of others finding out. She said we'd be taken away and hurt by people who didn't understand us, so we constantly lived in fear of slipping up and accidentally manifesting our powers in public.

The day I trusted Gabriel with our secret was the day I lifted a huge burden. It felt dishonest keeping a part of myself hidden from him when I loved him so much. Rather than running away or being afraid, he was even more determined to protect not only me, but my family as well.

He comes over and kisses my hand, looking at me curiously. "Why are you looking at me like that, *mi vida*?" he asks.

"You. I just love you," I say and kiss him.

"My favorite couple is here! Hey guys!" My sister Zo bounces into the kitchen. She is second to youngest, and she's been working as a hairstylist at a local salon with several other friends she's had since cosmetology school. She is the social butterfly of the family, often trying to convince us to go out dancing with her on weeknights.

She has the ability to control wind and air, even learning how to fly. Now that she knows how to fly with others in tow, we've used that to our advantage when we need to travel quickly. Conveniently, it saves time *and* gas.

She throws her arms around my neck and kisses us both on our cheeks. Gabriel and I give her a tight hug back. "Damn, Val! Isn't that soup ready yet? I've been waiting *all day*!" She shoots a look over at Val, who seems oblivious to the impatient tone in Zo's voice. Val is in her own world, singing off key and busting some moves I am not sure I've ever seen her bust before. I can't remember her being this enamored with a guy since middle school. Zo and I watch Val for a minute and then look back at each other, covering our mouths and giggling.

"Have you met the boyfriend yet?" I whisper to her.

Zo shakes her head. "Nope. I caught a quick look out the window a few times when he dropped her off. He never walks her to the door. He has a nice car though." She winks at me.

"Oh, a nice car? Well, in that case he *must* be a keeper," I say sarcastically.

Zo snickers. "I'm surprised he's actually showing up this time. I think this is his fifth invitation to family dinner. Poor Val gets her hopes up each time and then he bails last minute. Hope he was worth the wait." The doorbell rings and I hear a loud clang when Val drops the soup spoon into the *pozole* pot.

"He's here!" Val exclaims as she smooths her clothes down nervously, her voice a couple of octaves higher than it usually is. "Rory! Get the door!" Val yells as she tries to do some last-minute sprucing.

"Coming," Rory says with no sense of urgency as she emerges from what I call her hippie den. I'm not sure what my sister does in her room besides light incense and discover new ways to save the planet. Her ability is connected to the earth, so she can control things like stone, dirt, plants... pretty much anything derived from ground. Our baby sister owns the title "granola" proudly. She is working on her fine arts degree at The Evergreen State College, and I can envision her working as a full time artist one day. She is *that* good.

Rory shuffles to the door and says loudly, "Who is it and what are you selling?"

"RORY! *Open the damn door, cabrona!*" Val stomps out of the kitchen to give Rory the evil eye. Rory chuckles to herself and unlocks the door. We all wait with anticipation to get a look at this guy that has Val all aflutter.

Here's the thing. The list of qualities I expect from a guy worthy of my sister's heart is extensive. It's not just that she is strikingly beautiful, with her flawless cinnamon skin, full lips, and high cheekbones women would pay top dollar to have. She started shutting other people out around the time my father died. This is the first time since then that I've seen her let her guard down and allow someone into her heart. For that reason alone, as unfair as it may be, I'm expecting the man who walks through that door to walk on water.

With a fedora hat crooked to the side, he saunters in dressed from head to toe in black. His suit is a few sizes too large so that it drapes lazily on his skinny frame, like a sleepy stray cat. He smiles out of one corner of his mouth, the smile not reaching his eyes which are steely blue and unblinking, almost staring.

Holding out a bouquet of bright purple roses and a bottle of Cristal to Rory, he nods toward us in greeting. Rory seems to be experiencing an aversion to his generous spray of aftershave. She looks at him tentatively — not sure whether to push him out the door or take the flowers. She decides to accept his gifts since she was raised with some manners.

"Hello gorgeous. You must be one of Val's sisters. I can see that beauty runs in the family," he says with a half smile as he looks Rory up and down. "These roses are special. I know a guy who hand dips them in dye imported from Morocco. Just for my *Latina* queen because purple is for royalty."

"Thank you. Come in. Val is expecting you." Rory is being polite, but she is clearly disgusted by his synthetically dyed flowers, over the top and inappropriate compliment, and strong smelling cologne. I think she is going to throw those floral abominations out the second he turns his back regardless of how expensive they are.

I look over at Gabriel, who seems bemused by the whole thing, and on alert. He has a knack for reading people and I'll bet his Spidey Senses are picking up some interesting vibes. As I watch everything unfold, I wonder — *what does my sister see in this guy?*

Val rushes over and throws her arms around him, planting an enthusiastic and audible kiss on his lips. He kisses her back hard and then pushes her away and says, "Easy baby. We have company. Let's save that for later." He uses his index finger to bop her on the nose. She beams at him and flutters her long lashes. My sisters and I look at each other, shocked. Normally if a man tried to bop her on the nose, it would be followed up by Val giving him a swift slap to the face.

Val realizes we are all staring at her and grabs his hands, pulling him inside the living room. "Everyone, this is Jeffrey. He goes by Free. Hon, this is my family. You've already met Rory. She's the baby. And then there's Zo."

Zo holds out her hand and says, "Hi. It's good to finally meet you, I..." but she gets cut off as Free pulls her in unexpectedly for a bear hug. The force is so strong her head swings back. Her arms are pinned down as she endures his vice grip and winces a little.

"Sorry. I'm a hugger." Free laughs. Zo looks a little winded and disoriented. I brace myself because I know I'm next. Crap!

"This is Lina, the oldest. And her boyfriend Gabriel." Before Free can grab me, Gabriel intercepts and lays a big hug on him, causing my sisters and I to burst into giggles. Now it's Free's turn to be surprised and the look on his face is priceless.

Gabriel says, "We've been looking forward to meeting you, man." As he lets him go, he gives Free a single, swift smack on the back. He grins at me and puts his arm around my shoulders, protecting me. I look up at him in appreciation, taking a deep breath now that I can relax. He winks and kisses my cheek. My sweetie always has my back. Zo smiles at us both, knowing that Gabriel's little show was for her too.

Free's hat is disheveled and lopsided. Val notices and reaches her hand up to fix it. Right when she does, he grabs her wrist. "No! I got it," he snaps. I look at Zo and Gabriel in shock, and Gabriel's jaw clenches.

For a moment, Val locks eyes with Free until he lets her go and angrily puts his hat back in place. Holding her arm close to her chest, she rubs it gingerly and looks down. When she looks up again, she smiles at us and shrugs her shoulders. "I forgot. His dad gave him that hat a long time ago. It's very special to him." Biting her lip, she looks back at Free and puts her hand out tentatively on his shoulder. "I'm sorry, babe." The steely expression in his eyes softens and he puts his hand on top of hers.

"I know. It's fine." He says, kissing the top of her head. Her lips curl up in a smile and she peers up at him through her lashes.

"Umm. The food is going to get cold. Let's eat. Free, I can't wait for you to try it." Val says, trying to lighten the mood. She puts her arm around his waist and they walk into the kitchen with us following behind.

Before we follow Zo and Rory, Gabriel grabs my hand and turns me toward him with a serious look on his face. "Do you want me to say something to this guy? I'm ready to jump in if he touches her again," he says quietly. I smile and shake my head. My mind-mannered Gabriel is an Engineering Professor at a private university. He is also a highly skilled martial artist who has studied several disciplines since the age of three. If Free makes any wrong moves, Gabriel is ready to strike and Free won't stand a chance.

"*Gracias, mi amor.*" I smile at him tenderly. "I'll let you know." He nods and we head into the kitchen. Everyone is already seated. Gabriel and I sit in the two wooden chairs between Rory and Zo, across from Val and Free.

The kitchen smells heavenly. Val truly has a culinary gift. She cooks from the soul, so her food is always delicious. Maybe having food in our bellies is going to end the evening on a high note and we'll feel too lazy to care about what happened earlier.

We each have a bowl of piping hot soup in front of us, but they aren't ready until we add our own mix of toppings: cilantro, lime juice, radishes, onions, oregano, and cabbage.

"Wow. This looks delicious! My Mexican lady here is a culinary genius," Free says and gives a full-mouthed grin at Val.

She melts under his compliment. "It's called *pozole.* It's one of the few things I learned how to make from our mom. You can put any of these condiments on it. Do you want me to add toppings to your bowl?"

"Yeah babe, but no onions. We have unfinished business later." He cackles and my sister blushes. I glance over at Rory, who buries her face into her hands.

I chuckle quietly, trying to keep my amusement to myself.

Val sets Free's bowl in front of him and waits with anticipation while he tries it. He grabs the spoon with a heavy hand, takes a big dip, and buries his spoon into his wide-open mouth. "Mmmm. That is tasty. So good." He says while dipping his spoon back into the bowl. Val visibly relaxes and breathes.

The rest of us begin customizing our own *pozole*, coloring our bowls with various mixtures of toppings. No one in the family can make this soup the way Val does. People have tried and failed.

"So, Free what kind of work do you do?" I ask.

Free looks up from his spoon, interrupted from his nearly finished soup. He wipes his mouth with his napkin and starts playing with a big gold ring on his right hand. I notice there is an emblem of a bird in flight on the front of it. He chews for a moment and then interlaces his fingers together and places his elbows on the table. "I run my own business. I import goods and sell them through local retailers."

"Like what kinds of goods? Are we talking stuff that's legal or illegal?" Zo asks. Val shoots her a look. Zo never thinks she is being rude when she asks questions. She was born with a curious nature. But in a *Latino* family she would often get smacked for being a *metiche*, or someone who is too nosy for their own good.

In her defense, this is a good question.

"Oh. I have lots of interests... I have my hands in all kinds of things — antiques, handcrafted furniture, even science."

"Science? That's interesting." I say, only halfway

interested but making the effort for Val. She worked hard to make tonight special. Because I love my sister so much, I have to believe there is something redeeming about Free; otherwise, she wouldn't have fallen for him.

"Yeah. It's actually all very interesting," Free says as he scrapes the bottom of his bowl for the last bit of *pozole.* "I don't understand half of it myself. But the business side is what I'm interested in. Making money. The science part is somebody else's job. Like these roses, for instance." He points to the already wilted Franken-roses he brought. "The dye for those roses was made in a lab that I am a partner in."

"So how did you meet our sister?" Rory pipes up from the end of the table. She digs her spoon into her special vegetarian plate of hominy and veggie broth that Val made in a separate pot for her. Zo and Gabriel look up too, intent on learning how on earth our Val would fall for a short-fused guy who calls himself Free. Val brightens up and looks at Free and he smiles back at her. She notices his empty bowl and gets up to refill it.

"I'm a huge fan of her cooking. And her fire." Free smirks and nods at Val before dipping his spoon back into the bowl. Oh no. Does this mean he knows about her power?

"What do you mean, her fire?" I ask, trying to sound casual but feeling a shard of panic inside.

He laughs and says, "This one is full of spark and personality! The first day I met her I thought she was going to kill me." Relief sets in. Good. He doesn't know.

Val says, "He is part owner of the pub. I had never met him before so I didn't know who he was when he came in. It was a busy dinner service. His order came with a LOT of special requests... and I was a little... irritated..." She glances over at Free. "It was a double shift night, I had been on my feet all day, and then this customer comes in acting like he owns the place. I had no idea... he actually DID!" They both laugh. "I mean, the list of demands on this roast beef sandwich was long. I almost thought it was a joke. The waitress said: 'No, this guy is serious'.

So I said, 'fine'. And I did everything he asked. I cut the bread into 1 inch triangles. I used the three types of cheeses that he wanted. No mayo. Half sweet potato fries and half regular...and the list went on..." she shakes her head, laughing. Free grins like he did something brilliant. "I bent over backwards for this customer and when I finished I was proud. I thought, 'See? Even a diva customer can't beat this girl!'

I decided I wanted to take it to the table myself. I had to see who this was, and I thought for sure the customer would be happy. I put the plate down in front of him, told him I had made it myself, and I hoped he enjoyed it. I expected a smile, or even a 'thank you' for being so difficult. Guess what happened? He continued chatting with the table of guys he was with, and waved me away like I was bothering him."

In unison my sisters and I say, "Ooooooooh!" We knew Free was in deep trouble at that point. I am disappointed I didn't get to see her put him in his place. We've seen it happen time and again — and it can be extremely embarrassing when it happens in public. Believe me, I've seen her bring men to tears. She is not one to be messed with.

Free nods and laughs. "Oh yeah. She was a

firecracker! It was awesome." Val laughs too. Now I can see the chemistry between them. It is almost cute. "As you can imagine, she told me to go to hell and a few other places I won't repeat." Now all of us start to laugh, picturing Val telling Free off like he was just any other customer who made the mistake of crossing her on the wrong day.

"She stopped me dead in my tracks and made me notice her. Here I was, being yelled at by this beautiful, fiery woman and instead of being embarrassed or angry, all I could wonder is if she was single!"

He grabs Val's hand and she says, "Awww babe... I was just about to pick his plate up and throw it at him and then my boss Jax ran over to the table, red faced and sweaty. He looked scared. I mean SCARED! He grabbed my arm and started apologizing over and over again, calling Free 'sir' — *I'm sorry sir. Please let us make this up to you, sir. She had no idea you are a pub partner...*' and oooooooh damn. My face must have gone white when I learned who he was. Free never said a word. He just looked at me the whole time. And then he picked up one of the teeny sandwich triangles and started eating it. Jax and I couldn't say anything, we just held our breath."

"I tasted it, told her it was perfection, and I thanked her. I told Jax that she was a keeper and he should promote her." Free pats her on the back proudly.

"He really did! I couldn't believe it. Jax thanked him and we backed away from the table and into the kitchen where Jax let me have it. But he didn't fire my ass! He warned me. He told me who Free was and said to count my lucky stars that Free was in a good mood because he was the only reason why I was still there. That, plus I can 'cook like an angel' — his exact words."

"After I left that night I couldn't stop thinking about her. I went to the pub every night just to watch her cook. She was so confident and commanding in the kitchen. It was like watching a master. I had to get to know her better. One night I asked for her specifically to come to my table. When she did, I asked her to join me for a drink. She refused, saying she wasn't allowed to when she was working. So, I told her I'd wait."

Val smiles, rubbing his hand. "He actually did! He waited till past one in the morning for me to get off work. When it was time to close, we had the place to ourselves. He told me to sit down and he made me a martini." Val looks at Free with a dreamy look in her eye.

He adds — "Yeah, I was a bartender for a little bit back in the day."

Val continues, "We just talked. He asked me about myself — about my cooking, about what I want to do in my life, all kinds of stuff. By the time we stopped talking it was almost sunrise! He said he wanted to take me out to breakfast. This was the best first date I'd ever had and it wasn't even a date!" Free puts his arm around her and kisses her.

"Wow, that is a sweet story." I smile at both of them. Now at least I understand the attraction. My sister gets pursued by men often because of her beauty, but they usually don't seem interested in anything other than her looks or getting free food. Free actually seemed interested in getting to know her on a deeper level. By the sound of it, he was a perfect gentleman on that first date and he even sounds charming. It doesn't line up with the person we met today.

Val rests her head on Free's shoulder and he kisses the top of her head. "Dinner was out of this world, babe. Thank you." Free clears his throat, then says, "So…Val tells me you all are Marc Anthony fans. I have backstage passes and VIP seats for his concert on Saturday. Would you like to come as my guests?"

Zo is already on her feet. "Whaaaaaat? No you don't! Those tickets are impossible to get!"

Free winks and says, "I have some connections."

I look at Gabriel. He has been a Marc Anthony fan ever since his teen years growing up in Panama. I've heard him belt out "Hasta Que Te Conocí" a few times in the shower or in the car. He doesn't want to give in and let Free off the hook. I'm conflicted too. I can't shake this feeling of dislike towards Free. On the other hand, Val is obviously crazy about him. Perhaps that reaction of his was a one-time thing. Why would she want us to like this guy if he wasn't important to her?

I can see Rory and Zo's excitement to my side. It would feel rotten to deny them the concert. If we go I can keep an eye on Free and his interactions with my sister. Plus, I love Marc Anthony too, and it's been a while since Gabriel and I enjoyed a night of dancing.

"Thank you for the generous offer, Free. Yes, we would love to go," I say, holding Gabriel's hand. Rory and Zo let out a few squeals. Free smiles a Cheshire Cat smile and Val puts her head on his shoulder.

"That's great! I'll pick you up here at four and we'll grab a bite before the concert," Free says and looks at Gabriel again. Gabriel nods and slowly extends his hand over to Free's.

"Thank you Jeffrey. We appreciate your generosity." I can see Gabriel has a pretty strong hold on Free's hand. My honey is definitely letting Free know he isn't off the hook.

The girls are oblivious to the show of testosterone happening silently in front of us. They are chattering away about what they are going to wear. Gabriel sees them out of the corner of his eye and lets Free's hand go.

Val throws her arms around his neck and covers his face with kisses. "Oh babe! I'm so excited! Thank you!" He kisses her on the lips, then holds her chin between his thumb and forefinger.

"Anything for my lady." He says, his voice low and husky. "I have to meet up with an associate but it won't take that long. I'll pick you up in an hour." Val nods, eyes locked on his.

He stands up and grabs his coat from the back of his chair. "It was great to meet all of you. I'll see you soon." We each stand, keeping a safe distance from him so we don't get pulled into any dangerous hugs again. Val walks Free to his car and we all crowd around the window to watch. He has a shiny black sports car — maybe a Camaro? The windows are tinted so you can't see inside and there are purple and blue lights that turn on underneath his car. It looks like something straight out of *The Fast and the Furious*. She gives him a passionate kiss through the driver's side window before he speeds off, the bass on his rap music pounding so hard the house windows vibrate.

Val is still smiling when she comes into the house. She leans her back against the door, still in a revelry. All of us want to say something but aren't exactly sure how. She looks at us and the smile leaves her face. Sighing, she puts her hands up and says, "Look. I know what you guys are thinking. He is a little rough around the edges. But he really is a gentleman..."

"Val, I can see that you care about him a lot," I start out slowly. "It just scared us the way he lashed out at you like that. It was sudden and there wasn't any reason for it."

Val shakes her head, then wrings her hands. It's something I've seen her do when she gets nervous — which isn't often. "That hat. I forgot how important it is to him and I shouldn't have tried to touch it. It was my fault."

"First of all, screw his stupid hat. I don't care how much it means to him! He should never have grabbed you like that!" Zo's emotion has made her sky blue eyes an even brighter shade of blue. Her voice has risen an octave and her words come out like staccato bursts. "He was a few seconds away from having an air blast lay him down so hard his hat really would've flown off his head!"

Val glances down. "He's...not always like that."

Zo's anger has left her face and now all I see is concern. I lead Val to the couch, where I sit close to her, hugging her from the side. She avoids my gaze, looking down at the fabric on the couch as a single tear falls down her cheek. Zo and Rory sit next to us, embracing her quietly. Then Val's tears start flowing freely. I stroke her hair and just let her cry.

Gabriel disappears into the kitchen momentarily, then comes back with a glass of red wine for her. "Here, *hermana.*"

She sniffles and takes it from him, sipping quietly.

"He is good to me. He surprises me all the time with gifts or notes. He lets me know he's thinking about me during the day and he just...he makes me feel so special."

"Mmm hmm." I say, still stroking her hair. I don't want to interrupt her, allowing her the space she needs to share.

"No one has ever made me feel like this. He is successful and can have anyone he wants. And here he is, making *me* feel like a treasure."

"Please! He isn't so —" Rory starts in, but I give her a sharp look and she stops. We're all thinking the same thing, but it isn't what Val needs to hear right now. "Uh, I mean. You are a treasure."

"I know I'm not the easiest person to get along with. I like to argue and fight. I don't like other people's rules or being told what to do. I've done such a good job of keeping people away from me for so long that I was starting to think I was unlovable. And now for some reason, this person came into my life and makes me feel... accepted..."

My heart hurts hearing this. I've always admired my sister's strength and kind heart, as well as her beauty and brains. I didn't know she had feelings of unworthiness, but it is something I understand. I've lived with the same feelings, believing I wasn't good enough or lovable. Maybe those scars were created long ago when we lost our parents. Our father León was a soldier who died in the line of duty when I was in middle school. Less than a year later, our mother left us and never came back. A few stints in therapy gave me clarity around the damage this did to my self worth. I was so caught up in my own healing that I never realized that Val struggled with it too.

"Valencia, I wish you could see yourself the way that we do," I say, hugging her a little tighter. "You are fearless and strong. I have seen you jump out of a plane and skydive, screaming like a crazy woman and landing on your feet with a huge grin. You are a badass, showing everyone you can jump higher, be stronger, work harder. You beat up boys!"

"Come on, that was in elementary school...and that kid started something he couldn't finish when he called us beaners!" Val laughs, along with the rest of us.

"I remember the surprised look on his face when she punched him! Hahahahaha!" Zo almost chokes from laughter.

I remembered it too. This neighborhood boy was known for bullying other kids much smaller than him and had a big mouth. He often taunted kids on the bus ride home. My sister broke him of that the day she kicked his butt at the bus stop in front of all the other kids. She was like a bulldog, not showing any mercy. It took about four others including the bus driver to pull her off him, and she was still kicking and screaming when they did. She became a school legend after that.

"See? I've never seen you back down from a fight. I have always thought you were — that you ARE amazing." I hold Val's hand and look into her amber eyes. "Free is damn lucky to have you. It is NOT the other way around. You need to stop being so down on yourself. *Entiendes?*"

"Yes, I understand Lina," Val says quietly.

"Then you also need to understand that your happiness is important to us, Val. What he did tonight scared us — and it looked like it scared you too. Please, please promise me that you will tell me the truth if he ever lays a hand on you."

"You guys, he has a temper — kind of like me — but he hasn't hurt me. Like you said, I can handle myself. I beat boys up, remember?" There is something in Val's eyes as she says this, a glimmer of uncertainty that plants a seed of doubt in my brain. I'm hoping that he is a gentleman that adores her and loves her. But something is nagging at me, telling me that he isn't a gentleman at all.

"Can we move on now and start talking about the concert?" Val says, rubbing her hands together. My sisters and I begin excitedly plotting out our outfits and debating over the best Marc Anthony songs. Gabriel starts singing off key and we all burst into fits of laughter. I try to play it off and move on, ignoring the turbulence that remains in my stomach.

CHAPTER TWO

Val is falling into a black pit and I'm hanging on a ledge, grabbing her hands. The pit is full of a tar-like substance that moves with a life of its own. It is growing and covering her from her legs on up, slithering and consuming her. As it does, it seeps into her skin, turning her veins black. She is screaming and calling my name, her eyes full of terror. She keeps slipping as the black tar finds its way up her neck, black veins spreading through her skin like growing trees. Her eyes start turning black and she shrieks — a horrible piercing sound. I lose my grip.

I wake up in a state of confusion and panic, sweating and shaking. The room is dark with the exception of the alarm clock on the side table with neon blue numbers in blocky font. It's 1:15 A.M. With my head on Gabriel's chest, I listen to his breathing to try to calm down but I can't. My stomach is twisted into painful knots. I can't get the vision of Val's black eyes out of my head. And those piercing screams. It's upsetting me so much that I start feeling nauseated. I jump out of bed and head to the bathroom, just in time to vomit into the toilet. Tears rush to my eyes as I try to catch my breath. Then I start heaving again.

I hear a gentle knock on the door. "*Mi vida?* Are you ok? Can I come in?" Gabriel asks, his voice full of concern.

"No. Don't come in. I'm okay." I grab a towel to wipe the tears from my face.

"I'm getting you some water. Don't move." I hear his footsteps swiftly make their way to the kitchen. Within a minute he's next to me on the floor, handing me a glass of cool water. I know I said not to come in, but his disobeying my request this time is okay. I need him.

He wipes the hair from my face and kisses my forehead tenderly. "Drink, *mi angel.* You'll feel better." I drink, and the water instantly feels replenishing against my burning throat. That's the thing about me and water — it always restores and heals me. My sweet man knows me so well.

My stomach somersaults again and I heave into the toilet. I feel Gabriel rubbing my back as my whole body clenches from the next wave of nausea. He places a cold wet towel behind my neck, sending calming sensations throughout my body. I take another drink of water and lay my head on Gabriel's shoulder, inhaling him deeply and nuzzling into my safe place next to his neck. He wraps his arms around me as he kisses the top of my head.

"I don't know what's wrong with me. I don't usually get this upset over a nightmare. Maybe I'm getting sick," I croak.

"It must have been some nightmare. Was it about Val?" he asks. I nod my head. "Yeah, I'm worried about her too," he says, caressing my hair. His touch feels comforting. We sit that way for several minutes. "Better?" He asks, tilting my face up to look at him.

"Yes, better." I say, suddenly feeling tired again.

He takes the towel off my neck and whistles. "Completely dry. Looks like you needed that water." He shows me the towel and I shrug. I guess I did. "Come on beautiful, let's get you back to bed." He helps me to my feet and we walk back. I lay down and he covers me with the fluffy blankets. Crawling in next to me, he envelops me in his arms. Within minutes I drift off to sleep.

I wake up to hear the shower running and Gabriel humming cheerfully. I shrug out of my nightgown and walk into the bathroom, waiting to sneak into the shower. I tiptoe in slowly while his back is turned, just in time to massage shampoo into his hair. He jumps at first, startled, then chuckles and turns around for a kiss. "Good morning, *hermosa*. How did you sleep?"

I open my palm and divert the water so that it surrounds the both of us like a warm hug, gently pouring over his hair and rinsing the shampoo out.

"So much better. Thank you for taking care of me," I murmur and kiss him again.

He laughs and looks around at the unnatural patterns I am creating with the water. "I will never get used to seeing you do that. You are spectacular, do you know that?" He lifts his hand up, touching the cascading waterfall I created. It makes my heart sing to hear him speak about my abilities so naturally, after I've hid them for so long.

"We never need to invest in a fancy shower head!" I laugh and squirt water in his face. He yelps and rubs the water out of his eye, getting a mischievous gleam.

"Oh really? Want to play like that, huh?" He grabs some water and throws it back at my shoulder. I pour all of the water like a sheet on top of him, making him look like a wet puppy. I cover my mouth to stifle my laughter.

He grabs and kisses me suddenly, distracting me from my water sculpting and allowing the water to naturally come out of the shower head. I wrap my arms around his neck to deepen our kiss. My fingers twirl around the curls in his hair and he pulls me closer to him, his body warm and slick from the water. We melt into each other and forget all about the shower.

"I think we need to do that every morning. That was the best shower I have ever had... in my life." Gabriel is putting on his tie and looking devastatingly handsome in his work shirt and slacks, not to mention the sparkle in his eye while he reminds me of our eventful morning tryst.

"You need to stop looking at me like that, or else we both might end up late for work, professor," I say as I grab his tie and give him a quick kiss. He growls and puts his hands on my hips to draw me closer. "Hey, mister! I'm serious. I need to get ready too! I don't want to be late for our staff meeting." I giggle as he nuzzles my neck, his scratchy beard awakening the sensitive areas behind my ears. It takes all the strength I have to pull away and put my finger on his lips.

He sighs and looks down with a cute pout on his face. "To be continued, *querida*." He grabs my hand and kisses it cordially. "I will see you later, then. I love you."

I put my other hand on his face. "I love you, too. Have a good day." He grabs his leather work satchel and blows me a kiss as he heads out the door. Oh my heart. How did I get so lucky?

I look at the clock; I have about 20 minutes to get to the office. I chug the rest of my coffee and grab my shoes, leaving behind my half-eaten oatmeal. As I get to the door, I see a brown bag next to my keys with "Eat Me" written on the front. I look inside and I see that Gabriel has packed me a lunch to take to work. I smile and make a mental note to grant his request for another shower date tomorrow morning. He's made my heart melt several times today and it isn't even 8 am.

Our apartment is in the heart of downtown Percival Falls, about 10 minutes away from my office by bicycle. It's a bright but crisp spring Pacific Northwest morning as I ride to work. I don't see many people on the road at this time of the morning. Cruising downhill, the cool breeze whips against my neck, waking me up with its sting. As I turn the corner toward my building, I see children's chalk doodles on the street, left over from our city's art festival over the weekend. Then I pass my favorite cherry blossom tree, its petals blowing down around it like pink confetti. Jumping off my bike, I lock it up and make my way inside the building.

I work at a community center that serves low-income youth, families, and senior citizens. Our building isn't fancy, but it is a well-loved gem. The facility is hundreds of years old, with several facelifts along the way. The most recent iteration has provided us with ample classroom spaces, a board room, and a few offices overlooking East Bay Marina. I've worked at the center for about six years, starting as an intern when I was a college freshman. It has a special place in my heart because it was a safe haven for my sisters and I growing up. Between the caring staff and development programs, we not only found our voices, we also found the stability we needed at a critical time in our lives.

The Executive Director, Joyce Williams — lovingly called "Mama Joyce" — took an interest in us. Our mother often worked two back-to-back shifts as a nurse at St. Francis Hospital, trying to make ends meet after our father died. Mama Joyce knew we spent a lot of time at home alone, so she put extra snacks into our backpacks before we would leave at night and called to check in after we got home. We loved and trusted her long before she stepped in as our adopted mother, which happened unexpectedly when our mother left us. You could say she's been our angel.

When I was searching for internships, Mama Joyce offered me the opportunity to come to the center to build my career skills. She knew that I dreamed of one day running my own organization to support at-risk youth. I learned just about every aspect of the business. We worked together on several grants that have now allowed the center to expand programming and make much needed upgrades to the building. The day I graduated with my Master's degree last spring, she and the rest of the center staff sent me a huge bouquet of roses along with a note offering me a position as the Youth Arts and Music Program Director.

"Hey Lina! Good morning!" says Sydney, one of our front office staff. Her sunny disposition always has a way of making me feel cheerful.

"Good morning, Syd. I hope you had a great weekend." I wave back.

"Oh I did, thank you! I picked up some new plants at the Farmer's Market and went for a bike ride on the trails... Wow, I don't know what you did differently today Lina, but you are glowing! Are you using a new moisturizer or something?" My mind instantly flashes back to my early morning activities with Gabriel.

I feel the heat rising in my cheeks and I'm sure I'm blushing. "Oh, gosh. Uh, yes... I did try out something new. Thanks for noticing!" I say and then hastily escape up the stairs to the boardroom.

Joyce is pouring herself a cup of coffee. Calvin, Jaime, Sophie and Ben are sitting at the boardroom table chatting about their weekends. My colleagues and I are a close-knit bunch. Although we come from different backgrounds, everyone is committed to the mission of the organization and to operating as a unified team. Joyce hand picks people who are good-hearted as well as good at their jobs. She says it is the key to having a successful team.

"Hey guys! Good morning!" I say as I set my portfolio and purse down at the table.

"Hi Lina!" everyone chimes back.

I walk over to give Joyce a hug. "Hi Mama Joyce. Did you have a good weekend?" She is wearing a royal blue kimono over a gold tunic, which looks stunning against her dark chocolate skin. Her long white dread-locks are pinned up into a bun.

"Good morning, baby. Oh, my back is aching something fierce. I knew I shouldn't have gone crazy in the garden. Those weeds will be my downfall." She puts her hand on her back and rubs, a look of pain etched in her face.

"I thought the grandbabies were coming over this weekend," I say as I grab a cup that says *I hate Mondays* from the overhead cupboard and start pouring a steaming cup of coffee.

She nods and sips from her mug. "They did. Sadie brought the kids over and we had a fun trip to the children's museum. But I guess I just got a wild hair. Vernon and I were sitting on the back porch after they left and I just couldn't ignore the weeds anymore. They were starting to make their way to my tomatoes and I worked too hard on those masterpieces to let them get ruined." She waves her arms as she talks, and I smile, picturing her hacking away angrily at the weeds. "And of course, Vernon was no help with his bad knees and all. He just drank his lemonade and gave me a pep talk from the sidelines." We both laugh and I walk over to the refrigerator for some cream.

Vernon is a sweet natured man from Mississippi. He still calls Joyce his queen and every now and then will surprise her with flowers at the office, just because. Both of them are in their late 60s and so full of life; their work as community activists keeps them spirited and young. Vernon was a Civil Rights Movement organizer. He has told me chilling stories of things he faced as a young man growing up in a racially divided South.

"You know you can always call Rory, right? Weeds are her sworn enemy." Joyce chuckles.

Besides Gabriel, Joyce is the only one that knows about our powers. She figured out there was something different about us one day when we saved a cat that had fallen through a patch of ice at a nearby lake. We were so young. I was probably eight. She never saw what happened, but she could tell my sisters and I were hiding something when we relayed our story. Joyce has a nose for the truth.

When we came clean she didn't believe us at first, but then Zo, being the brazen girl she is, decided to show her what she could do. Grabbing a handful of paperclips from Joyce's desk, she made them levitate above our heads. Joyce looked as if she was going to pass out, but when she saw the fear in our faces she kneeled down to meet Zo's eyes and held her hand. "Thank you, my brave little one."

She looked at the rest of us and she said, "It's ok. You can trust me. I would never let anyone harm you." My sisters and I were relieved to finally find someone we could trust with our secret.

Val created a small fireball in her palm. Rory touched a wilted plant on Joyce's desk so the petals bloomed and the leaves grew bigger and greener. I placed my palm over a glass of water on Joyce's desk, lifting all of the water out and shaping it into a frozen rose. When I handed it to her, her eyes welled up with tears.

"I always knew you girls were special, but now I know you are extraordinary." And with that, she was our fierce mama bear. She went out of her way to make sure no one found out about our secret. When we told her it was a family curse she emphatically said we were blessed for greater things. She never told Vernon about what we could do, saying it was the one and only secret she ever kept from her husband.

"Oh, believe me I would have called Rory but I knew you had a special dinner planned. So...? Are you going to tell me about this man that Val is seeing? I've been waiting to hear how it went." Joyce's eyebrow is up and she leans in to get the scoop. I'm not sure where to begin.

I take a deep breath, not ready to delve into that drama this early on a Monday. "Ahhhh. Yes. We met him."

"...And?" She nudges me in the arm, her eyes probing mine for clues. I couldn't lie to her even if I wanted to. Joyce's superpower is seeing through bullshit.

"I'll have to tell you the story later. It's a long one. I'll bring you some ice for your back after the meeting and we'll talk." I wink at her.

Her eyes get big and she says, "Oh, you need to give Mama the T. You'd better not forget! I'll chase you down."

We set our mugs down on the boardroom table. When Joyce sits, everyone respectfully quiets down, eager to get started on this week's work plan.

Joyce's office door is open, so I knock on the wall next to the light panel. She is on the phone with what sounds like a vendor for our upcoming fundraiser gala and she waves me in. I shuffle inside, holding a bag of ice for her back and a small stack of donor letters for her to sign. I love listening to her work her magic on the phone. She has a perfect blend of professionalism, tenacity, and charisma. That's why our community center thrives and grows its capacity to help more families each year. I walk around the office, looking at all of the photos and children's artwork on her shelves and walls. There are a few photos of Joyce and Vernon with their daughter, Sadie and their grandsons, as well as photos of my sisters and I at different ages.

One photo catches my eye. It was taken at the center when I was about 12. We are hugging her so tightly that our cheeks are squished. Her eyes are glistening with happy tears. I remember that day. It was the day of the center talent show and we sang a song we wrote for Joyce called "Never Alone Again". Rory played a beat up guitar our father had left in our garage, Zo played percussion on some drums we made from tin cans, I played on the center's old off-tune piano and sang lead, and Val sat next to me and sang backup. It was our way to thank her for always being there for us. My eyes well up at the memory and the way she ran up and hugged us when we got off stage.

"Oooh you girls got me so good that day. Mama was ugly crying in front of everybody." Joyce is behind me, giving my shoulders a squeeze. "I think it's about time for my girls to write me another song," she says with a sentimental chuckle.

I look at her and smile. "You want a new song?"

"Naw, maybe not. The old song is perfect. I don't think you could ever top that." She starts humming the melody and rocking with me. I put my head on her shoulder.

I show her the bag of ice. "Are you still hurting?"

She stops rocking, remembering her back pain, putting her hand on her lower back.

"Yes! Work your magic, girl!"

Making sure her door is locked and the blinds are drawn, I place my hand in the bag and liquify all of the ice so that it surrounds my hand like a glove. "Ok, let me see." Standing up, Joyce turns towards her desk, one hand steadying herself on the desktop and the other pulling up folds of blue and gold fabric to reveal her lower back. As I inspect her skin, I can tell that the left side is slightly swollen and tender. Placing both of my hands on her back and starting on the side with the most pain, I move them slowly in a circle — radiating blue light to use the healing, cooling power of the water. With the water as extensions of my fingers, I feel the pockets of knots and tight ligaments. I radiate the healing glow deeper to flow over them, gently erasing the burning pain found there. Joyce visibly relaxes her shoulders down and lets out a deep breath. I can see now how much pain she was holding in her body. Poor thing. "Are you going to pass out on me?" I ask over her shoulder.

"No, baby girl. Just feeling the flow." She smiles back, her voice warm and serene.

I give her a kiss on her cheek and pull the water back to shape it into a frozen rose. "You're all fixed now," I say as I hand it to her.

She tilts her head and then places her hand over her heart. She looks at me intently for a moment, her eyes misting over. "I will never forget the day you gave me this. You and your sisters, my brave little girls. You survived so much, and you always did it together." She takes her hand off her heart and cups my face with her hand. "Like I said back then, you were meant for greatness. Every one of you."

Just then we get a knock on the door. "Yes?" Joyce says. She puts the rose down on her desk and walks over to the door. I quickly reshape the ice and put it back into the plastic bag. As she opens the door, we see a grinning Gabriel. My heart leaps.

"How are two of my most favorite women doing? Can I interrupt?" he asks.

"Gabriel! Come on in. Lina was just helping me with something." She gives Gabriel a warm hug. "Oooh, you are looking handsome as ever. When are you going to make Lina an honest woman and marry her? Y'all need to get started on some beautiful babies."

"Mama!" I say as Gabriel laughs.

"Believe me, you'll be the first to know," he says as he winks at her.

"I'd better be." Joyce crosses her arms in front of her and narrows her eyes at him. Gabriel hugs her from the side and puts his head on her shoulder, making her pseudo-stern look melt into a toothy grin.

"Can I steal my sweetheart away for a little bit?" Gabriel gives her another squeeze and then walks toward me, reaching out for my hand.

"Of course. Lina and I will catch up later. It's always good to see you, baby." Joyce waves us away. Standing in her office doorway, she watches us and says, "You two just warm my heart."

While we're in the hallway, I turn to Gabriel and give him a quick kiss. "Hi." I say.

"Hi", he says softly, holding both of my hands and looking at me intently. "My noon class is doing a field exercise today with my colleague, so I thought I'd come see you."

"I'm so glad you did. Let's go to my office." I say, tugging his arm and walking across the hall to where my office is. "YOUTH ARTS AND MUSIC DIRECTOR" is printed on the outside of the glass door, and my name plate next to it reads "Angelina Luna, M.F.A."Even though everyone I know calls me by my nickname, I like using my full name for professional purposes.

The other staff offices are smaller than Joyce's. Mine suits me just fine. It is better than the cubicle no bigger than a closet I had as an intern. I love the rustic feel, with the exposed brick walls and warm cherry wood floors. Rory set me up with succulent plants. I have a wooden planter with them nestled on my window sill. She knows I'm not so good with keeping plants alive but I love having greenery around me.

My office window overlooks East Bay Marina and the children's museum. Most days, I keep my window open so I can hear the bustle of happy children and feel the breeze coming from the water.

Hanging above my window is a dragonfly mobile Zo made me when she was ten. We've been obsessed with dragonflies since we were young; maybe it's because they always seemed to be around. Especially after our father passed away. The mobile is still one of my most prized possessions. She used her power to fuse together blue, green, amber and purple colored glass. As the pieces gently collide into each other, the glass chimes in various patterns, like the plucking of a harp. My favorite thing about the mobile is seeing the various colored images, like rainbow kaleidoscopes, across the room when the light shines through them.

As soon as we're inside my office, I feel Gabriel's hands on the sides of my hips, pulling me close to him. I turn around and put my arms around his neck, tilting my face up in anticipation of his lips. He kisses me deeply, melting all my insides and leaving me breathless. When I open my eyes to look up at him, the golden flecks in his honey brown eyes are sparkling. My hands caress his chin, playing with the stubble I find there.

"I missed you," he says, moving a strand of hair off my face.

"I missed you too. And thank you so much for packing my lunch. I guess you knew I was going to grab something that was nowhere near as healthy as this?" I smirk and bat my eyelashes at him.

"Well. I knew you had... a busy morning... and it probably would have slipped your mind." He smiles, then his expression changes and his eyebrows furrow. "You had such a rough night though. I wanted you to have something good to eat today. No eating on the run."

"Thank you." I kiss him again.

"How are you feeling?" he asks as he strokes the back of my hair, his eyes searching mine.

"Much better. I had this vivid and terrifying nightmare..." I shudder, remembering Val's black eyes from the dream. I shake my head, trying to reset the image in my brain. I turn and look out the window. "Hey, did you bring your lunch? Let's take a walk and eat at our spot near the water. Doesn't fresh air sound good right now?" I'd love a change of scenery and a good distraction.

"That sounds perfect. Lead the way, beautiful." He

grabs my messenger bag from the hook behind my door and we make our way downstairs and outside the building. I love springtime in Percival Falls. While it's true that fall and winter can be dark and dreary here in Washington, the spring and summer seasons always make up for it with the warm temperatures, lush flora and greenery. The sunshine is bright, a few fluffy clouds speckle the cyan blue sky, and a slight breeze prickles my skin just as it starts to feel too warm from the sun.

We walk a few blocks, passing a goth themed café that serves my favorite mochas, a retro record store with Gizmo and Monchichi toys in the window, and an herbal remedy store that always smells like dried lavender. Soon we get to the pier with a few scattered benches. This is one of my favorite spots to visit. No matter what kind of day I've had, I always seem to find my serenity here. The smell of sea life invigorates me, connecting me with the marine creatures and plant life that thrive underneath the surface of the water's ripples. Sometimes I get to see a sea lion or blue heron. Most days I just see schools of tiny fish and algae.

"Is right here ok?" I ask Gabriel. He nods and puts my bag down. I dig into the middle compartment and take out the brown lunch sack he packed me. When I open it, I find a set of sandwiches and a container with freshly cut vegetables. Wait. This looks like a meal for two people.

"I was hoping I could see you for lunch today. I wasn't 100% sure it would work out, but I prepared just in case." Gabriel puts his hand out, palm up.

"That is my man. Always prepared." I laugh and hand him one of the sandwiches.

"I do my best." He says.

I realize these are his amazing caprese sandwiches, but with chili flakes in there the way I like them. He always tells me he didn't start using *picante* before he met me and now that he's in love with a Mexican he has learned to appreciate spicy food.

My mouth is watering already and I go in for a big bite. The bread is lightly toasted for just a slight crunch, and the brightness of the tomato cuts through the rich fresh mozzarella, finished by the herbaceous basil. I close my eyes and savor all of the explosion of flavors, chewing appreciatively.

"What do you think? Adequate?" He asks me as he finishes swallowing his own bite.

"Yes. Totally adequate." I say, leaning over to bump him with my shoulder. "It's really delicious and just what I wanted."

He grins at the compliment and takes another bite, looking out at the bay. I take a deep breath and feel a wave of calm wash over me. In the distance I can see a few boats sailing further away, making me wonder about the magnificent views they are treated to from their vantage point. Seeing the South Puget Sound by boat is on my bucket list.

"Have you heard from Val yet?" he asks, breaking me from my daydream. "Isn't she supposed to let us know what the plan is for the concert? Is *that Jeffrey* picking us up?"

I cock my head and give him a playful look. '*That*' Jeffrey. He says it with disdain but I can't help but find it endearing.

"No, I haven't. But I'm sure she'll be in touch. Everybody is pretty excited about the concert. Even you." I poke him playfully on the arm. "I'm going to be watching him like a hawk and I know you are too." I pause, watching an older couple walking a cocker spaniel down the path close to the water.

"Do you remember our first date?" I ask, feeling suddenly nostalgic. "One of the first songs we ever danced to was "Nadie Como Ella." Remember? It was that little dance club on the westside?"

Gabriel smiles and nods. "Could you tell how nervous I was that night?" He takes a sip from his water bottle and looks at me. "I felt so lucky that you agreed to go out with me. I thought, 'This beautiful goddess is finally close enough for me to hold her hand.'" He places his fingers under mine, bringing my hand up so our hands are together, palm to palm.

I look at him in disbelief. He is the most gorgeous man I have ever laid eyes on. It doesn't surprise me at all when women openly gawk at him, whether it is his students or complete strangers. He's *that* stunning. Aside from his lean, muscular physique, his chiseled face is framed by a faded beard that only makes him more ruggedly handsome. His golden brown eyes are so bright, as if they were lit from behind. The golden flecks in them dance when he smiles, accentuating the laugh lines around his eyes. And that mouth. I remember being mesmerized by his lips during our first few conversations. Every time he talked I just stared at his mouth, wondering what it would be like to kiss him.

And me? I've always felt so awkward around guys and embarrassed by their attention. When people told me I was pretty, I drowned out their voices with self doubt. I've been told I look like one of my favorite actresses, Angelina Jolie. Aside from our first names

I'm not sure if I see any other similarities. Maybe the eyes a little? Mine are aqua and hers are more a striking blue — closer to Zo's eye color. I wish I had half of Angelina's charisma, fearlessness, and magnetism. To me, she is the embodiment of a goddess. My sisters have always been more confident around men. Well, maybe except Rory who isn't really comfortable around people in general.

I almost didn't accept when he first asked me out on a date, but there was something so sincere and sweet about him that I just couldn't resist. He surprised me that first night. I was expecting someone that gorgeous to be shallow or a womanizer who was ready to pounce on any pretty girl that walked by. He was none of those things. He was a perfect gentleman, holding his arm out for me to grab hold of and offering his jacket as we walked into the cool evening air.

We had a conversation about family and dreams. He told me about growing up in Panama and about how important his family is to him, especially his sister Serena who still lives there. He showed me his magnificent heart that night and I fell for him right away. Who wouldn't?

"You are kidding me, right? I never knew that! I mean...look at you!" I scoff. "Girls are always staring at you in front of me as if I wasn't even there. I would be jealous but I don't blame them." I say. He shakes his head in amusement, brushing a breadcrumb from my lips. "I wouldn't be surprised if you dropped me for an upgrade. I know I can be moody, plus I have a lot of drama with my sisters..." I say this jokingly but in the back of my mind, it is one of my deepest fears.

"*Preciosa...* Guys are always looking at you too. But

I *am* the jealous type and give them The Look so they back off. You see, it's not just that you are so dazzling that you take my breath away..." He interlaces his fingers with mine, massaging my forefinger. He looks up at me and his eyes are wide and full of emotion. Suddenly I'm no longer hungry, my heart pounding like it is going to burst out of my chest. "I have never met anyone in my life with a heart as pure and loving as yours," he says. "There is no one on this earth that compares to you. I have been yours since the day we met." My eyes well up with tears.

"I don't mean to make you cry. I just want you to know that you are it for me. You are my soulmate. I'm yours, *mi vida.*" Now the tears are easily flowing. He has told me many times how much he loves me, but hearing him say this today, in this way, makes me feel like I've won the lottery.

"How did I ever get so lucky to find you?" I ask, shaking my head. "I love you more than I can express. You are it for me too." I throw my arms around his neck and nuzzle into him. I wish I could stay here forever and not have to go back to work.

Reluctantly I pull away and grab a napkin from our lunch bag. "Great. Now I'm going back to the office like a mess." I sniffle and dab my eyes with a napkin, giggling at myself in the process.

"You could never look like a mess, *mi vida.*" He smiles and kisses my forehead. "Come on, let's take you back to the office before you get into trouble."

CHAPTER THREE

ABRIEL WALKS ME INTO THE lobby at the center, where I see Sydney perk up and wave at us while she talks to a customer on the phone. "Are you going to stop in before your class tonight?" I ask him. He teaches a youth martial arts class a few days a week at the center. One of our favorite rituals is having dinner together on the roof of the community center where we can watch the sunset. Sometimes our schedules don't allow us to do it, so it's a treat when we can.

"Hmmm. I don't know. I think we've seen enough of each other for one day." He strokes his chin and looks up, in a mock pensive pose. I smack him playfully on his chest. "Hey! *Mala!*" He laughs and kisses my cheek. "I wouldn't miss it. Thai food?" Oooh one of my favorites.

"It's a date, handsome." I kiss him fully on the lips while slightly aware that we're probably being watched by everyone in the lobby. He smiles and lets go of me so I can head back to my office. He waits until I get to Sydney's desk and turns to walk out the door. A slight pang touches my heart as I watch him leave. Part of me wishes we didn't have to go to work and could spend all day together. I realize I'm still smiling when I turn around and see Sydney and Callie, another of our front lobby staff, grinning at me.

"You two are the most romantic couple I know. Seriously. You make me hopeful for the day that I find my Mr. Right." Sydney says. Callie nods dreamily in agreement.

"Does he have a brother?" Callie asks with wide eyes. Sydney nudges her in the stomach with her elbow. "Ow! What? It was just a question." She looks at Sydney with a pained look on her face, rubbing her belly where Sydney poked her.

"Actually, he does. But Ramón is already taken," I say. Gabriel's older brother Ramón lives about 15 minutes away with his wife Cecile and two kids, in a tudor home he designed and built himself. He is one of the most successful architects in Percival Falls.

Callie and Sydney both sigh with disappointment, making me laugh as I walk up the stairs to the office floor. We usually keep our office doors open unless we have meetings, so I wave at all of my colleagues as I walk by. Joyce's door is closed, so she must have a meeting going on. As I get into my office I hang my bag on the hook behind my door, then walk over to my computer to start checking messages. I realize the message light is blinking on my phone, so I pick up the receiver and dial the passcode to listen to my voice-mail. Three messages. I grab my pen to start jotting down notes.

The first two messages are follow up calls about an upcoming theater camp. The last one is from Val. Hearing her voice instantly reminds me of the nightmare I had and I shut my eyes tightly. I can hear the sound of pots and pans in the background and I know she is calling me from work. She seems slightly distracted so she is probably holding the phone between her head and shoulder and using her hands to cook. I've seen her do this a million times and I'm always impressed with her ability to multitask. She says she wants us to go shopping to pick outfits for the weekend. I hear her boss Jax yelling at her in the background — telling her it isn't break time yet and he needs his French dip... NOW.

"Does it look like I've stopped cooking? No! So stop breathing down my neck! You'll get your sandwich when I'm finished making it!" Yep. Typical feisty Val. It makes me smile. If those two didn't love and respect each other the way they do, I'd be worried for my sister's ability to keep that job. Jax has a soft spot for Val and she knows it, which is why I'm sure she'll give him a big kiss on the cheek as soon as she is off the phone. "Call me back." I hear more yelling in the background. "Or better yet, text me. This fool is getting on my case about being on the phone. Byeeee!" The phone clicks and the robotic voice mail lady asks if I want to replay, save, or delete the message.

I hesitate before I hit the delete button, unsure why. It's a mundane message and I'll be seeing her soon. Maybe it's because her voice sounds so normal. Hearing it helps erase the memory of her screams in my head. I decide to save the message.

I scan this week's calendar for the best evening for a sister shopping date. Looks like Wednesday for me — no late meetings. I have a general idea of my sisters' weekly schedules, so it's a safe bet. I pick up my phone and start texting a group message to my sisters.

"HEY LOCAS. SHOPPING DATE THIS WEDNES-DAY. PICK YOU UP AT 5:30. ☺ "

I have to include an emoji of some kind or Zo will think I'm angry. Millennials and their emojis. My phone vibrates immediately and I see a text message from Zo:

"Damn, why U yelling in ALL CAPS? 😜 😂 Just messing with U. C U soon sis. ♥ 😘"

I text: "♥♥♥ you back"

It's our sister code. It means "I love, love, love you". Zo started saying it when she was three and it's been integrated into our Luna sister language. We usually say it before we hang up the phone. Out of all of my sisters, Zo is the most affectionate. She's the sister to see if you're having a bad day. Her hugs are magic. She's also the most mischievous. When we were growing up and I lived with her I was always on edge, anticipating the next practical joke she had planned for me.

My phone buzzes again with two more messages. Val and Rory are both in for the shopping trip. It's officially a sister date.

I look at the clock and realize it's almost time to set up for the 3 p.m. meeting with my youth camp staff. I grab my camp binder and a pen from the top of my desk and head out the door.

"Thanks for your work, everyone! I'm excited to see the final versions of your brochures on Friday. Don't forget to check in with the Graphics office this afternoon about approved photos to use." Everyone starts picking up their gear and shuffling out of the conference room.

It's almost time for our afterschool programs to start. One of the favorite parts of my job is greeting the kids as they come off the bus. I want all of them to know me by first name and feel comfortable here, just the way Mama Joyce made us feel when we were young center participants.

Today is the start of our Willy Wonka themed week. The counselors will teach the kids some songs, lead cooking experiments that involve candy, and transform our large auditorium into a chocolate factory. I run upstairs to grab my Willy Wonka hat and jacket from my office. As I walk past each office I see my colleagues getting ready, too. Calvin and Sophie are Oompa Loompas and Ben is a Wonka Bar. We're always game to dress up and make fun of ourselves for the kids.

Jaime clearly went overboard with the orange Oompa Loompa face paint and I have to stop myself from laughing out loud. None of the other staff decided to paint their faces, so she gets points for going the extra mile. I yell out, "Looking good, lady!" and wave at Jaime, who is trying to figure out her suspender situation. I'm very impressed with the level of detail she has in her outfit. I think back to the day she suggested the theme at our staff meeting, explaining that it was her all-time favorite movie. No wonder she has every detail of her character executed perfectly.

She looks up and grins. The orange paint makes her skin look jaundiced against her white teeth. "Thanks, Lina!" Jaime yells back, then starts humming the Oompa Loompa song. I hum along as I head into my office and open up the tall wooden cabinet next to my door. I find the purple velvet jacket and put it on, brushing off a couple of dust specks, then put on the orange top hat. Looking at my watch, I see that we have 15 minutes until the first bus arrives. I shut the cabinet and head out into the hall.

"Everybody ready?" I yell out.

"READY!" They holler in unison. One by one, Calvin, Sophie, and Ben walk out into the hallway in full costume. They are giddy with excitement, checking out each others' outfits. Ben's Wonka Bar costume is fascinating to everyone. He launches into a description of the amount of cardboard boxes and aluminum foil he used. Jaime opens her door and everyone stops talking, completely stunned. She almost looks unrecognizable. She is wearing a green wig, her skin is bright orange, her eyebrows are painted white, and she has every detail of the outfit down to the buttons and white gloves.

Calvin breaks the silence first, exclaiming "Good God, woman! You look amazing!" Everyone else nods enthusiastically. She made our other Oompa Loompas look like cheap imitations. Jaime is embodying the character, walking out with her hands up and bow legged like she is going to break into a dance. Calvin has a not-so-secret crush on Jaime, and practically has cartoon stars blasting from his eye sockets as he marvels over her costume. I don't know how she doesn't see it. She is single, but maybe she wants to keep their work relationship uncomplicated. Or, perhaps she just isn't into him the same way.

Suddenly I'm blinded by a flash of light. When I stop blinking, I see Joyce holding a camera and snapping pictures of the other four who are posing and smiling. She is also dressed like Willy Wonka, only she has a curly wig on so she looks more like Gene Wilder.

"Oooh! Y'all look great! The kids are going to love it." She pats Ben on the back of the box, causing him to step forward to secure his balance. "Let's go open this chocolate factory!" she says, heading down the stairs. The others follow except for Ben, who can barely move.

"Uhh. Guys? A little help?" Ben says as he tries to move without falling over. His balance is going to be challenged today. The team comes back up the stairs. Calvin stands on Ben's left side and Sophie stands on his right. Ben puts his arms around their shoulders and they both pick him up and ease down the stairs. I walk behind them, ready to help if Ben falls back.

As we reach the bottom of the stairs I can see the bus pull up. Sydney is beaming as she admires everyone's transformation. Callie runs up behind her holding two baskets full of candy. "I found them!" she says, out of breath. Sydney hands one to Ben and Callie gives the other one to Jaime, who is still doing her funny Oompa Loompa walk. There is a roll of red paper "carpet" that leads into the main gymnasium where all of the activities are set up. Joyce and I link arms. She winks at me and tips her hat. We open the double doors together and walk out to the bus. Jaime and Calvin follow us and hold the center doors open for the children.

Earl, the bus driver, waves at us from inside the bus. The children pile up on the inside right, peering at the center. Joyce walks toward the back of the bus and Earl hits a button so that the wheelchair lift shaft opens at the back. Celia, a sweet-natured redheaded seventh grader, waits in her wheelchair in anticipation while Jamal, one of our older students, wheels her onto the platform. While Earl secures her on the lift, her hands bang the sides of her wheelchair anxiously.

"Hurry up Mr. Earl! I want to get to the chocolate factory!" she squeals. The platform whirs loudly, shakes for a second, then starts descending toward the curb.

"Well hello, Miss Celia! Are you ready for an adventure?" Joyce leans down to Celia's eye level and softly puts her hand on top of Celia's shoulder.

"Yes Mama Joyce! I can't wait to see the factory! We watched the movie seven times last weekend!" She is speaking in high pitched bursts, clearly unable to contain her excitement.

"That's so good, baby girl. You are going to love what we have planned for you." Joyce unstraps the wheelchair from the bus harness to take her inside, using the pathway of the red carpet. "VIP with a golden ticket, coming through!" Joyce announces as if she were announcing the Queen's arrival. Celia is eating it up, relishing the attention.

Earl opens up the front bus doors. With a grand flourish of my arms, I say "Welcome to the chocolate factory!" The kids start cheering and bounding down the bus steps toward the center. Inside, Calvin and Jaime hand out candy as the kids walk through. Seeing the glee on their faces makes me feel positively sparkly. I couldn't erase this smile from my face even if I wanted to.

Jamal is the last one off the bus and walks down the steps to meet me. He is so tall his head almost hits the top of the bus. "They are all out, Miss Lina." He says in his baritone voice.

"Thanks, Jamal. I appreciate you taking care of everyone. Are you ready to check it out? I think you're going to like it." I say as he steps onto the sidewalk next to me. "Thanks Earl!" I wave at him as he closes the doors behind Jamal and drives away. Jamal peers into the center with a half smile. The lobby is full of sugar-loaded bouncing children, giddy from the candy we've given them.

"It's almost like the fizzy lifting soda pop," he says as he crosses his arms and puts his hand on his chin.

"I'm impressed, Jamal! I thought you said you didn't like old movies," I say with mock surprise.

"Miss Lina, I might have seen it once or twice. Back in the day, you know, when I was a little dude." He puts his hand closer to the ground to illustrate how small he was.

"It's okay. I won't tell anyone your secret." I say, then move closer and say in a softer voice, "The truth is, I think that's pretty cool. It's nice to appreciate classic cinema." He purses his lips and nods.

"Ok — let's get in there before our littles fly away from all that fizzy lifting magic," I say and we both follow the red carpet into the community center.

I'm still smiling when I put my jacket and hat away in my office. The staff had as much fun as the kids did in the activity stations we created. I don't know if it's my own sugar high or the euphoria from a successful staff collaboration. I can't wait for our grand finale at the end of the week, when we put all of the kid's crafts together to recreate the chocolate factory inside our gym.

My phone buzzes in my purse. I have a message from Gabriel.

"Can you meet me on the roof? I'll be ready for you in a few. xoxo"

I smile and put the phone back inside my purse. I'm looking forward to telling Gabriel how it went today. It might also be good to warn him that some of his martial arts students will be squirrely, now that they've eaten their fill of candy.

I close my office door and walk to the stairwell that leads to the upper floors and roof. I hear a cacophony of different music blasting from the third floor rooms as several high energy workout classes go on at once. The next floor up is where our yoga and tai chi classes are held. Here the music is serene and the lights are dimmed in some of the classrooms. I have two more storeys to go until I have roof access. My limbs are feeling a little fatigued and I'm starting to break a sweat as I get to the final floor. I tell myself this is a good way to work off those candy calories from this afternoon.

The last floor is secured to protect our younger members from getting lost or putting themselves in a harmful situation on the roof. I enter the pass code on the keypad and open the door leading outside.

I blink, trying to make sure what I'm seeing is real. The roof has somehow been transformed into a lush garden paradise I have only seen rivaled in luxury travel magazines. The walls are completely covered in green — ferns, succulents, and tall shrubs, accented by eucalyptus. Hellebores, poppies, lilacs, sterling roses, and anemones are scattered throughout creating a watercolor-like tapestry of colors. The sweet intoxicating perfume from the lilacs and roses permeates the air. Toward the right side of the roof is a white linen covered table with votive candles and roses. How did he do all of this? I almost can't take it all in. This is the most spectacular sight I have ever seen.

Then I feel the air shift around me as if a force is pulling me to the right. I look and nearly fall over as I see Val, Rory, and Joyce being lifted onto the back end of the roof by Zo, who is gliding alongside them. They're all looking at me with big grins on their faces.

"Did you guys do this? It is beautiful!" I say as I rush over to hug them. They all close in for a big group hug, a cocoon of warm bodies and tightly wrapped arms. I notice that nobody is speaking. I step back and look at them, puzzled by their silence. My sisters are NEVER quiet. "What's going on, you guys? Aren't you going to say something?"

They look at each other conspiratorially, as if they're all in on some big secret. With eyes aglow, Mama Joyce lifts her hands up and cups my face. "Baby girl, turn around." She whispers.

I hear footsteps behind me and turn around to see Gabriel, who takes my breath away. He has a blue dress jacket over the white shirt and tie he wore this afternoon, which makes him look even more handsome. He walks toward me slowly, deliberately. The look of love in his eyes makes my heart stop. I put my hand over my chest, reminding myself to breathe.

It feels like we're the only two people in the world, and all I see is his adoring face. There's a crinkle at the sides of his eyes and his full lips are turned upward into a soft smile. I realize that he's holding a bouquet of wildflowers, roses, and lilacs. I want to rush up and throw my arms around his neck and cover his face with kisses, but I'm frozen and lost in the magic happening around me. He stops a few steps away from me, his head tilted.

"*Querida,* I hope it's okay that I surprised you," he says quietly. All I can do is nod. He looks down at the bouquet, pauses and takes a slow, deep breath. When he looks up at me again I see glistening in his eyes — tears not yet shed. My breath catches in my throat and I feel tears start to prickle the edges of my eyes. He hands me the bouquet carefully, as if every petal is fragile. I slowly take them from his hands, staring at him.

"Angelina Luna. My phenomenal, brilliant Angelina. The day that you came into my life is the day that my life began. It's as if I was stuck in a gray and dark world, then I started seeing in bright colors. The world suddenly became vibrant and alive. I wake up and I go to sleep every day with joy in my heart, feeling like the luckiest man in the world because I am worthy of your love. The only regret I have is not meeting you sooner so that I could have saved you from ever knowing what heartache was like..."

As I listen, my body feels like it's vibrating from all of my emotions. My breaths are coming in short bursts and my heart is racing.

"You are the most incredible woman I have ever met. Beautiful inside and out. You have a generous heart, you are intelligent, unbelievably talented. You fiercely love your family and friends, you are passionate about helping people, and you fight for what you believe in — even if it means you're fighting with me. I love the way your nose crinkles when you laugh — which is the best sound in the world, right next to your singing."

I giggle. It comes out as a hoarse little gasping

sound. I sniffle as the tears continue to flow. His eyes are misty with sincere emotion, his voice cracking at times.

"There is nothing that I would rather do than spend the rest of my life making you happy. I want to hear about your dreams and help them come true. I want to be the one to lift you up if you fall down. I want to take care of you when you're sick. I want to protect you from any harm that comes your way. You have the ability to heal those around you, but I want to be the one who gets to heal you. *Mi Angelina hermosa...*" He pauses, smiles, places his hands on his left knee and bends so he can get down on his right. My heart is pounding in my ears but I can still hear sniffles behind me from my family. Gabriel never loses his gaze, looking at me intensely, a tear finally making its way down his stubbly cheek.

"I promise with all of my heart, I will love you beyond my last breath... Will you please do me the honor of being my wife?" He reaches his hand up to hold mine, which is shaking. I start feeling movement in my hand that's holding the bouquet and I realize the flowers themselves are moving. Rory must be working her magic behind us, making them bloom. Inside a pale pink rosebud makes its way out from behind the others. The petals start to twist and open, revealing a heart shaped diamond ring inside. I gasp and almost drop the bouquet. The diamond is a pale pink, surrounded by smaller diamonds lining a double platinum band. It sits nestled around the flower's stigma. I grasp Gabriel's hand even tighter. I can't control my sobs any longer. My whole body shakes, completely overwhelmed.

The ring starts to float above the rose — no doubt Zo's handy work. Gabriel stands up and takes the ring, clasping it between both his hands.

"Answer him, stupid!" I hear Val yell. I laugh and turn around to see my family holding each other. Mama Joyce is dabbing her eyes with a handkerchief. Val smiles, wiping tears away with the back of her hand. Zo and Rory have their heads on each other's shoulders.

"Thanks, girls." Gabriel smiles at them, then turns his attention back to me. "Well, *mi Angelina*? What do you say?" He raises an eyebrow and holds the ring up in front of him.

My lips are trembling but smiling. I swallow the knot in my throat so I can speak again. Stepping closer, I caress Gabriel's cheek with my hand, fingertips moving over his beard and chin, feeling moisture from his tears.

"I don't know what I ever did to deserve you. You are the most amazing man, Gabriel, and I love you so much. I don't have enough words to say just how much I love you..." I shake my head and tangle my fingers into the hair at the nape of his neck. His eyes soften and he pulls my hand to his lips, kissing my knuckles gently.

"Nothing will make me happier than having you as my husband. Yes, of course I will marry you!" I say, probably a little too loudly, kissing him with a grin on my face. I hear cheers and clapping behind me along with some sniffles, and a collective "awww!"

My bouquet explodes in a million petals showering down on us as Gabriel and I continue kissing. I pour all of the emotion I'm feeling into this kiss, allowing the love to rush over us until we come up for air. We rest our foreheads against each other with our eyes closed, reveling in the moment.

"I love you," I whisper.

"I love you more," he whispers back. The moment feels intimate in the middle of a joyous celebration. When I open my eyes, I tilt my head back to look at him and wipe away a tear from his cheek. He reaches his hand up to wipe a tear from mine, then moves his hand over my shoulder. He glides the ring into place on my left hand and kisses it.

Through blurry tears I look at my hand and the token of promise that adorns it. It looks new but as if it belongs there, like I was always meant to wear it. I stroke it softly with my fingertips, feeling all of the ridges of the diamonds and smoothness of the band. Gabriel has his arms around my waist, watching me discover my ring.

"Do you like it?" He whispers into my ear.

I nuzzle into his chest and kiss the spot between his neck and collarbone. "It is perfect. You are perfect. I would have loved it no matter what — because it's from you." I say between kisses.

"Alright, time to break it up. We're dying over here! Let's see this rock!" Zo exclaims, linking her arm with mine, pulling me away while Val and Mama Joyce hug and kiss Gabriel. Zo and Rory are oohing and ahhing over my ring, moving it around to see how the light catches it.

"Wow, *hermano!* Great job on the ring!" Zo shouts over my shoulder. I feel arms hugging me from behind and I know it's Val.

"Did we surprise you or what?" she asks softly as she gives me a squeeze.

"Surprise doesn't even describe it! You guys just about killed me." I look at all of them now, my best friends, my sisters. I shake my head, thinking of the fantasy that just unfolded before my eyes. "You guys..." My throat tightens up again. "This was the most amazing thing I have ever seen. You created this paradise that I couldn't have imagined!" I swallow again, trying to get the words out as emotion threatens to steal my voice. "This is the best moment of my life and it's even more special because all of you were here to share it with me ..." The girls are all crying now, reminding me of the many times we've lost it watching romantic comedies together.

"Gah! You're ruining my makeup!" Zo says, using the inside of her blouse sleeve to dab at her tears. She tends to use a lot of mascara to make her "baby blues pop", as she puts it. Now the inky black streaks are running down her face. "I have a client at the salon tonight. I don't want to look like a hot mess."

"Actually..." Val jumps in. "You should wear your makeup like this everyday. Now the inner punk rock girl you were always meant to be has surfaced."

That was all we needed to hear to burst into laughter. Even Zo is laughing. I hold on to Rory's arm, almost losing my balance. The moment itself isn't that funny, but we're all a little off balance from the emotional rollercoaster. Val slaps me on the back hard as she laughs, jolting me forward and making me snort, which makes everyone roar even harder. I'm bent over my knees and holding my stomach. Zo slumps onto the floor next to me, rolling to her side into a fetal position.

I kneel down, my legs feeling wobbly and unstable. Pretty soon we are all on the floor in hysterics, lolling around like drunken fools.

As I struggle to catch my breath, I see Gabriel and Mama Joyce watching us in amusement.

"We haven't been drinking. I swear." I hold my hand up, pledging the truth.

"That better be true. You've been working all day," Mama Joyce says jokingly, her hand on her hip.

I look at Val, who is wiping tears of laughter from her face and chuckling. She looks up and gasps. "What is it?" I ask.

"Look!" She points above our heads. We all look up at a floating spherical form about the size of a baseball. As it slowly spins, inside I can see a small raging fire, an ocean wave, a green jungle, and dragonflies. Our fits of laughter stop and we help each other to our feet. The last time we've seen this was... maybe ten years ago?

"It's the Care Bear Stare..." Rory whispers.

"The what?" Gabriel asks cautiously.

"We don't know exactly what it is. That's the name Rory gave it when we were little, when it happened the first time." I whisper.

"It's only happened a few times. It seems like it's tied to our emotions. If we're all feeling something together, like a really strong feeling, our powers manifest into this. Rory called it the 'Care Bear Stare' because our hearts were all focused on the same thing at the same time. She loved that cartoon as a little girl, so that made sense to her."

"That's incredible..." Gabriel says, marveling at the orb. "But I still don't understand the 'Care Bear' reference. I remember the cartoon. In Panama they were called *Los Cariñosos*. Does it turn into a bear shape?"

Rory smiles and lifts her hands up. "This is why."

The rest of us put our hands up in unison, toward the orb, and focus our gazes on our elements inside it. As we do, the bones within our hands begin to glow, continuing throughout the rest of our bodies. My glow is a bright turquoise, Val's is amber red, Zo's is light blue, and Rory's is green. We look almost like Day of the Dead *calaveras*, brightly painted skulls adorned with decorations. Our skulls are glowing and our eyes are radiating with the same lustrous light.

My heart and mind feel like they're expanding to envelop everything around me, connecting me to my family as well as to the earth and sky. It feels powerful and infinite. The orb grows, engulfing all of us within it, including Gabriel and Mama Joyce. They look frightened, unsure of what to do.

"Don't be scared. You aren't in any danger," I say to Gabriel. He looks at me, puzzled.

"Lina... I hear you... in my mind." He puts his hand up to his temple.

"In here, we are all connected," I say.

"Your glow looks different this time, Lina," Zo's voice says inside my head. Looking down I see there's a white glow radiating out from my core, swirling into the turquoise light surrounding it. I'm mesmerized as I watch the lights interact with each other, almost the way ocean waves ebb and flow.

"This is like a dream!" Mama Joyce exclaims, reaching up to touch the walls of the orb. As she touches it, the wall ripples like golden water. Gabriel puts both of his hands into the wall, manipulating the liquid type substance and allowing it to flow between his fingers.

Looking down at the flower petals to the side of us, I get an idea. I create a whirlwind and start picking all of the flower petals and stems up, reshaping them into whole blossoms. Gabriel gasps. "Lina! Are you doing that?"

"Mama Joyce, hold out your arms," I say with a smile. She looks puzzled but does as instructed. I shift the wind to bring the newly materialized floral bouquet into her arms.

"Oh my! You've shared your powers!" Her eyes are wide as she grasps the flowers to her chest.

Zo opens her hand and blows into it, manifesting a small fire. Rory begins floating. She giggling as she kicks her feet and arms as if she were swimming.

"I'm going to put Lina's power to good use. Where's that champagne so I can do some cool tricks?" Val says as she looks toward the table. "Ah yes! I see it!" She turns back to me and suddenly my blood turns cold. For one fleeting moment, Val's eyes are pitch black.

My mind flashes back to the nightmare, those terrifying black eyes and the moving tar consuming Val. A piercing scream jolts me out of my vision and I realize it's Zo. Rory comes back to the ground with a crash. The orb dissipates instantly, leaving everyone confused and disoriented.

"What... What was that?" Zo asks shakily, her chest heaving and her hand on her forehead. Oh my god. She couldn't have seen it.

"What was *what?*" Val asks, concerned but seemingly unaware of what happened.

"Zo, what did you see?" I whisper back, hoping she only saw a small glimpse of what was in my head.

"It was Val. Her eyes... They were black... Her body was almost covered by horrible black liquid. Almost like it was eating her," Zo says, shuddering.

"I saw it too," Rory says quietly, rubbing Zo's shoulder.

"You guys are scaring me." Val says, alarm raising in her voice. "Why didn't I see it?"

I take a deep breath. "I had this nightmare last night. A vivid, scary nightmare. It was about you, Val." I look at her, then at Zo and Rory. Gabriel is now beside me, holding my hand and stroking my hair. Mama Joyce hands a glass of water to Zo.

"You guys! We've never done that before — seen the exact same thing telepathically... But why didn't Val see it?" Rory pipes up, more confused than scared. I'm at a loss as to why any of this happened. Our manifested gifts blended in a much more powerful way than it ever has. My glow was different this time. Val's eyes. Rory and Zo seeing the memory of my dream. All of this is completely new territory.

"Sis?" Val's amber eyes are focused on me. "Hey. I'm right here and aside from being slightly freaked out, I'm okay. And you know what? We're supposed to be celebrating one of the best days of your life here and we haven't even gotten to the delicious dinner I made for you!"

I hug her tightly, whispering, "I love you, V."

"I love, love, love you too, Lina Luna." She whispers back, stroking my hair. Zo and Rory wrap their arms around us in a giant sister hug.

Zo lets us go and claps her hands together. "Ok

chicas, this is way too much drama for one night. Let's get back to celebrating Lina and Gabriel! Mama Joyce, let's go get our drink on!" She and Joyce laugh and start heading back toward the table. Val kisses me on the cheek and winks, then grabs Rory's arm and walks toward the others.

Gabriel and I watch them for a minute, then turn to look at each other. His eyes are searching mine, warm and comforting. "Are you okay, *querida*? You looked like you'd seen a ghost."

"I don't know. This time it felt different; it was more powerful than before. And I saw something..." I look back toward my family, who have successfully opened a bottle of prosecco and are pouring it into glass flutes. Val puts on her chef's apron and starts setting up her cooking station.

"I'm so ready to get back to having the best night of my life. Aren't you?" I kiss him and flutter my lashes.

He kisses me back and nods, then shouts, "Hey! Don't start the party without us! We're coming!"

"Oh no! I forgot about your martial arts class tonight!" I sit up in my seat in a panic, dropping my fork and the piece of grilled Chilean sea bass attached to it. In our excitement we lost track of time and Gabriel's class has already started.

Gabriel kisses my cheek and laughs. "It's okay. I found a substitute. I've been planning this for a while." Mama Joyce nods and continues digging into the delectable coconut rice with chickpeas.

I relax back into my seat and pick up my fork again.

Val flavored the moist, buttery fish with a mixture of lemon, capers, and dill. It's tangy, fresh and zesty.

Rory grins at me across the table, mid-bite. "Did you like the flowers I made you?" she asks.

"They were the most spectacular flowers I have ever seen *in my life*, Rory! You really outdid yourself. The ring inside the rose, and the explosion of petals?! It was straight out of a movie!" Rory is practically gleaming from all of the compliments.

"All of you had an important role in this day. I'll never forget it." I look across the table at all of them, my heart swelling with gratitude.

Val lifts her glass and the others follow suit. "To Gabriel and Lina!"

Everyone says in unison, "To Gabriel and Lina!"

Val continues, "Gabriel, I couldn't have chosen anyone more perfect than you as my sister's soulmate. I know you'll take good care of her. Welcome to the crazy *familia*, bro." We cheer and click glasses.

Just as I think the night couldn't get any better, I see a streak of pink peek out from behind a cloud, signaling the sunset. Within moments, the entire sky is painted in pinks, purples, and oranges. As the sun sets and the air cools, Val points her fingers toward a few nearby tiki torches and ignites them with small bursts of flames.

CHAPTER FOUR

G ABRIEL SLEEPS LIKE A BABY, a hint of a smile on his face. After we got home from our engagement dinner and I had him all to myself I pounced on him with every ounce of affection in me. It led to a few hours of lovemaking that left him blissfully tuckered out. As I listen to his content breathing, I smile to myself.

I hold my hand out so I can see the ring on my finger. I still can't believe everything that happened tonight. Some days, like today, I wish my parents were still here. I close my eyes and think back to one of my last memories with my father. It wasn't a milestone or a special event, but a regular day at the park. We were having a picnic. He was alternating between pushing Val and I on the swings, and Mom was sitting on the blanket with Rory and Zo. It was a summer day and we were surrounded by a field of daisies. I still remember the sound of Val's infectious laughter as he pushed her higher and higher.

I still remember the day two soldiers came to our house to deliver the news to our mom about our father's death. They looked so official in their crisp military suits, which were different than the green uniform

I saw my father wear many times. Their faces were grim and they were formal with my mom, calling her "ma'am". They handed her an official letter and offered their condolences. She knew before she opened it. She crumpled to the ground like a folded piece of paper. We stood paralyzed watching from the living room, not sure what was happening. The sound of my mother's cries still haunts me to this day.

The last time I saw my mother was the day she disappeared, almost a year later.

I've played the memory in my head a million times as I've struggled to understand how a mother who obviously loves her kids would leave them and never look back.

I had just turned 12. That year changed everything for us.

It started out like any other day. She made us breakfast, then sent us off to the bus stop. In retrospect, she did hug us all a little tighter before we walked away. She stood out on the sidewalk a little longer to watch us as we left. When she told me, "Look after your sisters, Lina", a phrase she said to me every day, there was something different about the way she said it — a tinge of sadness in her voice.

We were unaware she was gone at first. We came off the bus and walked home together, just like we always did. Mom's hospital shifts usually ended late, so we hadn't expected her home until close to bedtime. Rory and Zo went into the living room and turned on the television to watch whatever after school special was on. Val headed into the kitchen to find something in the refrigerator to eat. I had homework that day, so I went to my room and put my bookbag on the bed. I was sifting through my materials when I heard Val shout my name from the kitchen. I found her with her head in the refrigerator and the door wide open. She was ecstatic.

"Lina... Mom hooked us up!" she shouted. "Look at how many meals she made us! We have chicken *molé*, rice and beans, pork chops..." Val read each meal title off and pulled packages from the fridge. Mom left us foil-wrapped meals with descriptions and dates on them — all of them made that day. The freezer had even more. It struck me as a little odd since Mom was always too busy to make any substantial meals. That's how Val learned she loved to cook so much — out of necessity. She was fed up with eating Top Ramen every day.

"How did Mom have the time to do this if she is supposed to be at work?" I wondered. When she came home from a double or triple shift, she was exhausted, usually heading to her room to sleep. Sundays were her only day off, which were the days she had time to make us something other than frozen waffles or canned soup.

Val was unfazed by the abundance of food. She was excited to get a break from cooking, but I had an uneasy feeling in my gut. I knew how stressed my mom was about money, and over the past several months she had an even shorter fuse. I thought maybe something happened with her job. I decided to check the house for clues. Val grabbed some pork chops and rice, getting the container ready to put into the oven while I started walking around the house. I wasn't sure what I was searching for, but I knew something was off.

In the bathroom, I discovered that mom's makeup

and toiletries were still there. When I got to her room, her suitcase and clothes were still there. Her purse. Her car and keys. Everything was still in its place.

Looking through her closet, I found a picture frame with broken glass on the bottom. It was my parents' wedding photo. There was also some black powder on the floor next to the bed. Aside from these things, though, nothing in her room seemed out of the ordinary. I tried to convince myself that everything should be fine. I remember thinking, *Maybe she just went out for a walk and she's planning on coming back soon.* But I still felt it. Something was wrong.

Walking back into my room, I slumped down on my bed. The side of my cheek touched something hard underneath the pillow, making me sit up and look. It was an envelope. When I pulled it out, I saw my mom's handwriting on the outside: "To Lina". Opening up the envelope, I found a folded letter inside with cash tucked behind it. A lot of cash.

My darling Lina,

I can't tell you where I'm going. You can't follow me and I don't want you to look for me. It won't make sense to you right now, but I'm doing this for all of you.
You and your sisters are stronger than you know. Take care of each other always. You are the best parts of me and your father. I love you and I hope you can find it in your hearts to forgive me... Mom

I folded into myself as the reality sunk in. She

wasn't coming back. We were alone now. I read that last line again.

I hope you can find it in your hearts to forgive me... Mom

How was I going to tell my sisters? How was I going to provide for us all? Were we going to be split apart and sent into foster care? My middle school brain scattered into a million directions as I was forced to start thinking like a grown up. We didn't have any family to call on. Our father's parents died in Mexico in a horrible house fire the year he joined the military, and his only sibling died as an infant. His voice cracked when he spoke about them and the adobe house of his childhood. My mother, on the other hand, never shared memories about her family. All I knew was that they were estranged and it was so painful she never spoke of them.

I crawled up into a fetal position and cried until I had no tears left in me. All I wanted in that moment was to fall into my Mom's arms and beg her to stay.

"Lina! What are you doing?!" Val yelled from the kitchen. The sound of spraying water and the urgency in my sister's voice snapped me back to reality. The explosions of emotion I was experiencing manifested throughout the house, water spilling from faucets in the kitchen and bathroom.

I wiped my tears and took a few breaths. Focusing inward, I normalized the water and stopped the spraying. I resolved then and there to be strong for my sisters now that I was going to take care of them. That was the last promise I made to my mother.

Our lives were never the same after that day, but we figured it out together. It was Zo's idea to call Mama Joyce, since she was the adult we trusted the most. Joyce and Vernon came over right away. While Vernon made a fresh batch of lemonade and fried up some hush puppies, Joyce sat with us in the living room. She reassured us that she wouldn't allow anyone to break our family apart. True to her word, she was our advocate and helped us navigate the system. She and Vernon took us in and adopted us into their already big and loving family.

It turned out that our father left us the house and his military retirement in his will, and our mother had set aside all of the paperwork for us to find. We moved into Joyce and Vernon's home. They kept our original house as a rental to generate income for us, holding those funds in an account we could access when we were of age. Being able to move back into our childhood home when we became adults was a blessing, and the money helped put me through school. I'll always be grateful to Joyce and Vernon for being our adoptive parents, and for preparing us for our futures.

Suddenly, I realize that my mom *was* there tonight. Mama Joyce has been the best mom we could've ever wanted. She's been our guardian angel. I don't know where we'd be without her and Vernon. There will still be a hole in our hearts left by our real parents, but we were four very lucky girls to have a generous adoptive family with unconditionally loving spirits.

Gabriel mumbles something in his sleep. I peer into his face, wondering what he's dreaming about. His face is serene and even more handsome, his long black lashes fluttering every now and then. I wonder what our children will look like. Maybe we'll have a little boy that looks just like him with dreamy eyes and curly hair? The thought warms my heart and I kiss his cheek. He smiles in response and nuzzles his face into the pillow. I reposition myself so that my head is next to his, then close my eyes and slowly drift off to sleep.

After starting out the week on such an incredible high, everything else feels anticlimactic. Aside from Mama Joyce excitedly telling everyone about how romantic our engagement was, work goes on like normal. The camp kids are still enjoying Willy Wonka week. Our staff is getting prepared for next week's camp theme: mad science. Calvin is beyond thrilled; he's idolized Bill Nye the Science Guy since he was a kid.

Gabriel and I have made a few calls to spread the news about our engagement. His was to his siblings. My phone call was to my closest friend since grade school, Jade, who lives about two hours south in Portland. Being able to share and hear the excitement in other people's voices makes it even more real. She almost blew out my eardrum with her high pitched scream, followed by a list of questions.

"When did this happen? How did he do it? What was he wearing? When is the wedding? When will you have babies?" The conversation makes my head spin. She is even more inquisitive than Zo. We both get emotional as I go over Gabriel's sweet gestures and my family's involvement. Even though Jade is like a sister to me, she doesn't know about our magical gifts. It's hard to keep some of the most important details of myself from her, but the knowledge comes with a huge burden.

"I wish I could have been there, girl. I'm so happy for you both. Gabriel is a lucky guy." I hear Jade wiping away tears. She and I have seen each other through many heartbreaks, including the loss of my parents. We met in our old neighborhood when we started elementary school together. The bus driver assigned seats and I was paired up with Jade. We bonded over my Strawberry Shortcake lunchbox and had a deep and animated discussion about our favorite characters and scents. Always the romantic, she followed her boyfriend out to Portland before I started college. The boyfriend didn't work out, but she created a successful career as a food blogger. I still get to see her around the holidays when she comes to visit her parents at their home in my old neighborhood.

After I hang up the phone I feel drained but happy. Now all of the important people in our lives know the news and we can move on with planning. We still aren't 100% on the date, but we think a summer wedding next year will be lovely.

My Wednesday shopping trip downtown with my sisters is a chance to rehash the events we experienced a few days before, plus gush about the Marc Anthony concert. Zo, of course, has to try on a million outfits before she decides on *the one*. We give her a hard time about it, telling her Marc Anthony isn't going to pick her out from the audience and declare his love for her. She shrugs and says, "That's what you think."

Finished with her dress shopping, Rory heads to a nearby bookstore, while Val, Zo, and I continue shopping at a locally owned boutique known for retro and eclectic styles. Zo disappears into the dressing room with an arm full of gowns while Val and I make a beeline for the wall of accessories. Val spots a long rose gold necklace with a straight pendant and holds it up to herself in the mirror, tilting her head as she poses and scrutinizes. I look at the earring collection, zeroing in on some drop earrings that might look good with my dress.

When I look up, I see Val looking at me.

"What is it?" I ask.

"I just can't believe you're going to be a married woman soon," she says with a sad twinge in her voice.

I chuckle. "I know... it sounds so... grown up."

"Yeah... grown up..." She pauses, biting her bottom lip and thinking. "You're going to have your own family. You'll be busy, you know, being a wife and having kids. I don't know if I'll get to see you as much."

"Val! Nothing is going to break this family up. Gabriel is now an official part of it and he knows that I'm a package deal. You will never lose me."

"You promise? We'll still have sister dates?" Her eyes are wide and hopeful.

"Promise. I'll write it into our wedding vows. Mani pedis and chick flicks twice a month." I giggle and hold up my pinky finger. She smiles and wraps her pinky around it.

"He really has adopted us, even with all of the crazy, right? He's felt like my brother for a long time. I wish Free would spend as much time with you guys. He's so tense when he's nervous..." She looks wistful, her eyes focused on my engagement ring.

Thinking back to our first interaction with Free, it's hard to picture him being as integrated into the Luna family as Gabriel, but maybe he'll surprise us.

"Well... the concert is a great start, right? For us to get to know him better?" I say, trying to sound cheerful. Val brightens up a bit at the mention of the concert.

Zo finally emerges out of the dressing room holding a black dress, adorned with lace and beaded details at the top of the form fitting bodice. Val lets out a whistle and I put my hand over my mouth, imagining how stunning she will look. "This is the dress that I'll be wearing when Marc Anthony falls in love with me," she says playfully. "Let's eat!"

After we pick up Rory at the bookstore, we walk a few blocks south on 4th Avenue to our favorite restaurant, a Korean BBQ place that makes the best beef short ribs in town. We are such regulars that the owner, Mrs. Kim, always makes a point to come out and greet us with hugs. She even remembers our names. We find a table next to some large live ferns. Rory sits closest to it so she can touch its leaves and secretly give it some love. When our food arrives, the ferns have perked up and turned a more vibrant shade of green. "*Cuidate, mija.* We don't want to draw attention," I say, quietly jabbing her under the table with my toe.

She whispers, "Poor baby. Hope you feel better now." While she spoons her stir fried broccoli and rice into her mouth, the rest of us look at each other and roll our eyes. She is so much more affectionate with plants than humans.

I dig into my short ribs and rice, famished after a

couple of hours of shopping. Val is spooning chili paste onto her plate of japchae noodles. Zo blows carefully on her bowl of dumpling soup, effectively cooling it down in just one puff.

Before we finish, Mrs. Kim surprises us with a plate of brightly colored sugar cookies. They aren't on the menu, but Mrs. Kim has spoiled us before with special treats. Zo's eyes light up and she immediately grabs a pink one from the top, popping the entire confection into her mouth.

"Good, but not as good as Fifi's," she says with her mouth full.

"Fifi?" Rory asks. "Is that a person or a place?"

"FIFI!" Val and I say in unison. Rory stares at us like we've sprouted horns from our foreheads.

"You may not remember her, Rory. Fifi was Mom's friend. She took care of us sometimes." Val says, noisily slurping the last of her noodles. Rory's eyebrows furrow as she struggles to remember. After a moment, her face lights up.

"Cookies! I do remember!" she grins proudly. "They were the only sweets we ever had in the house. I used to sneak some in my backpack before I left for school."

I laugh and throw a napkin ball at her. "No wonder they always disappeared so fast. You little rascal!"

"She wasn't the only one," Zo says with a laugh. "I *lived* for Fifi's cookies! She always made my special requests too." Val and I shake our heads.

"Hmm. It's been a long time since I thought about her. We haven't seen her since... well... since Mom," I say. A hush comes over the table as everyone starts thinking about the days when our original family was whole.

"You know what's weird? I found a picture of Fifi the other day. It was on the bottom of the wardrobe. Not sure how it got there. It was tucked behind an old pair of boots I decided to wear that day. She and Mom were sitting on the back porch, you remember that white wicker bench we had forever? I was next to Fifi eating a cookie with a big cheesy smile on my face. I guess the picture left me with a craving..." She giggles and holds up her second cookie, half-eaten. "Fiona. That was her name. 'Fiona, Sylvia, and Zoë.' Dad wrote it on the back of the photo."

"Everything happened so quickly after Mom left. We went to live with Joyce and Vernon. I wonder if Fifi ever tried to find us?" Val says, looking at us. Her question makes me wonder, too.. She was my mom's best friend. I wonder if Fifi was also left behind.

As we drive home, Rory leans forward and asks, "Sooooo Lina...who are you picking as your Maid of Honor? No pressure, but you should know that if you pick me I'll make floral arrangements that will make your guests faint from awesomeness."

Next to her, Zo opens her mouth to come up with a rebuttal. "Well — I can do some cool stuff too! Like a million butterflies spelling out your names!"

"None of us are going to be Maids of Honor! She has a best friend. Jade gets the job automatically," Val says matter-of-factly.

"You guys... I haven't even thought about it!" I laugh. "But... There's no way I could possibly choose.

I need all of you up there with me. I'll have multiple Maids of Honor. I can do that, right?"

Val looks at me with her eyebrow cocked. "I don't think that's how it works — according to tradition."

"Forget tradition. It's my wedding and I say I want every single one of you to have a place of honor, including Jade," I say with resolve in my voice. Everyone else is quiet for a moment.

Zo holds her hand up. "Next order of business! Who gets to plan the bachelorette party?"

Val gives her a high five, "Oh yeah! Bring on the strippers!" She and Zo start dancing and mimicking a disco beat with their voices.

Rory groans, covering her face with her palm. "Gross! Why do you *cochinas* always have to go to the dirty place?"

"I agree with Rory. Absolutely NO strippers." I lock eyes with Zo in the rearview mirror and she stops dancing.

"Awww, come on. Isn't that the whole point of a bachelorette party?" she whines. Val pouts too.

"No. Gabriel and I are both on the same page about how stupid it is that people feel like they have to lose all control before their wedding. If I needed to engage in debauchery, then I shouldn't be getting married," I say firmly. Rory crosses her arms and grins.

"Fine. It will be boring as hell, but whatever you want..." Zo rolls her eyes and sulks for a moment, then her face brightens as she gets an idea.

"Drag queens!" She blurts out. Everyone starts chattering excitedly and I smile. I took my sisters to their first local drag show last year. I've been in love with the artistry, illusion, and glamour that goes into drag ever since I saw RuPaul's video for "Supermodel". A night of drag with my closest girlfriends sounds like the perfect evening.

As we round the corner to my sisters' house the girls have already decided on a venue in Portland so that Jade won't have to travel far. There are plenty of spa resorts nearby where we can stay. Val and Jade are texting back and forth and throwing out ideas. Operation Bachelorette Party is underway.

The girls are still in planning mode when they leave the car to head toward their front door, barely noticing when I say goodbye. It makes me happy to see them taking on an active role in the festivities. We haven't even figured out the actual wedding yet, but I know I'll have plenty of help.

Rory stops before she gets to the door and comes back to the driver's side of my car, reaching in the window to give me a quick hug. "Don't worry, sis. I'll protect your wishes and make sure they don't go rogue."

I give her a tight hug back, touching her spiral curls. "Good, I'm counting on you. Goodnight."

"Goodnight." She reaches behind her back for a second, then hands me a sterling rose. "I know they're your favorite, she says.

"You know me so well, Rory. Thank you." I inhale the sweet rose perfume. She walks toward the house, turning to wave before she reaches the front door. I start the car and head back home.

The rest of the week feels like a blur. Gabriel and I work late hours, so our dinners on top of the roof at the community center are a welcome time to reconnect. Mama Joyce kept Rory's paradise of greenery, making the roof a popular break spot for our employees. She told everyone that an anonymous florist generously donated the lush garden to the center. Vernon built a few wooden benches and placed them around the perimeter where staff members eat, read a book, or enjoy the view of the cityscape and marina.

I stand in front of the mirror, putting on a coat of peach-colored lip gloss as a final touch. I told Gabriel to stay out of the bedroom while I get ready so I can surprise him. I want to look special for him tonight. I haven't even let him see the dress I chose for the concert. My hair is halfway down so that it cascades over my left shoulder. I feel very exposed and out of my element with this dress, which is probably why Zo insisted on me buying it. She tries to get me out of my comfort zone, which I'm grateful for because I am such a creature of habit. The dress shows off my curvy figure with a mermaid silhouette, draping black lace over a nude colored bodice. The cap sleeves are slightly off the shoulder, exposing my collarbone.

I look at the faded scar above my right elbow and touch it gently. It's a childhood injury. Val accidently burned me when she lost during a game of Connect Four. She was only five at the time and was still learning how to control her powers. It's been a regret she has carried into adulthood. She keeps telling me she will pay for me to get it fixed or covered up with a tattoo. I told her it's a part of her that will always be with me, so I want to keep it.

The dress flares out at the bottom and blooms

out around me as I spin, perfect for salsa dancing. I feel a little giddy thinking about Gabriel's reaction. I don't think he will know what hit him. My daily style is typically demure and business casual, with jackets over sundresses or tunics with slacks.

While I've been getting ready, my sisters and I have been texting each other and sending photos. We decided to get dresses with similar black lace details but in different styles. Val's is an off-the-shoulder frock with a short skirt. Zo's dress is backless, with a high neckline. Rory's is an A-line dress with bell sleeves. Everybody looks absolutely dynamite, even Rory, who never dresses "fancy". She allowed Zo to put mascara on her, which makes her light gray eyes look even more striking. Her hair is pinned up, showing the dyed emerald locks of hair that usually only peek through her curls.

"Damn, we are going to be the hottest sisters there! 😎" Zo texts.

"You might just grab Marc Anthony's attention, Zo. 👀" Rory writes.

"See you hot chicas soon. Love you. 🤍🤍🤍" I write, then put my phone away. I giggle, thinking about how they're texting each other in the same house.

I quietly open the door. I don't see Gabriel in the hallway, so I tiptoe on the pads of my high heels so I don't make too much noise. I see him in the kitchen pouring two glasses of red wine. He looks gorgeous in a black dress shirt and slacks, his physique accentuated by the form-fitting shirt. His shirt sleeves are rolled up almost to his elbow and he is wearing a black leather cuff on his right arm. I pause, tilting my head as I admire how handsome my future husband is. I hope we never stop getting butterflies when we're around each other.

"Is one of those for me?" I ask coyly to get his attention.

"Yes, I..." Gabriel's words stop as soon as he sees me. "*Dios mio...*" he says under his breath, standing still while he puts his hand over his heart. His warm brown eyes are drinking me in, wide and unblinking. I almost shrink back from the intensity.

"Angelina you... are an exquisite masterpiece. I don't think I want to share you with anyone tonight. Especially not Marc Anthony." He walks toward me. My breath catches in my throat.

He stops inches away from me and I look up at him, not sure if I should touch him; we may not end up going to the concert if I do. I can smell his clean masculine scent, woodsy amber with a hint of citrus. The top buttons on his shirt are open to reveal enough of his heaving chest and the pulse at the base of his neck. Our bodies are so close, I can feel his heat.

"How did I get so lucky?" he whispers, his fingers reaching forward to touch mine. The sensation feels like a little shock, making me jump.

"I feel like the lucky one," I whisper back.

His fingers find my ring and he caresses it, bringing my hand up to his lips. With eyes never leaving mine, he kisses my knuckles tenderly, making my knees go weak.

"*Mi vida,* if I kiss you right now, I'm afraid this beautiful dress won't make it to the concert," he says huskily. I feel a flush rising in my cheeks. He swallows and I see the muscles in his jaw clench. The incredible amount of control he has right now makes him even more irresistible.

Holding my hand, he leads me back to the kitchen island and our glasses of wine. Handing me one and keeping the other, he says, "Cheers to a magical night with the woman of my dreams." We clink our glasses together to toast.

"Cheers, handsome." I bring the wine glass to my lips. The smell of the wine is heady and intoxicating with notes of oak and black cherry. As I take a sip I realize how dry my mouth is. The wine's astringent burst wakes up my palette, followed by a fruity finish. Just as I am about to take my next sip, the doorbell rings.

"Our carriage awaits, my beauty." Gabriel smiles.

CHAPTER FIVE

I OPEN THE DOOR AND SEE an official looking man in a black suit and hat. He appears to be in his early 20s, with sandy blonde hair neatly styled under his chauffeur's hat. Although he looks formal in his uniform, there is a kindness and sparkle in his hazel eyes that shines a little brighter when he smiles.

"Miss, everyone is waiting for you in the car. There is chilled champagne ready to serve. Is there anything I can store in the back for you?" Gabriel and I look at each other with wide eyes. This is fancier than anything we've ever experienced. The shiny black stretch sedan with jet black tinted windows looks enormous in front of our apartment complex. People walking down the street look on curiously, probably wondering if there is a famous person inside.

"That is very sweet of you to offer. Thank you, but I'll carry my shawl and purse." I say, holding my hand out to shake his. He looks puzzled, as if no one has ever done that before. "My name is Lina, and this is my fiancé Gabriel. What's your name?"

"Well...uh. My name is Sam, Miss. It will be my

pleasure to drive you to the concert and anywhere else you wish." He tips his hat and shakes my hand.

"Sam, pleased to meet you. Thank you for driving us and those *locas* in the car tonight. I hope they don't get too wild for you." I wink. He shakes his head and looks back at the limo.

"Not at all, Miss Lina. They are delightful." He smiles broadly, puffing his chest out a bit. I instantly know I'm going to like him. Gabriel holds my hand and leads me toward the limo with his other hand on the small of my back. Sam hurries to get in front of us so he can open the door. As he does, I hear the tropical sounds of Marc Anthony and La India's "Vivir Lo Nuestro" blasting through the speakers. Val and Zo are singing and drinking champagne gleefully, dancing in their seats with over exaggerated shoulder action. I look over at Gabriel and he shakes his head.

"*Hola hermanas!* Looks like the party's already started, eh?" he shouts over the music.

In unison, they lift their glasses and cheer.

"After you, *amor.*" Gabriel holds his hand out for me to steady myself while I climb into the car. I look around in awe. The inside is so roomy that we could probably fit 15 people comfortably on the U-shaped leather couches. Electric blue neon is illuminating everything so it resembles an upscale lounge. Not only is there a bar, there is also a huge monitor and a state-of-the-art entertainment system.

As I settle into the seat next to Rory, I see Sam lean over to say something to Gabriel, which makes him smile. I can't hear what they are saying, but Gabriel pats Sam on the back and climbs in next to me.

"What was that about?" I lean in close to Gabriel's ear.

Gabriel puts his hand on the base of my neck to pull me closer to him, sending shivers unexpectedly down my spine. "He says I'm a lucky man. I agree." He kisses me on the cheek, making me melt. Aww. Sam is going to get a big tip.

Val and Zo are already tipsy and I can see why. The open bottle of champagne is more than half empty. Rory looks at them and rolls her eyes. She is drinking a bottle of guava kombucha — not only because she is 19 and underage, but also because she sees no value whatsoever in drinking alcohol. She says it poisons the bodily temple.

"Lina! Gabriel! Your glasses are coming right up." Zo yells over the music. Val grabs two glasses out of the bar and Zo uses her powers to air lift the bottle of champagne from its ice bucket to her hands so she could pour. She hands them to us with a smile. "You both look amazing!" She yells again.

As much as I love the music, it's way too loud and I can't imagine driving all the way to Seattle like this. My ears would be ringing so much I wouldn't be able to enjoy the concert. "Can we turn this down?" I ask as I point to my ears. Rory nods and adjusts a knob on the wall behind her. "Whew. That's much better." I nudge her with my shoulder to thank her. She gives me a thumbs up.

"Val, where's Free?" I ask now that I can use my normal voice.

"Oh, he had a meeting in Seattle. He said he'll meet us later. He arranged for us to have dinner before the concert so he'll meet us at the restaurant." Secretly, I'm relieved to not have to ride in the limo with him.

We have so much fun in the car that time goes by quickly. Before I know it, Sam has parked and is opening the door for us. I blink to adjust to the bright sky after being sheltered within black tinted windows for an hour. We are in front of one of the swankiest Seattle restaurants I've never experienced but read about. Michelin star chef, Josefina de la Palma, is known for her farm-to-table Latin cuisine. We saw it highlighted on Food Network and Gabriel and I made a pact to try it one day when we saved up the money. After I watched the featurette I dreamed about tasting Chef Josefina's food.

"Oh my gosh! I've wanted to come here!" I exclaim. I'm practically clapping like a cheerleader because I'm so excited. The surprises just keep on coming. Free is definitely pulling out all the stops, perhaps to compensate for his lackluster first impression.

Zo whistles as she looks up at the glass building in front of us. "Whoa! Free is hooking us up!" She nods appreciatively at Val, who gives her a half smile in return.

Walking into the restaurant is like walking into a chic modern hotel. The walls are floor to ceiling glass, with spectacular views of Elliot Bay, Mount Rainier, and the downtown Seattle skyline, depending on where you're seated. The floor is sleet gray tile, offset by cream and charcoal colored high back chairs and teakwood tables. A small bouquet of white tulips in black vases adorns each table.

The maître 'd is dressed in a black suit with a crisp white dress shirt and dark gray tie. As we approach his post, he looks at us impassively. "Do you have a reservation?" he asks.

Val steps in front of us. "Yes, it should be under Jeffrey Simon."

He looks down at his book, using his finger to go down the list in his black appointment book. He finds Free's name and his eyebrow goes up.

"Yes indeed, Miss. We have a very special place set for you in our sky lounge. Please follow me." I notice that his tone has changed from uninterested to caring very much, as if we were upgraded to first class.

We walk through the dining room to a spiral black iron rod staircase leading to the next floor, which is even more spectacular than the first. I notice a rock wall with cascading water, which gives it an expensive day spa aesthetic. The floor is made of thick glass, so it creates the illusion of floating. The black marble bar is stocked solely with top shelf liquor.

A young, male-model type bartender smiles broadly at us as we walk by. He is wearing black from head to toe with the exception of a white towel over his shoulder. His light brown hair is pulled back in a small bun with a few strands framing his chiseled face. Zo flashes a megawatt smile right back, turning on the charm and fluttering her long lashes at him. He looks at her with a mesmerized expression. Her effect on men is always fascinating to witness. It's safe to say that controlling air is not her only superpower.

We are led to a table facing the waterfront with a large cream-colored couch. The table centerpieces on the top floor are all white roses, a gorgeous contrast against the black table linens. As I sit, I marvel at the view of the waterfront. The backdrop of mountain ranges makes it look like a photograph you'd find at an art gallery.

"Your server will be with you shortly. Enjoy your evening," Mr. Maître 'd says cordially as he leaves leather bound menus in front of us.

Chef Josefina's signature, etched in gold, adorns the front of the menus. It epitomizes decadence. With fingertips grazing the golden lettering, I open it up, excited to read about the exquisite cuisine she has created that I'll probably never get to try again in my life.

Mr. Cute Bartender has just appeared at our table. I look over at Zo, who is focusing all of her attention on him, drawing him in with her gaze. He looks familiar. I wonder if his other job is modeling since I've heard that many models bartend or serve tables when they aren't working on photo shoots.

"Good afternoon. My name is Paulo and it is my pleasure to personally welcome all of you to Josefina's sky lounge." He pauses when he looks at Zo. "My compliments on how impeccably all of you are dressed. Are you going to the opera tonight?"

"We are going to a concert!" Rory says brightly.

"Ah, well I have no doubt that your entrance will be a memorable one," he says, still looking directly at Zo. "Before your server gets here I would like to take care of your drink orders." He has a thick accent that sounds... Italian, maybe? Zo noticed too and she is making sure he keeps his eyes on her by touching the necklace on her collarbone and tilting her head. I glance over at Val and Rory, who are both amused and fascinated at the masterful seduction happening before our eyes.

She asks, "Paulo, you have an interesting accent. Where are you originally from?"

"I'm from Italy. Tuscany, actually, Miss..?" He raises his eyebrow to indicate asking her what her name is.

"Zoë Iliana Luna. *Encantada.*" She says, holding her hand out to shake his. Wow, she is even tapping into the few Spanish words that she knows. "I've never been to Italy but I've always wanted to go. You are so lucky to come from a place so famous for its natural beauty." And just like that, Zo hijacked our bartender for the next several minutes, engaging him in a lively conversation about growing up as the son of winemakers in a small village in Tuscany. The rest of us smile at each other over our menus — listening to the show unfolding before us with great interest, all the while pretending not to.

Val loudly clears her throat then asks, "Paulo, when you have a moment, I'd love to get a Jalapeño Mojito." She smiles sweetly, knowing full well she just interrupted her sister's game. Paulo looks slightly embarrassed, realizing he hadn't fulfilled his work duties. He nervously runs his fingers through his hair, moving a couple of strands out of his face.

"Of course. We have some fresh mint and peppers we just harvested this afternoon from our chef's organic garden. What can I get for everyone else?" He has regained his composure, taking our orders without writing anything down.

"Well, I'm not sure. What would you suggest for me?" Zo asks him, of course, pulling him back into her web of seduction. The rest of us roll our eyes. Oh no, not again.

Val leans over and whispers, "Man. We are never

getting our drinks…" Making me giggle. Gabriel nudges me with his elbow. Aside from not wanting me to ruin this for Zo, he is also a bit of a romantic. I kiss his cheek.

Paulo gives Zo different options, and Zo reacts to each suggestion as if she is captivated. Finally she settles by asking him to make something special just for her, which seems to delight him. He nods, looks at Zo and says *"Con piacere, signorina."* With pep in his step, he heads back to the bar to make our drinks. Zo waits until he gets to the bar before she pulls out her phone and starts Googling like a madwoman. When she translates his phrase, she sits back and smiles.

"He'll get a good tip if he remembers all of our drinks after that rendezvous, Little Miss Magnetism," Val says dryly as she looks over at Zo, who feigns innocence and pouts.

"I can't help it if men sometimes find me…alluring." She says the last part in a breathy whisper like Marilyn Monroe.

Rory raises her hands up and pretends to bow. "Masterful, Zo. You are the queen."

"I'm happy to teach you some moves, grasshopper. You can bring home one of those hot male models from your drawing classes. He'll be putty in your hands!" Zo rubs her hands together as if she is molding clay.

Rory frowns and looks down. "I don't think so, sis."

"Oh, why not? You're gorgeous, insanely talented, you have a heart of gold, and want to save the world. There is no reason why you can't land any guy you want. Our town has a ton of tree huggers to choose from. You know, now that I think of it — it's been a long time since I've seen you with anyone! Lina, who was the last boy you saw Rory with?"

Zo looks at me but I can see Rory out of the corner of my eye shift uncomfortably, fidgeting with her hands. Obviously this is not something she wants to talk about, and I think I know why. I've caught signs here and there that she has been drawn toward women ever since her early teens. I'm just waiting for her to tell us when she feels comfortable.

"Oh, leave her alone, Zo. Rory is a serious college student and she doesn't have time for relationships." I wink at Rory, who smiles at me gratefully and mouths the words "*Thank you.*" "Besides — don't you remember how I refused to date for years? Then I finally met Gabriel and that was it." He holds my hand up to his lips and kisses it.

"When Rory finds the right *person,* she'll know..." I say, looking at Rory. Her mouth slightly opens and I give her a reassuring smile. I kiss her hair above her forehead. When I look at her again, tears have welled up in her gray eyes.

"Thanks Lina..." She whispers.

Zo softens. "Okay, okay. But Rory, seriously. When you are ready, talk to your girl." She pats herself on the chest and forgets all about giving Rory an inquisition.

Val's phone starts ringing in her purse, making her jump to fish it out. "Oh! It's Free. I'll find out when he'll be here." She hurries away from the table to take her call. As she leaves, Paulo brings our drink tray to the table. Impressive! He got all of them right.

"Fresh raspberry juice spritzer for the young lady." He sets down a highball glass with skewered raspberries and lychees, garnished with a sprig of mint. Rory lets out a little squeak when she looks at it.

"Jalapeño Mojito, mineral water with lime, and an Amber Ale." He sets down Val's mojito, then my mineral water and Gabriel's beer.

The last drink looks like something out of *Food and Wine Magazine*. Inside a margarita glass is a creamy light blue concoction — almost a robin's egg blue — with coconut flakes around the rim. All eyes are on the special drink as he presents it to Zo.

"This is something special. I wanted to create a drink in honor of this *bellissima signorina* with the dazzling blue eyes. It has blueberry juice, blue curaçao liqueur, coconut cream, and rum. I took a risk and guessed you like coconut," he says as he hands the drink to her. Zo looks flushed and stunned, as if she might cry from the sweet gesture.

"I... *love* coconut... it's one of my favorite flavors!" she gushes. All of us wait with baited breath as she takes a sip from the glass. She closes her eyes and smiles dreamily. "This is absolutely delicious or should I say, *molto delizioso. Grazie* Paulo." She looks up at him through thick black lashes, proud that she was able to incorporate some of the Italian phrases she researched on her phone while he was busy in the bar. It paid off, because he puts his hand over his heart — probably to keep it from bouncing out of his chest like a cartoon character.

She licks her lips and goes in for another sip. He smiles, bows his head, then returns to his work station. Zo watches him the entire time. Perhaps the seduction tables have turned. He found Zo's weakness: her taste buds.

Val comes back into the dining room in a huff, looking irritated. She throws her phone back into her purse as she sits. "Good, our drinks are here," she says and grabs her mojito, taking a few big chugs. Zo looks at her with wide eyes, offended that she didn't care to savor the spectacular drink her new boyfriend worked so hard on. Val slams the drink back on the table, then wipes her mouth with the back of her hand.

"So, Free isn't sure he'll make it. His meeting took a bad turn — whatever that means — and he said he needs to stay and try and fix things with his buyers. He's still in Tacoma. He said if he can, he'll join us at the concert."

"Valencia, it's going to be okay, *hermana,*" Gabriel says with forced cheer, trying to lighten Val's mood. "We're still going to have a good time. And hey, I'm happy to pay for the meal. We don't need him."

Val perks up and a mischievous look spreads across her face. "Actually, you won't have to, Gabriel. Free gave me his gold card before I left and told me everything was on him tonight. I say we make it a night to remember." She grins and pulls out the shiny gold card from her wallet.

After probably the most decadent three course meal of our lives, we're all in our own food comas. I don't know if I'll ever get another chance to taste the things I tasted tonight. Wagyu beef tacos with homemade flour tortillas, lobster tail and sea urchin paella, and Mexican Chocolate marbled flan topped with macerated huckleberries? To die for.

Hopefully when we get to the venue, we'll be ready to work some of those calories off on the dance floor.

I peer out at the Seattle cityscape. The sun is starting to set, morphing the skyline into pinks, purples, and ambers. I put my head on Gabriel's shoulder, feeling a sense of gratitude and wonderment. I wish I could capture this moment somehow in a photograph.

"What are you thinking, *mi amor?*" Gabriel asks as he strokes my hair.

"I'm thinking I might not mind so much if we stayed here even longer and missed the concert. Is that a bad thing?" I ask.

He chuckles. "I know what you mean. I felt that way earlier when you surprised me with that amazing dress." I smile and nuzzle into his neck.

When the check comes, Val drops Free's gold credit card into the portfolio as if she was dropping a microphone. "Boom!" She says, a little too loudly for a fancy pants place like this.

Before we leave, Zo makes her way back to Paulo's station. I can't hear what they're saying, but I see him write down something on a cocktail coaster and hand it to her. She takes it between her fingers, smiles and walks away without looking back. He watches her every step, captivated. I start singing under my breath, "Whoa here she comes...she's a maneater..." Val and Rory both snicker.

The limousine is waiting for us as we depart the restaurant. Sam smiles, holding the door open for all of us. "I hope your dinner was delicious, Miss Luna," he says cheerily as I approach the limo door.

"It was unbelievable, Sam. Thank you." I climb into the lounge on wheels.

"Is anyone else having a food crash?" I ask.

Gabriel nods and rubs his belly. "I will remember that meal for a long time. That ceviche was dynamite. Everything tasted so fresh and vibrant. It might be better than my mama's ceviche, which is saying a lot." He laughs. "Plus we got to see Zo turn a young man into jelly." He waves over to Zo, who immediately grins.

Val slumps herself down next to Zo, who fans her jokingly. "He sis, are those drinks catching up to you?" she asks. Val mumbles something and shakes her head. "Are you feeling bad about spending Free's money?" Val looks up defiantly.

"Nope. Not at all. He said he was going to pay for everything. All I did was get a few extra things to try," she says, crossing her arms. Of course, those were the most expensive items on the menu. "The thing is, money is nothing to him. I'm sure it'll be fine. He won't even care. He's always trying to get me to spend his money and it just feels weird. Today was the first day I spent money like a drunken sailor."

"Is that what's upsetting you? Spending money with gusto?" Rory asks.

Val pauses, then says, "No... I'm disappointed. I wanted for all of you to get to know him tonight." Zo wraps her arms around her.

"But he said he still might meet us. Isn't that what he said?" Zo asks as she bends her head down to meet Val's eyes. "And if not, then there will be other times, right?"

"I know. I just wanted tonight to be extra special. We had it all planned out," Val says sadly. Rory pulls a petal out of her purse — it looks like it's from the restaurant. She places it in the middle of her palm, then puts her other hand over it. When she opens her hands, a dark maroon rose is revealed. She slinks over to Val's side of the seat and tucks it behind Val's ear.

"Val, everything *has* been extra special. No matter what, it's going to be an amazing night, okay? I promise," I say, reaching over to put my hand on hers.

A moment later, the limousine stops and Sam opens the door for us. I can hear faint music coming from somewhere else. Gabriel looks at all of us. "Well, I get to be the very lucky man who walks you three beauties in. Shall we?" He reaches his hand out to Rory. She grins brightly, showing off perfect teeth against rosy lips.

Gabriel steps out first, then pulls out Rory, Zo, Val, and finally me. "I wanted the best for last." He whispers against my lips as he gives me a quick kiss. The girls all say "awwwww."

"Thanks, Sam. See you later!" Gabriel waves to Sam, who tips his hat. Then he puts his arm out for Val, who links her arm in his. His other arm is around my waist. Zo and Rory have linked arms and are walking behind us.

There's a huge line around the building leading to the front. To the side is a roped off area with two large men in suits. They are both bald and look like ex-military: huge, muscular, no-nonsense, and mission-focused. I can barely tell them apart, making me wonder if they're related. Val tugs at Gabriel's arm. "Come on, bro. That's our entrance. We're going VIP all the way today."

She walks up to the two men with an air of authority. She looks at one with a name tag that says SMITH and says, "We are with Jeffrey Simon". Without a word,

Smith pulls out a tablet and proceeds to look at his list. The other man, whose name tag reads DALE, looks straight ahead. Smith taps Dale on the arm and he opens the rope, handing us some lanyards with "Backstage" in large black letters.

"Right this way. Enjoy the concert." Behind us, I can hear the clickety clack of Rory's heels jumping up and down.

CHAPTER SIX

"THANK YOU." VAL SAYS DRYLY, then she turns and looks at us, mouthing "Oh, my God!" The rest of us can barely contain ourselves. Not only are we about to see one of the best Latin singers of our time, but we might actually get up close and personal.

We head into the venue, which is like the ballroom fantasies are made of. There are cream colored marble touches everywhere. Several crystal chandeliers hang from the high ceilings, giving it a sense of royalty and grandeur. We take in the surroundings with eyes as big as saucers, so overwhelmed with the beautiful architecture and the fact that we're really here. The VIP entrance leads to a lounge above the main floor, which has its own bar and dance floor. Everyone else on the bottom floor level is standing, surrounding the stage, but our floor has tables and chairs within a stone's throw distance to the stage.

Off to the side of the lounge is a door with a sign that reads *Backstage Passes Only*. Rory nudges me in the ribs. Both she and Zo hold up their lanyards proudly to show nothing is off limits to our crew. We'll probably make our way there after the concert. For now, we are just getting settled in and looking around. Everyone on this level is dressed to the nines, women in formal gowns and men in suits. There aren't many people up on this level, but enough for us to make our way to one of the tables and stake our claim.

Marc Anthony isn't on stage yet, but a DJ off to the side is playing some music to warm people up. I look over the balcony at the salsa dancers spinning and twirling beneath us; it makes me want to dance with Gabriel. We've always had smoldering chemistry on the dance floor. Gabriel cozies up to me from behind, wrapping his arms around me. We start moving side to side to the music. I turn my head to kiss him and rest my head against his chest.

Zo, Rory, and Val come up to the balcony next to us, peering down at the dance floor below.

"Wow! So this is what it's like!" Rory exclaims, looking around like a kid in a candy store. She is marveling at everything in sight — the dance floor, the stage, the bar, the people. She has wanted to experience a Latin dance club ever since she saw the movie *Dance With Me* with Vanessa Williams. The club is allowing under 21 patrons entry with a special "NO BOOZE" stamp, which she is wearing proudly.

Zo pipes up, "Actually, this isn't what it's usually like. I've been to a few salsa clubs, and I've been to lots of concerts. This is the swankiest concert hall I've ever been to. I read that Marc Anthony specifically requested this place because he wanted people to dance rather than sit down. Plus..." she points up, "Badass crystal chandeliers!"

Rory is studying the dancers with interest and

moving her shoulders to the beat. I whisper to Gabriel that he should ask her to dance. He smiles and nods.

"Can I have this dance?" He offers his hand to her like a gentleman. She opens her mouth wide and then grins from ear to ear. She looks at Val, Zo, and me, who cheer her on and give her a thumbs up. She grabs his hand, practically skipping as he leads her out to the VIP lounge dance floor. Except for a few other couples, there is plenty of dance space.

Gabriel is such a skilled dancer that he immediately puts Rory at ease by leading her smoothly into each move. I can hear her infectious laughter above the music. When he spins her the first time, her squeals of delight make Zo and I laugh out loud.

I notice Val seems anxious. She looks around, then checks her phone. "Anything from Free yet?" I ask her.

She shakes her head and throws her phone back into her purse. She looks over her shoulder at the dancers below, then over at the bar. "Where are the waiters in this place?" She flags down a waitress near the bar, who walks over with a friendly smile.

"Can I get you ladies anything to drink? We have complimentary wine and well drinks tonight as well as tapas at the bar."

"Actually, I would love to get a bottle of champagne for our table." Val says and points to our table a few spaces down, before any of us can say anything.

"...and some water too, please!" I say to her quickly before she leaves. Val has been drinking excessively tonight, which is starting to worry me. I'm hoping I can get her on the dance floor to sweat it off so we don't have to carry her home.

After the song ends, the lights flicker, signaling the

start of the concert. The stage area goes dark. Gabriel and Rory come back and we all head over to our table. Rory looks exhilarated and her cheeks are flushed.

"Salsa dancing is my new favorite! This is so much fun!" she says breathlessly. Our waitress arrives with a bottle of prosecco, glasses, and two carafes of water. "Ooooh, just what I needed!" Rory says and starts pouring herself a glass of water.

When the stage lights come on, a full orchestra complete with conductor, horn section, percussion, pianist, strings, flutes, and guitarists is revealed. The conductor lifts his baton up, then the intro to "Hasta Que Te Conoci" begins, and the audience starts cheering. The unmistakable voice of Marc Anthony starts singing and the crowd goes wild.

I look over at Gabriel and he is yelling and clapping just as loudly as anyone else. I think he's checked several items off his bucket list today. He notices me watching him and I blow him a kiss. He smiles, then closes his eyes and starts singing along.

The rest of the concert is spent mostly at our table watching the show, enthralled with Marc Antony's golden voice and emotional delivery. The show doesn't depend on theatrical lighting or special effects. It's all musicianship and soul. The acoustics are so perfect that I feel the bass in the instruments reverberate through my chest. We dance, sing along, and even find ourselves in tears at times.

About halfway through the concert I notice that Val has started enjoying herself, getting swept up in the music. When the orchestra plays a particularly uptempo song with a hard thumping *reggaetón* dancehall beat, a gentleman wearing a white guayabera shirt and dress slacks comes up and taps Val on the shoulder. "*Bailamos*?" He asks with his arm out to the side. He nods his head toward the rest of us in greeting.

Val takes a swig of her prosecco, then grabs his hand. "Why not? This is my jam." He leads her to the dance floor and the rest of us are right behind them. Zo and Rory are dancing together with smiles on their faces.

Gabriel and I dance perfectly in sync. I know when to anticipate his turns just by the position of his hands, and we are twirling and spinning all over the floor. I start noticing people watching us, which makes me feel a little self-conscious but also gives me motivation to put on more of a show. Gabriel looks at me and as usual, can tell what I'm thinking. He knows the one place I get competitive is on the salsa dance floor.

With a twinkle in his eye, he pushes me into a spin with a flourish, then grabs and dips me. He leans in for a quick kiss, then lifts me up and spins me again. My sisters start applauding and cheering, along with several other onlookers. We now have a circle of people around us except for a few other couples, one of which has just closed proximity and is performing some impressive twirls a few feet away from us. Gabriel and I continue dancing, lost in our own world. Every now and then I see a glimpse of my sisters and the man that initially had asked Val to dance, who are shouting us on above the music.

When the song stops, Gabriel pulls my arms around his neck and slowly drags his hands down the sides of my arms and stops at my waist. I get so caught up in the moment that I pull him close and kiss him passionately. When I start hearing clapping, I abruptly stop and giggle, embarrassed. I'm not usually into public displays of affection. The moment felt right, and Gabriel was so irresistible, that I honestly forgot where I was. He smiles, kisses my hand and then bows to the crowd, taking in all of the accolades with a sense of humor.

As we head back to our table, people move to the side to make space for us to walk through. We get a lot of high fives and compliments from the other patrons. I was starting to think I was getting rusty since Gabriel and I don't go out dancing as much as we used to. We're both still catching our breath when we sit down, guzzling down glasses of water. Mine immediately seeps into my pores, cooling me down and making me feel as if I just took a refreshing dip in a pool on a hot day. Gabriel still looks a little overheated, so I discreetly absorb the water into my palm, placing it on the back of his neck to allow him to feel the water's cooling sensations.

"Ahhhhh. That feels incredible." He closes his eyes and lets his head roll forward, allowing me more access to his neck and shoulders. I let my hand rest so that water can permeate deeply into his muscles. His breathing normalizes and he puts his hand on top of mine. He leans over to whisper in my ear. "*Gracias, mi amor.*"

"So Rodolfo here is from Costa Rica. Isn't that close to Panama, Gabriel?" Val asks, gesturing to her dance partner, who's now sitting at our table. Gabriel brightens up and shakes Rodolfo's hand and they begin an animated conversation in Spanish about their villages and the things they miss from their original home lands. Listening to them reminds me how much

Gabriel misses Panama and the people he left behind. He's taken me to visit his family twice and it always feels like a privilege to see this part of him, the part that helped shape him into the man I fell in love with.

While the music plays and the conversations continue, the hairs on the back of my neck start standing up. I get the strange sensation that someone is watching me. I look around, wondering if I'm just imagining it.

Then I see him.

Free is standing in a dark corner across the room, next to the hallway leading to the bathrooms. His icy gaze is unblinking, focused on Val and Rodolfo. I fixate on him, watching him and trying to determine how long he's been watching us.

He sees me and then his expression changes, he smiles and waves. The smile doesn't reach his eyes, which are still piercing and dark. I force a smile and wave back, hoping my smile is a little more convincing than his. As I do, I say, "Free is here." My voice sounds a little more deadpan than I intended it to. Val immediately turns around, following my gaze. She is actually thrilled to see him, not picking up on any of the warning in my voice. She gets up from her seat and runs across the dance floor, throwing her arms around him and kissing him. He kisses her back, watching Rodolfo out of the corner of his eye.

Gabriel is on alert, his hand tense behind my back. The air in the room has changed and now it seems like the carefree night we were having is gone. I don't even hear the music anymore.

Free and Val come back to the table. Still standing, Free stares down Rodolfo, who cowers under the stare and stands up to offer his seat. "I'm sorry, I didn't mean to take your seat. Here, please sit down," he says respectfully.

Zo and Rory look at me, then back at Val and Free, startled by the sudden transition from fun to serious. Free acts as if he doesn't hear him, turning to all of us and reaching his hand out to shake Gabriel's hand. When he grabs Free's hand he says, "Good to see you again. Glad you could make it."

"I'm sorry I got caught up with some business. I hope all of you have been enjoying your night," he says. I notice that Rodolfo has retreated back to the bar. Free glares at him for a split second, then focuses back on the table. "How was the restaurant?"

"It was amazing!" Val gushes. "The food was like it came out of a dream. Zo might have even found a new boyfriend." She laughs. Free's eyebrows go up as he regards Zo.

"I'm not surprised. Beauty runs in this family. It would be hard not to fall under the spell of any of the Luna sisters. Am I right, Gabe?" Free says, as he sits down with legs spread wide, pulling Val down onto his lap. My sisters and I glance over at Gabriel, who cringes a little bit at the familiarity Free is attempting to forge.

"That is true, Jeffrey," he says curtly. I put my hand on his, feeling his knuckles harden as his fingers curl into a fist.

"Who's your friend?" Free asks Val as he pulls out a cigarette, which Val instinctively lights for him.

"Oh, Rodolfo? He isn't a friend. We just met," she says, her voice trailing off at the end as she realizes that Free's question has an accusatory tone.

"Actually, he's my friend, Jeffrey," Gabriel chimes

in, trying to save Val. "We grew up around the same area and I haven't seen him in a while."

"Oh, that's great that you connected with an old friend," Free says nonchalantly. I can still sense a steely quality in his voice that's making me uneasy. "I'm glad all of you have had a good time tonight."

"Um, thank you, Free. This has been a wonderful experience and we appreciate it," Rory says.

"I'd be happy to get you a real drink, if you want." Free looks over at Rory's glass of water and taps the glass. Then he waves at the waitress.

"No. No thank you. This is perfect for me." She says, grabbing her glass possessively. He laughs.

The waitress comes to the table and smiles. "Hi there! What can I bring you?"

"Cognac for me. And another round for the table," he says as he makes a little circle with his pointer finger.

"Right away," she says and saunters back to the bar.

"I'm so glad you're here, Free. I missed you," Val says. Free takes a puff from his cigarette slowly, not showing any sign of affection or emotion.

"Did you?" he asks coldly. Her eyebrows crease, his words visibly making their impact on her.

"Yes. I wanted you here. With me," she says, softly.

"Oh yeah. You should have seen how upset she was when you couldn't come to the restaurant," Zo says matter-of-factly.

Free taps his cigarette on the ashtray in front of him, and I see the gleam of his gold ring with the flying bird emblem. He twists his ring around for a moment, then looks at Val and asks, "Is that true?"

"Yes. I was. All I wanted tonight was for you to spend time with me and my family," she says with sadness in her voice. Free's harsh demeanor softens and he lifts her chin up to kiss her.

"I'm sorry, baby. I wanted to be here, but you know I had a mess to clean up at work."

"I know." She nuzzles into his hand. Whatever anger Free had, it's melted away. His arms are wrapped around her. His mouth is no longer a taut line, but a crooked smile.

"I have a surprise for you," Free says. "I'm going to take you away for the rest of the weekend. I have some business up in the San Juan Islands. Don't worry about Jax, I've already worked it out with him so your shifts are covered." His mouth opens into a big toothy grin. Val looks shocked.

He traces a finger down her arm. "Did I tell you how hot you look tonight? I bet you had so many men giving you attention." The waitress comes and sets down Free's cognac, then another bottle of prosecco. "Thanks, hon," Free says with a wink.

"I...I haven't packed or anything..." She stutters, still trying to wrap her head around the idea of being whisked away at a moment's notice without any preparation. The rest of us are no help. We're just as surprised as she is.

"I can get you whatever you need. Just say yes." Free holds her hand and watches her expression earnestly.

"Just go, Val. You've never been there," Zo says. "You work too hard. It's about time you relaxed a little bit."

Val chews on her lower lip, considering her options.

Finally, she says, "Let's do it." Free kisses her hard on the lips and she laughs.

"Hold on," Free says, reaching into his pocket to pull out his phone. He looks at the display. "I have to take this. Be right back." He starts walking toward the balcony to have his conversation outside.

"How are you feeling, Val?" I ask, now that Free is out of earshot. "You look a little…"

"Deer in the headlights?" Rory offers.

"I don't know! I was supposed to work this weekend, and I'm sure Jax is probably pissed. Free is technically his boss, so it's not like he's going to say no to him. I just feel unprepared. I wish I had time to go home and pack, or to look up where we're going. It's all totally out of my control. And you guys! We've been having the best time! I feel bad leaving you."

"Well, you are kind of a control freak, so I'm sure this has gotta feel weird for you." Rory laughs. Val sticks her tongue out at her.

"It's okay, Val. You can leave if you want. We'll be fine," Zo says.

We hear Marc Anthony address the crowd. "Seattle! Thank you for welcoming us tonight. You are beautiful! This last song is in honor of someone I have admired my entire life and who I was honored to call my friend, *La Reina de la Salsa,* the late Celia Cruz!" The orchestra starts playing "La Vida es Carnaval" and everyone cheers. The patrons in the tables around us are on their feet, next to the balcony. Even Gabriel is singing along.

Free comes back and stands next to Val, observing the crowd. "We have to get going. Our car is here and waiting outside," he shouts above the music. She looks confused.

"But — the concert isn't over." She looks at the performance below and the sea of people dancing and singing.

"It almost is. And if we're going to beat the traffic we need to head out now," he says firmly, as if speaking to a child. "You guys don't mind if I steal her from you, right?" He grabs her hand and looks at us impassively.

Stepping forward to give her a hug, I whisper in her ear, "Call me later." Gabriel and the girls say their goodbyes quickly, then watch as Val and Free hastily go to the exit. Free pushes through the crowd, making some people stumble back and look at him angrily. He almost drags Val behind him because he's walking so fast. We watch them frozen, no longer a part of the reverie surrounding us. We wait till they're completely out of our line of vision before we turn around. Gabriel puts his arm around me and I lay my head on his chest.

The mood has changed from joy to melancholy. Rory and Zo both look down at the concert expressionless and I feel a heaviness in my heart. I nudge Rory and she smiles wistfully. Leaning forward so they both can hear me, I ask them, "Do you want to stick around and meet Marc Anthony?"

They look at each other. Zo shrugs. "You know, I was pumped to meet him and experience the whole VIP thing but, it just won't be the same without Val..." Rory nods slowly. Zo verbalized what we were all feeling. We aren't going to finish out the night together and it didn't feel right to stay without Val. We didn't realize she was leaving so soon.

"I know what you mean. Val should be here. She

planned this whole night and she should be part of it. What do you think about giving these passes away and heading home?" I ask. They brighten up, nodding their heads.

"Let's find Rodolfo and his friends," Rory says.

"That's a perfect idea! Especially after the rude way Free treated him. I really want to apologize to him, too," I say. Gabriel smiles and kisses me on the cheek.

The song finishes and everyone starts clapping and cheering. I look around for Rodolfo and can't spot him but I see his friends at the bar. I tap Gabriel on the shoulder and point so he knows where I'm heading. Walking through the crowd carefully, my family follows close behind.

When I get to the bar, I approach Rodolfo's group of friends. "Hey, we were looking for Rodolfo. Do you know where he is?" I ask Santiago, a tall, dark skinned Dominican that Rodolfo introduced us to earlier.

"We've been looking for him. We thought he was in the bathroom but it's been a while. If you see him, can you tell him to come find us?" Santiago says with a thick Caribbean accent.

"Actually we wanted to give these to all of you." I show Santiago and his other two friends my VIP badge. They look stunned.

"*En serio?*" Santiago asks, his voice rising above the music.

"*Si, amigos.* We are serious." Gabriel smiles broadly, taking his VIP badge off his neck and handing it to him. I give mine, Zo's, and Rory's over as well.

"Please give one to Rodolfo when you find him, and tell him it was a pleasure to meet him." The guys start chattering with animated hand movements, before giving us tight hugs and thanking us profusely.

Seeing the joy on their faces is exactly what we needed to cheer up. "I'm texting Rodolfo to let him know. Wherever he is, that news will get his attention! *Muchisimas gracias, amigos.* This is such a generous gift!" He pats Gabriel on the back and shakes his hand. The other friends start heading toward the VIP lounge, proudly holding out their badges. We wave at them and proceed outside.

The brisk air hits us immediately, reminding us just how humid and stuffy it was inside the concert hall with all of the warm bodies and activity. I take a deep breath and fill my lungs with the cool, cleansing air. There aren't too many people outside since many are still inside dancing.

Sam the limo driver is parked in front of the building waiting patiently. He jumps out of the driver's seat and opens the passenger door for us.

"Hi Sam!" Zo waves and heads over quickly. "Woo! It's cold out here!" We're all walking behind her when Rory suddenly stops dead in her tracks.

"Rory?" I ask. She closes her eyes and kneels down, touching the concrete below.

"Someone is hurt," she says quietly. She opens her eyes and looks to the right. Rory senses when someone is wounded or close to death because of her connection to the earth. It only happens when she's in close proximity, so whatever happened can't be too far away. Gabriel and I look at each other before we walk toward the right side of the building.

"Can you wait for a minute, Sam?" Zo steps out of the limo and joins us. My pulse quickens as I consider the possibilities waiting for us. I hope we aren't going to find a dead body.

After we get around the corner we see a couple of dark shadows in an alley. It looks like two men kicking something on the ground. "Oh my God!" I whisper hoarsely. As my adrenaline kicks in and clears up my vision, I see it is actually a person on the ground. Not just any person. Rodolfo.

CHAPTER SEVEN

"*Nooooo! Por favor!* I didn't do anything." Rodolfo's cries are weak but desperate. His shaking hands are bloodied, covering his face. The men are relentless, brutally kicking him. Rodolfo is attempting to protect himself, crunched into a fetal position on his side. Both men are dressed in black from head to toe including gloves and masks. I can't see any distinguishing characteristics. Only their eyes and mouths are visible.

Without hesitation, Zo throws powerful blasts of air at the men from her outstretched hands, forcing them back against the wall behind them. Stunned, they shake their heads. We run to Rodolfo's side in just a few strides, surrounding him in a protective circle. Rory and I bend down to soothe Rodolfo while Zo and Gabriel remain standing. Gabriel steps in front of us to face the two men, ready for their next move.

One picks up a brick and the other pulls a knife from his pants pocket. "Gabriel! Watch out!" I yell. Both men move in to attack Gabriel. Before I can blink, Gabriel shifts his weight to grab the knife holder's wrist, spinning him so that he punches the brick the other man is holding and sending it flying. He yelps in pain and drops the knife. With her left hand out, Zo brings the knife flying toward her so she can catch it. Before he has a chance to see what happened, Gabriel follows up with a swift punch to the man's jugular, making him stumble backward gasping for air and clutching his throat. The other man grabs Gabriel in a headlock. Gabriel punches him in the ribs before using the wall to run up and flip over the man, reversing the headlock. Gabriel throws him to the ground with a single push.

Both men look at each other then scramble to run away. Before Gabriel and Zo can chase after them, Rory puts both hands on the ground and screams, forcing a wall of rock to spring from the ground in front of them. Without time to stop, they both run straight into the wall at full speed, knocking themselves unconscious. The wall immediately goes back into the ground next to where they lie. Gabriel runs up to check their pulses.

"Still breathing. Good. They need to face the police. Rory, can you find a way to tie them up?"

"Gladly." Rory gets up and surveys the ground quickly. After locating a twig, she holds it in her open palm, making it stretch and transform into rope. Standing over the two men, she places the rope on their wrists. With fingertips touching the top of the rope, she makes it move and twist itself around them so that their hands and feet are bound. "You are going to pay for what you did to our friend," she kneels down and whispers to their sleeping bodies before she walks back to where we're tending to Rodolfo, who is also now unconscious.

"Did they hurt you?" I inspect Gabriel's face and hands. His face looks unscathed but his knuckles are cut and bleeding. Gathering the humidity in the air to create a thin cushion of water around my hands, they begin to glow bright blue. I gently massage the tissue around his knuckles, taking the bruising and blood away with the water's healing energy.

"They didn't get the chance to cause any real damage. *Gracias, mi vida.* How is he?" he asks after placing a gentle kiss on my lips in thanks.

Zo kneels next to Rodolfo on the ground, stroking his hair. She shakes her head. "I don't think we should move him. His ribs are probably broken..." Looking up at Gabriel, she adds, "Damn, bro. You really *are* a ninja!"

Gabriel shrugs and looks down, shaking his head. "I don't like fighting, but sometimes that's the only option. *Pobre Rodolfo.* I wish we got here sooner."

Rory has her arms crossed, looking over Rodolfo's bloodied body. Wiping a tear from her eye, she takes her phone out of her purse and dials 911. While she tells the police what happened and where we are, I hold Gabriel's hands up to inspect them one last time and ensure they're healed. I kiss them then kneel down to inspect Rodolfo's injuries now that the fighting is over and I can focus. Using the power of the water still on my hands, I hold them over him to scan the damage. It's bad. Aside from the broken ribs, his face has multiple lacerations, his eye is swollen, and his nose and left foot are broken. It would take me days, and much more water energy, to heal him completely. We don't have that amount of time, so I decide to heal his ribs so he can be transported to the hospital.

Needing to gather as much healing energy as possible, I pull my hands apart slowly, creating a big

O as I gather droplets of water from the misty night air. The glow in my hands is even brighter and spreads throughout my upper body. I begin penetrating his chest, carefully guiding his ribs back into place. The image of the men brutally kicking him moments ago comes to mind. I shut my eyes tight and shudder. "I've never seen violence like that. Why would they do that to him? He's such a gentle soul."

Rodolfo stirs, whimpering like a wounded animal. Zo strokes his hair softly and murmurs, telling him he's going to be okay.

"They're here," Gabriel says, walking toward the red flashing lights. I'm not done with Rodolfo's ribs but I have to stop before the first responders arrive. Closing my eyes, I take a deep breath and make the water disperse so that my hands and body can normalize. Two police officers get out of the car, flashing a huge bright light from their patrol car toward the scene. Gabriel and Rory walk over to meet them while Zo and I stay with Rodolfo.

While the police interview each of us and gather information, an EMT team arrives to tend to Rodolfo. The police wake up the two assailants and handcuff them, cutting the rope from their hands and feet. When their masks are off, it's the first time we get to see their faces as well as the damage done during our encounter. One man is Caucasian with steely blue eyes. He must be in his mid-20's. His hair is shaved and he has a gold tooth in the front of his mouth. His face is locked in a permanent sour scowl. He has a cut under his eye and a big purple welt underneath it. He looks strangely familiar. He spits blood out on the ground as police ask him questions.

The other man looks much younger, maybe even late teens. He looks like he could be multiracial, with shortly cropped curly black hair and an earring in his left ear. His nose is bleeding and his chin is scraped, probably from the fall to the ground.

The medical team cleans their wounds as the police continues asking them questions. Both attackers are refusing to say anything. Finally one of the officers says, "Ok, since you guys have been so chatty, I guess we're done here. Time to take you downtown and you can talk through your lawyer. You have the right to remain silent..." He continues reading them their rights, grabbing them by the nape and putting them into the police car.

Sam has been waiting with us since the police arrived, sweetly offering to wait and take us in the limo wherever we need to go afterward. Before going away in the ambulance, Rodolfo wakes up, shaken and disoriented. After he had time to get his bearings, he started to tell police what happened. He said he was given a note by one of the waitresses which indicated his car was being towed. When he ran out to see his car, there was no tow truck. He approached the car and was hit over the head from behind, losing consciousness.

He woke up in the alley with two strange men. "They told me I made a big mistake. I didn't understand. I told them I didn't do anything. And then they started hitting me and wouldn't stop," Rodolfo says, breaking into tears.

"Thank you, sir. We have enough to go on for now. You have my card if you remember anything," the interviewing officer says, tapping the side of the gurney next to the ambulance. "He's good to go," she tells the

EMT before she walks back to the police vehicle. The men in black sit watching us from the back of the police car with cold expressions. Zo flashes her middle finger at them as the police car heads away.

We turn back to Rodolfo to say our goodbyes. Gabriel puts our phone number in Rodolfo's pocket. "*Amigo*, please let us know how you're doing and if we can help you with anything."

Crying, Rodolfo calls us angels and blesses us in Spanish before the ambulance doors close.

The trip home in the limo is deathly quiet as we process what happened. Someone did this to him and it wasn't just an accident. Why would someone want to hurt him?

Zo finally says, "They somehow got a note to him in the bar, so they were watching him. And then they told him he made a mistake."

"I don't know why, but one of those guys seemed familiar. Maybe he was in the club and I saw him," I say.

"Yeah, I thought so too!" Rory says. "The taller one, right? I couldn't place it but he did seem familiar." Pretty soon we're stopped in front of the girls' house. Sam opens the door. He has his hat off, over his heart. It's a kind gesture to show his acknowledgement for the rough way our night ended.

"Thank you, Sam. You've been wonderful tonight and we appreciate it." Zo kisses him on the cheek. Sam blushes. Rory surprises him by throwing her arms around him before heading up the steps to the front door.

Before he closes the door, he looks at us and says, "Is there anywhere besides home you'd like to go? It would be my pleasure to take you. I'm on the clock for another few hours." Gabriel and I look at each other. I'm tired, but now that we're alone it would be nice to enjoy an extended trip in the limo.

"How about the pier? It's one of our favorite places. I can use a moment next to the water." I say, smiling at Gabriel. He nods and smiles back.

"Right away!" Sam grins and shuts the door.

Within minutes, we arrive and Sam has the door opened for us. "As requested, the pier. It's a chilly night, so please take this." Sam hands Gabriel a folded blanket from the front seat.

Gabriel pats him on the back. "Thanks, Sam. We won't be long."

"Take your time." Sam tips his hat and gets back into the driver's seat. Gabriel opens up the blanket and throws it around my shoulders, hugging me close.

"Let's go get some fresh air, *preciosa*," he says as he kisses my forehead and pulls the blanket around me. I ease onto the boardwalk, careful not to catch one of my heels in the cracks. The pier at this time of night is completely free from its normal traffic — passerby, shoppers, restaurant patrons, boat residents. The air is still and the waters are dead calm.

As I approach the waterfront I see several boats parked at the marina below, a few with soft lighting inside. The water looks black with the exception of the moon's reflection, golden and luminous. The breeze hits my face and I close my eyes and take a deep breath of the marine air. Gabriel puts his arm around me, keeping me warm with Sam's blanket.

"I wonder what kind of view Val is getting from her

hotel room right now." I muse. "Maybe she's seeing the same reflection of the moon that we are."

"Mmm. Probably is. Good thing she missed out on all of the action," Gabriel says, then chuckles. "It would've been hard to explain any burn marks to the police."

My thoughts return to Rodolfo's attack and the way Gabriel and my sisters stepped in to save him. Looking over at Gabriel's sculpted profile, I am struck by his beauty and his heart. He gazes out at the water, his eyes twinkling from the moon's reflection. He notices me looking at him and turns toward me. His eyes soften as he caresses the side of my cheek. I put my hand over his and continue to hold his gaze.

"You really are a superhero, you know that?" I say. His eyebrows go up, surprised by the compliment.

"I think all of us were tonight. *We* saved that man. Together. I am the proud sidekick of The Amazing Luna sisters." He caresses my cheek with the back of his fingers — bloodied only an hour ago.

"*You* amaze me, Gabriel. You are the kindest, most gentle man I know. Then at the same time you are a warrior! My sisters are right, you're a ninja." I say, kissing his fingers. "I can only imagine the can of whupass you'll unleash one day if someone ever hurts our children."We both start laughing. It feels therapeutic to laugh after such a stressful end to the evening. Before I know it, tears are running down my cheeks, partially from laughter and partially from the trauma we faced tonight.

Gabriel sees the tears and his laughter stops. He tilts my face up with his hands. "Hey," he says, wiping the tears away with his thumbs.

"I'm okay. I just needed to...let go. Tonight's been a rollercoaster."

He pauses, looking at me with reverence before kissing me, fully claiming my mouth and lips with his. My hands move up to his neck and pull him closer, grabbing his thick curly hair. Every inch of me tingles in response, awakened. I inhale him as we kiss, relishing in his intoxicating scent.

His hands move from my face to the small of my back as his kiss becomes more urgent. For a moment, we are completely immersed in each other, oblivious to the risk of being discovered in this public place.

The sound of people's voices awakens us from our magical moment and we end our kiss. I smile up at him, my breath ragged. He smiles back. He kisses me on the forehead and pulls me into the crook of his neck, where I snuggle in and look out at the water. A young couple walks past us, conversing loudly, still adjusting their voices after leaving the deafening music at a nightclub. The man acknowledges us with a nod and Gabriel nods back.

With his lips against my hair, Gabriel murmurs, "I think we need to go home and finish this conversation."

"I agree. Take me home. Right now," I say, looking up to him seductively through my lashes. Gabriel's desire reveals itself as his pupils dilate and his lips part. He grabs my hand and pulls me back to the limo. Sam jumps out of the front seat and opens the door when he sees us coming. "Home, please, Sam. And step on it." I say with conviction as I head into the limo, pulling Gabriel in behind me and kissing him again.

Our hands are all over each other, emboldened by our privacy. We start making out like teenagers, almost too lost in our activity to realize the limo has stopped. "Uh. We should put this on hold," I say, with my finger against Gabriel's lips. We're both out of breath and flushed. My face is tingly and numb. I quickly smooth my hair down to look presentable before Sam sees us.

When he opens the door, I smile as if we were doing absolutely nothing out of the ordinary. He reaches for my hand to help me out of the car. Gabriel is close behind me.

"Sam, thank you so much for all you did for us. It was an unforgettable night." I reach out to hold his hand. He bows his head cordially.

"Miss Lina, it was unforgettable for me too. The pleasure was all mine. Oh, by the way. I wanted you to have this." He hands me a card. It is the card of one of the arresting officers we met tonight, Sgt. Shelby Lightfoot. "I also wrote the name of the hospital they took your friend to on the back of the card. I know how scary things were for you. I wasn't sure if you were able to get that information."

I turn it over and see "Seattle Medical Center" written on the back. I hold it to my chest. I was so stunned by everything that happened that I forgot to ask where they were taking him.

"Oh, Sam! Thank you. I don't know how we can ever repay you." I hug him tightly. Gabriel hugs him, too. Sam laughs then pats us both on the back. "Here, Gabriel and I want to give you a tip for tonight. You went above and beyond." I start looking through my purse quickly to pull out whatever cash I can find.

Sam puts his hand up and shakes his head. "No, Miss Lina. I've been well compensated for tonight. It's all been taken care of by Mr. Simon."

"Mr. Simon?" I ask, puzzled.

"Jeffrey Simon, ma'am. Miss Val's significant other," he says. "But... if you ever need a limousine service again I would be honored for you to consider me." Sam hands us a business card for his company.

"We'll be in touch." Gabriel smiles broadly.

Sam grins and shakes both of our hands. "Please do!"

"Goodnight, Sam. Thank you for everything," Gabriel says. "Now if you don't mind, I'm going to take my beautiful fiancée inside." Sam tips his hat and waves goodbye as he climbs back into the driver's side of the limo. Gabriel looks over at me and whispers, "Hold on." I smile and put my arms around his neck, then he picks me up and carries me into the apartment, where we waste no time in picking up where we left off.

I open my eyes, faintly hearing salsa music and smelling something delicious coming from the kitchen. I stretch lazily and look at the clock: 8:55 AM. Our usual Sunday morning ritual is getting up at 7:00 AM so we can get freshly made scones and coffee from the bakery down the street. My sweet man let me sleep in. I yawn and pull myself out of bed and head to the bathroom to brush my teeth.

Peeking into the kitchen, I see Gabriel plating up crepes topped with strawberries and cream. My stomach growls in anticipation. Gabriel sees me and grins. "*Buenos dias, hermosa.* Perfect timing! Did you get enough sleep?"

I walk over and throw my arms around his neck,

covering his face in kisses. "Yes, sweetheart. You are the best. Thank you."

"You are so beautiful and peaceful when you sleep. After that crazy night you deserved extra rest. Ready to eat?"

"Yes! This looks wonderful." He hands me a glass of juice and we bring our dishes to the dining table.

I dig into the crepes. He put a layer of Nutella inside. The chocolate hazelnut flavor pairs beautifully with the vanilla crepe and fresh strawberries - a perfect marriage of sweet and tart.

"Like it?" Gabriel is watching me from across the table with amusement.

"It's adequate." I smirk back at him.

"I can tell, *mala,*" he says as he winks at me. I giggle before I put another piece into my mouth.

After we finish eating, I go to the kitchen island to find Officer Lightfoot's card. My plan is to call and see if I can find out more about those men that attacked Rodolfo. I dial the number on the officer's business card.

"Seattle PD non-emergency line. How can I help you?"

I clear my throat. "Uh, good morning. My name is Angelina Luna. I would like to speak with Officer Light-foot, please?"

"Officer Lightfoot works evenings, ma'am. I can put you through to her voicemail if you want to leave a message."

"Well, before I do that, perhaps you can help me? Two men were arrested last night by Officer Lightfoot, near the Palace Ballroom on Broadway and 5th Avenue.

I wanted to know if they were still in custody." I say, biting on my lip.

"I can check, please hold." The phone clicks over to music — a Muzak version of Christopher Cross's "Sailing." Before the song finishes, it clicks over again. "Ma'am. Those men were booked on a felony charge. They were appointed a court date this morning by our County Judge and are still in custody as of this time." I scribble furiously as she directs me to the website where I can look up more information.

After ending the call, I enter the website address in my phone's internet browser. Before long, I find the names of the men in custody: Steven James Simon. Age 22. Darius Raymond Smith. Age 19. Booked on felony assault charges.

Writing down the names, my hand stops at Simon. Same last name as Free. I gasp and drop my pencil. Gabriel walks over to see what I've written down. His eyes widen.

CHAPTER EIGHT

A SICK FEELING WELLS UP IN my belly. My thoughts start racing, putting the pieces together. I thought there was something familiar about that man last night: he has similar facial features as Free's. What if Free has something to do with this? The way he reacted when he saw Val dancing with Rodolfo sent a chill down my spine. They said Rodolfo made a mistake. Could he be capable of something so malicious?

Looking down at the words I've written on the paper, I am numb and unsure of what to do. "We need to find out for sure if one of the men that attacked Rodolfo is related to Free." I walk over to the table and open up my laptop screen to begin my research. I discover a social media account for Steven in Washington state. Bingo. His profile picture is of him holding up a beer in one hand and a joint in the other. It's definitely the same guy. I scroll down to his other photos. A few have Darius in them, solidifying their relationship and their identities. I notice they're both wearing rings similar to the one Free has, which strikes me as odd.

Then I see a photo captioned, "Thanksgiving with the fam." Steven is standing among what looks like friends and family — and in the back, with those piercing eyes, is Free. "It's him." I say. Most of the people in the photos are tagged, but it doesn't look like Free is. I type "Jeffrey Simon" in the profile search and don't find him, then try again with "Free Simon". Nothing. It looks like he keeps a low profile online.

Going back to Steven's photos, I continue searching and eventually land on one with the two of them alone in front of a black SUV from four years ago. They're both holding up a couple of red Dixie cups. A bottle of Hennessy is on the car hood behind them. The caption says, "My big bro hooked me up with a new ride today. #crew4lyfe #rideordie."

Brothers. That would explain why he'd be willing to do whatever his older brother told him to do, including attacking someone he believed disrespected him.

My belly flips over and I suddenly feel sick. I hunch over and close my eyes to steady myself. Gabriel's hands are on my shoulders. "Baby? Are you okay?" He strokes my hair. I take a few moments until I finally sit up and find Gabriel's concerned brown eyes watching me.

"Can I get you something?" he asks. I shake my head no.

"Now we have proof. They're definitely related." Gabriel looks at the screen. When he turns to look at me there is a fire in his eyes.

I immediately dial Val's cell phone number and wait. No answer. I hear her voice mail message, "Hey. This is Val. Tell me who you are and I might call you back." Then a beep.

I hang up without leaving a message. "Shit..." I say. "Gabriel, we have to get a hold of Rodolfo. We also need to let my sisters know what happened." For someone to coordinate an attack like that means that Free is capable of anything. Val is hours away with him and I don't know if she's safe.

"I'll call Rodolfo. Why don't you start calling your sisters?" Gabriel says. "Don't worry. We'll make sure everyone is safe." I start dialing my sisters' phone number while Gabriel calls the hospital from his cell phone. I walk into the bedroom and sit on the bed while I wait for my sisters to answer my call.

"Yo!" Rory picks up the phone on the second ring. Caller ID told her it's me.

"Rory! Is Zo with you?" I ask.

"Uh. Yeah. We're both having breakfast here at the table." She sounds uneasy, sensing the urgency in my voice.

"Good. Put me on speaker phone," I say.

I hear a click, then Rory says, "It's the party line! What's up, sis?" I swallow hard, not exactly sure where to begin.

"You guys, I just got off the phone with the Seattle Police Department. I wanted to learn more about the two men who hurt Rodolfo."

"Good," Zo pipes up. "I hope those bastards rot in jail for a long time."

"They're still in custody. They were booked on felony charges and are going to be in at least until they get a court date and possibly post bail. But...that isn't everything. I found out their names and looked them up. One of them is Free's younger brother. I'm texting Zo a screenshot right now." I send her the photo I found of Free and Steven.

"Hold on..." Zo says. I hear a few seconds of silence until both girls shout out expletives.

"I knew he looked familiar," Rory exclaims. "When they were in the car and had their masks off. It was the eyes."

"Poor Rodolfo!" Zo says. "All he did was dance with Val, and look what happened? Free is a psycho!"

"Gabriel is on the other line with Rodolfo. We're going to visit him soon. Do you want to come with us?"

"Yes!" They say in unison.

"We'll be ready in twenty minutes. But wait! What about Val?" Rory asks, panicked. "We haven't heard from her at all since she left. Do you think she could be in danger?"

Swallowing the lump of fear in my throat, I say, "Oh no, I'm sure she's fine. Just get ready and I'll work on connecting with her."

"Thank you, Lina. See you soon," Rory says, then I hear the phone click as she hangs up. I call Val again. I don't know what I'm going to tell her, especially if she's left with Free.

I just need to hear her voice and make sure she's okay.

Dialing her number, I still get no answer but decide to leave a message this time. "Val, hey. It's Lina. I just wanted to see how things are going and if you're having a good time. Call or text me as soon as you can. Love, love, love you." As I hit the end button, I feel a looming sense of dread. Would he hurt her? He has the capacity to try. I have to put my faith in Val because I know how powerful she is, but then again, she may not be prepared to handle an attack from someone she loves.

Gabriel sits on the bed next to me and starts

massaging my neck. I hadn't realized how tense I was until now. He says, "I talked to Rodolfo. He's still recovering in the hospital. I didn't tell him what we know. I just want him to focus on getting better. He said he's excited to see us today. How did your sisters handle the news?"

"They took it the same way I did. Shock and fear. I told them we'll pick them up soon so we can visit Rodolfo in Seattle. I just left a message for Val..." my voice trails off.

"Lina, don't worry. I'm sure she's fine." Gabriel wraps his arms around me. I nod. The pit in my stomach says otherwise, but I just have to trust that she's okay, and that if Free dares lay a hand on her she'll fight back the way I know she can.

"Let's get dressed and get out of here. I want to see how Rodolfo is doing," I say.

After picking up my sisters, we drive an hour north to Seattle Medical Center where Rodolfo was taken. While Gabriel drives, I talk with my sisters and piece together the information that we have, going back to Free's response when he saw Val dancing with Rodolfo. We remember him taking a phone call before he whisked Val away — that could have been when he planned the attack. Or he could've planned it way before, when he was watching her from the sidelines. We have no idea how long he'd been watching her.

Zo's other power, of being a super sleuth, is coming in handy. She uses our time in traffic to look up all she can on Free and his brother on her phone. I don't know how, but she finds Steven's criminal record. Theft. Assault with a deadly weapon. Drug charges. In other words, he's no angel, and this won't be his first stint in jail.

"Look at this!" she says, zooming in on a portion of the report that says: KNOWN ACCOMPLICE OF DRUG AND WEAPONS DEALER KNOWN AS 'FREE BIRD'. REAL IDENTITY UNCONFIRMED BUT SUSPECTED TO BE JEFFREY A. SIMON, BROTHER.

Free Bird. Free's ring with the bird emblem was the same kind of ring Darius and Steven were both wearing in those photos. "What can you find on Jeffrey?" Gabriel asks over his shoulder as he drives.

"I'm already on it," Zo says, her fingers moving furiously. Scrolling over the results, she looks confused. "Hmmm. No criminal record. Not even a traffic violation." She searches again, this time typing FREE BIRD in the search engine. "Well, aside from a lot of Lynyrd Skynyrd references, there are some local police reports referencing Free Bird. Yep. Drugs. Weapon dealer. Assault. He's one of their most sought-after criminals, but they've never been able to make any charges stick. He's very connected. His associates are obviously loyal because they continue to take the fall and clean up after him."

"Jesus!" I say, shocked. This is way worse than I could have imagined. I look at Gabriel, who is staring straight ahead at the road. His knuckles are white from his grip. "What are we going to do?" I ask, completely at a loss. No one says a word. Val is in even more trouble than we thought and we have no idea how to get this guy out of her life.

When we arrive at the hospital, Rory gets out of the

car first and picks a yellow wildflower from a crevice in the sidewalk. Looking around to make sure no one sees her, she encases the flower between both of her hands. When she slowly pulls her hands apart, the flower has grown and multiplied into yellow, orange and red Gerber daisies. "Can you find me a twig?" She asks Zo, who starts scanning the ground around her feet.

"Ah. There's one!" Zo says as she picks up a tiny broken twig next to the car tire and hands it to Rory. As Rory rubs it between her fingers, the twig transforms into something resembling raffia. When it gets three inches long, she ties it around the bouquet.

"Great colors, Rory. I'm sure he'll love them," I say, patting her back. She looks pleased with her creation, admiring it from all angles.

The hospital is a cavernous, modern building that feels more like a mall than a hospital. The waiting lounge has a flat screen television and beige chairs, accented by pops of teal and peach. We head toward the information desk, where four different staff members are stationed.

"Hello, Ma'am," Zo says to the woman closest to us, a 50-something woman with dark skin and eyes the color of mocha. "We're looking for our friend. He was brought in here last night by ambulance. Rodolfo Madrigal."

"Yes, give me a moment and I will look him up," she says. "Mad. Ri. Gal... here we go. He's on the third floor. Looks like he's in a recovery wing. The elevators are straight ahead and to the right. I'll let Darla upstairs know that you're coming to visit. I'm sure your friend will appreciate having so many smiling faces to cheer him up." She smiles and points toward the path to the elevator. I look at the name plaque on her desk: "Gena."

"Thank you, Gena. Have a good day," I say, smiling back at her. Zo and Rory move with purpose toward the elevators, leaving Gabriel and I behind. We step up our pace. There are a few other people in the elevator when we get there: a woman with an elementary school-aged daughter, and a man on crutches with a cast on his leg. As we get inside, Rory pushes the button for the third floor.

The little girl looks up at us, fascinated by the flowers Rory is holding. Gabriel notices and picks a bright orange daisy from the top. Looking at her mother, he gestures toward the flower and the little girl, silently asking for permission. She smiles and gives him a silent thumbs up. Stooping down so he can be at the girl's eye level, he offers the flower to her. She beams and immediately reaches out to take it. The bell rings for our floor and we step off. All of us wave at the little girl, who excitedly waves back and grins so we can see a couple of missing front teeth.

When we get to our floor I kiss him on the cheek and whisper, "You are such a prince."

He puts my hand up to his lips and kisses it. "*Y tu eres mi princesa.*"

Zo and Rory are several paces ahead of us, walking toward a smaller reception desk where a blonde with red glasses is seated. Her name plaque says DARLA, so this must be the right place.

She looks up and smiles as we approach her desk. "Hi there! Are you the folks that Gena sent up to see

Mr. Madrigal?" She has a Southern twang that endears me to her right away.

"Yes, we are!" Zo says.

"Wonderful. Please sign in right here, and I'll get you some tags with the room number." She hands us a sheet attached to a clipboard. While we sign in she prints four tags with 'B13 MADRIGAL' on them. "Here you go. Please wear these while you're visiting. The room is down this hall, on the left side."

We thank her and head down the hall, reading the numbers to the side of the doors. Finally we get to B13. The door is slightly ajar. We knock softly. "Hello?" Zo says brightly. "Rodolfo?"

We hear something stir inside and then Rodolfo's voice, "Yes, come in." We push the door open and see Rodolfo sitting up in bed, watching television. When he sees us, he perks up and says, "Hey!"

In the light of day, his injuries are even more appalling. His face is puffy and most of it is covered with dark purple bruises. One eye is swollen shut. He has a two-inch stitch on his eyebrow which is partially shaved, a bandage keeping his nose stabilized, and a neck brace. His leg is in a cast up to his knee. Despite all of this, he smiles from ear to ear, excited to see us. It brings a tear to my eye, remembering his cries of pain and desperation last night.

Rory carries the flowers in front of her, putting them on his side table before carefully hugging him. He puts his arm around her, patting her. "Thank you, *chiquita*. The flowers are beautiful."

"We were so worried about you!" Zo and I come to the other side, joining in on the hug.

"How are you feeling, *compa?*" Gabriel asks, moving

over to Rory's side and patting Rodolfo's hand. I move sit down near the side of the bed, careful not to disturb any cords or injuries.

"I've felt better, *amigo. Pero gracias a Dios,* I'm happy to be alive." He looks up at Gabriel with a twinkle in his eye and a slight smile. I shake my head in awe.

"Oh Rodolfo. They hurt you so bad," Rory says. She hands him a glass of water from his side table.

He takes a few gulps, then says, "*Muchisimas gracias.* I tried to protect my face, but as you can see, I wasn't very good at it." He smirks and motions toward his battered and bruised face. "You know, I remembered something else from last night..."

We look at each other, bracing for the possibility that we'll need to explain away a glimpse at our extraordinary abilities.

He continues, "There was a point when they were kicking me that I felt like I was falling. Like I was in a black hole, just falling. I think that's when I fainted. But I heard voices in the dark — friendly voices. The police told me that all of you found me. I was dreaming about you when I fell asleep. You told me I was going to be okay." His eyes well up with tears and he puts his arm around Rory, hugging her close. "*Ustedes son mis angeles.* I don't know what would have happened if you didn't find me. How did you get them to stop?" His eyes are wide as he looks at each of us, then Gabriel.

"Gabriel kicked their asses," Zo says quickly. "He isn't just a pretty face. The man has serious fighting skills." Excellent strategy, Zo. By giving all of the credit to Gabriel there won't be any suspicion about us.

"*En serio?*" Rodolfo smiles up at Gabriel. "I don't know how I can ever repay you. I am grateful to God that He put you in my life, right when I needed you." He reaches out to shake Gabriel's hand. Tears flow down his cheeks and the rest of us begin to cry too.

"Rodolfo, you're among friends now. We're grateful we got to you in time," Gabriel says.

He sniffs and wipes his eyes with the back of his hand, still attached to multiple cords. "You are family. From now on, you are my family. I owe you my life. If there's ever anything I can do for you. Anything. Just say the word."

"You don't owe us anything. But we would be honored to call you family." Gabriel says, patting him on the shoulder.

My phone buzzes in my coat pocket. I look at the number. "Oh, it's Val!" I say.

"Oh, please tell her hello and that I enjoyed meeting her," Rodolfo says. The rest of us look at each other, communicating our shared worry silently.

"I will. I'll be right back." I walk out the door and hit the receive button. The hallway is basically empty with the exception of one or two nurses milling about. One of them smiles as she walks by and I wave.

"Hey, sis! Sorry it took me a while to get back to you. Somehow my phone was turned off and I didn't notice until right now." She sounds like she's in a good mood. I let out a sigh of relief. She's safe. At least for now.

"It's okay Val. Are you...doing okay? Having fun?" I say, trying not to sound weird. Hopefully she can't tell I'm sitting on a whopper of a secret.

"You have to visit this place, Lina. For one, it's completely surrounded by water. The view from our room is spectacular. We saw Orca whales from our balcony! And it's so calm and peaceful here. I wish I could stay longer." She continues on about the bed and breakfast, the sights, the activities. I half listen, half debate in my mind whether I should tell her about what happened. The safe bet is to wait until she's here to tell her; Free's reaction is the big unknown. I hear a pause and say, "Uh huh. That sounds wonderful."

"What the hell? Have you been listening to anything I said?" Val sounds annoyed and a little hurt.

"I'm sorry. I'm distracted. Gabriel and I are visiting a friend in the hospital. That's where I am right now."

"Oh shit! Why didn't you tell me that before you let me ramble? Who is it?" she asks.

"It's a friend of Gabriel's. Nobody you know." I feel a stab of guilt for lying.

"I'm sorry, sis. I didn't know. Do you want to call me later?"

"Actually, when are you coming home? I miss your face," I say with complete sincerity.

"I miss you too. And the other brats. We're leaving in a few hours. We should be back sometime tonight. Do you want me to text you when I get home?"

"That would be perfect. I'll come over and you can tell me all about your trip. This time with me listen-ing." We both chuckle.

"Ok, I'll see you soon sis. Tell the girls and Gabriel I said hi."

"Val?" I say before I catch myself. I want to spill and tell her everything, and I wish more than anything she was next to me right now.

"Yeah?"

"I love you..." I say.

I can almost hear her smile. "I love, love, love you

too, big sis." Then I hear a click as she hangs up. I'm glad I was strong enough to stay quiet. I hate keeping secrets from her, but I know I have to. Back in Rodolfo's room, everyone seems engrossed in a Spanish language version of *America's Funniest Home Videos*.

"Val says hello, Rodolfo. She hopes you get better soon." I say, putting on my best smile. The lies keep coming. I don't want him to think she doesn't care. Gabriel, Rory, and Zo look at me inquisitively, waiting for an indication on Val's status.

"Oh, she is so sweet," Rodolfo says. "Your family told me she's on a trip right now. The San Juans? I hear they're beautiful."

"Yes, she told me she has a view of the ocean from her room, and she actually saw some Orca whales." I say, hoping he can't see through my thin veil of secrets. Thankfully, he seems oblivious. My family isn't buying it, though. They continue staring me down, analyzing me for clues.

"Wow! I can only imagine." Rodolfo says, looking out the window. "She deserves it. She's a kind person, just like all of you." He looks down with a slight frown. "I got a bad impression from her boyfriend at first. I could tell he was upset. I was afraid that I got her into trouble." The girls and I look at each other. His instincts are right on. For a stranger to pick up on Free's volatile nature confirms again in my mind how dangerous he is. Rodolfo continues, "But I had it wrong. He just took her on the most amazing trip and is treating her like a queen. I'm sorry I doubted him."

Zo is about to speak, but I shoot her a warning look. She doesn't have much of a filter and I don't want her to spill the beans to him. I see that Gabriel is having a hard time not saying anything either, especially about Free.

"Rodolfo, we'll have you over for dinner when you're feeling better," I say, patting his hand. "Just rest and heal, okay? We can't wait to see you up on your feet and dancing again," I look over at my purse, hinting to my family that it's time to leave. "Is it okay if we keep checking on you? Give you a call to see how you're doing?"

"I'd love that! And please, let me treat you to dinner," He says, grabbing my hand. "I insist. My family owns a restaurant in town."

"That sounds amazing. We wouldn't turn that down."

We hug Rodolfo and say our goodbyes.

"*Hasta pronto, amigo. Cuidate.*" Gabriel says. Rodolfo smiles and waves as we head out the door.

As soon as we get into the hallway, Zo goes into detective mode. "What did Val say when you told her?"

I sigh. "I didn't tell her. She's having a great time and she has no idea about anything that happened. Plus I have no idea how Free will react. If he's capable of this, imagine what he could do to her? I told her I'd come see her tonight when she gets home. I need to tell her in person when she isn't with him."

Zo purses her lips and considers what I just said. "Okay. Yeah, that's a good plan. And then we don't let her anywhere near that bastard anymore. Just let him *dare* to lay a hand on her..."

Rory nods solemnly. "He would not walk away from that fight." Hearing my hippie baby sister — who normally wouldn't hurt a fly — talk about harming someone proves how far she's willing to go to protect Val. Any of us would.

"Hey." I say, grabbing both her and Zo's hands. "We are not going to let him hurt her, okay? When we explain what happened to Rodolfo, I know she won't go back to him."

CHAPTER NINE

AFTER DROPPING OFF RORY AND Zo at home, Gabriel and I head back to the apartment so I can wait for Val to contact me. "Do you think I handled that the right way?" I ask.

Looking forward at the road, he nods. "Yes. Rodolfo needs to heal and we shouldn't burden him right now."

"What about with Val? Should I have told her?"

"You trusted your instincts and I agree. It's better to tell her when she's away from him." He puts his right hand on my knee and looks over at me. His words reassure me a little bit. Now I just need to talk to my sister so that this knot will leave my stomach.

When we arrive at the apartment, Gabriel asks if I'm hungry. "No. I can't eat anything right now. I'm going to take a shower and freshen up." I kiss him on the cheek and head into the bathroom.

When I emerge from the shower, I smell something irresistible cooking. With a towel around my hair, I walk into the kitchen to find Gabriel frying plantains and fish. The smell of fresh garlic and lime immediately makes my mouth water, reminding me I haven't eaten for several hours.

He looks up from his frying pan and asks, "Feeling better?"

"Yes, the shower was exactly what I needed. That smells delicious!" I say, towel drying my hair. He smiles and plates up our lunches, then we walk to the dining room table. My first bite of the flaky white halibut is bursting with flavor from the spice mixture and pop of lime. I follow it up with one of the crispy plantains, salted to perfection.

"Ohhhh this is so good," I say in between bites. "Thank you, my handsome fiancé. I think I'll keep you." Gabriel smiles and winks at me as he chews.

"I knew there was something you liked about me," he finally says.

My phone buzzes in my purse across the room and I get up quickly to grab it. "It's a text from Val. She says she's about 15 minutes away from home," I say.

"Let's go, then." Gabriel says, getting up from the table. "Are you ready?"

I take a deep breath and frown. "I'm going to have to be."

When we drive up to my sisters' house, the first thing I see is Free's car in the driveway. A wave of turmoil hits my core. "Oh no..." I say, looking at Gabriel. His mouth is a thin line and his hands grip the wheel. We park in the driveway but don't move, staring ahead. My mind is racing, trying to come up with a way that this doesn't end horribly. The only saving grace now is that we're here to protect my sister if Free acts out.

I put my hand over Gabriel's, still clutching the

wheel. "Okay, let's get this over with. Maybe we'll get lucky and get to do some more ass kicking today." I smile wistfully at him. He gets a gleam in his eye.

"I'm counting on it."

We walk into the house quietly, not sure what to expect. In the living room we see Free right away, his back toward us as he looks through the book collection. I hear voices in the kitchen. Rory and Zo must have intercepted Val to try and talk to her about what happened. The voices are starting to rise in volume and intensity, causing a lump in my throat. Oh no. Rushing in, I move past Free without saying hello. He turns and notices me, saying "Hey!" and I wave quickly. Gabriel is right behind me.

"What is wrong with both of you? Why in the hell would you say something like that?" Val's arms are crossed and her back is against the sink. Zo and Rory stand closely in front of her. All of them look exasperated. When we walk in, they turn to look at us.

"Lina, tell her." Zo says.

Val looks at me with wide eyes. "What? You're in on this, too?" she asks, shock and disbelief all over her face.

"Val, you need to listen to us. Rodolfo was attacked, and it wasn't an accident. It was by two men — one of whom is Free's brother..." I say, trying to sound calm despite the agitation I feel from my sisters. Val covers her face with her hand, groaning.

"I don't believe this shit, Lina! After everything Free did to try and make sure you guys had the best time. He paid for *everything!* He wanted you to have total VIP treatment. And then he takes me on this unbelievable trip. This is how you repay him?! I'm sorry about what happened with Rodolfo. He's a very sweet guy and he didn't deserve that. But Free had *nothing* to do with it! You can't stand for me to be happy, can you? You don't think I deserve to be happy?"

I open my mouth to say something, but I'm so taken aback that I'm speechless. I wasn't sure what to expect from Val but it wasn't this. She's reacting like a cornered animal. Her face is flushed and her voice has risen an octave. I notice Free behind me, quietly listening. His face is unreadable — cold and blank. Gabriel moves over to my left side, positioning himself between Free and me.

The temperature in the room is starting to feel uncomfortably warm. I know Val is losing control of her emotions. She needs to calm down before she sets something on fire.

"You are so quick to accuse him, after all he's done to try to gain your approval." Tears of frustration have pooled in her eyes. They've turned light amber, the color they get when she's angry. Beautiful but dangerous. I know I have to tread lightly if I'm going to keep her calm.

"Val! Of course you deserve to be happy. You deserve every good thing in the world..." I say, my voice wavering. "And yes, we did appreciate the concert, and the limo and the dinner! We loved spending time with you. It was an amazing night, it really was. But you didn't see what we saw. The way those men beat Rodolfo as he was lying in the street..." I close my eyes again as Rodolfo's terrified face flashes through my mind.

When I open my eyes, Val's expression has softened a little by my reaction to the memory. "It was one of the worst things I've ever seen, and he did not deserve it." As I say this, Rory and Zo give Free the evil eye. He seems oblivious to their anger; his arms are crossed and he remains emotionless. "We got there right before he lost consciousness and we dealt with those two criminals. Believe me, they were sorry they laid their hands on him."

"Yeah, those two punk bitches got their asses handed to them by my brother," Zo says. "And then we saw their faces after the police took their masks off." She walks closer to Free, staring him down. He momentarily looks away, uncertain. "Steven Simon. Ring a bell? He is the spitting image of this guy right here...who also goes by a lame ass alias. *Free Bird.*" She puts her hands on her hips, looking him dead in the eye. Free glances away nervously, taking a step back for some added distance from Zo.

Within seconds, Val is in front of Zo, standing between her and Free. The two look like they're about to spar.

"Val, don't," I say, grabbing for her arm. She pulls away from me ferociously. The rejection stings, making me blink in confusion.

"No! Step the hell away. Right now. I'm sick of listening to this. Free has been a complete gentleman not only to me, but to all of you." Zo doesn't back away, instead staring her down, matching the intensity in Val's eyes.

"Oh, really? Is that how you felt when he got to the ballroom and treated you like a little girl in big trouble because you were dancing with someone else?" Zo asks sharply. "Because I remember having a damn good time up until he showed up and started acting like someone else touched his toy. And you just played into his hands, allowing him to make you small and weak." Val's eyebrows shoot up and her mouth drops open, hurt registering in her eyes. Her hands ball up at her sides.

Zo looks down at her balled fists and then back at her face. "You want to hit me? Go ahead and do it. I know you have the balls that your boyfriend here doesn't, because clearly he always has other people do his dirty work for him." Zo hisses in Val's face.

Before anyone can stop her, Val's hand swings up, slapping Zo's face so hard that she loses her balance and almost falls before Rory catches her. Val's eyes are full of rage, her chest heaving. Zo's hand is rubbing her face, which is red. She's still staring at Val in shock, tears rimming the edges of her red eyes.

Free moves behind Val and holds onto her shoulders. She is still breathing heavily and holding her hand close to her heart. I notice a ring on her index finger. It looks antique and even though it has a dark stone, it shines and catches my eye.

"Come on, baby. Let's go," Free says into Val's ear. She nods sadly and looks around.

"No, Val. Don't leave," I plead. "Not like this."

"I'll get my things later," she says, her voice strained. Free grabs her hand. I don't know if it's my imagination, but I see a hint of a smug smile on his lips. The rest of us stand frozen while they walk out the door and slam it shut.

Gabriel and I step forward to hug my sisters. I feel warm tears on my shoulder as Zo heaves and sobs. "It's okay, sweetheart. It's okay," I say soothingly. When she finishes sobbing, she looks at me, her face flushed and tear stained. I place my hand on the side of her cheek where Val slapped her. Cupping my hand and moving it over her face, I gather her tears. When I have enough, my hand glows bright blue as I heal her face, taking away the sting and emerging bruise.

"Thanks." She sniffs, wiping her nose with her sleeve.

"Eww. I could've gotten you a tissue for your boogers, *mocosa.*" Rory says, trying to lighten the mood and make Zo smile. She does, just a little.

"I can't believe she did that." Zo whispers. "I mean, we've had arguments before but...the way she got so protective of him so quickly made me angry. She wasn't listening to anything we said. And then — she slapped me! I know I dared her but I didn't think she'd *actually do it!*" Behind her, Rory smirks.

"That's what you get, *cabrona.* You shouldn't have told her to." Rory says. Zo sticks out her tongue in response.

"I'm still trying to understand the whole thing..." I say, looking up at Gabriel. He looks just as stunned as the rest of us. "What happened before we got here?"

Rory sits down in a chair at the dining room table. "Well, we were surprised when we saw Free come in with her. They were both happy. She was practically bouncing around the living room. He sat down on the couch like he owned the place — you know, legs and arms spread open taking up the whole seat. Val went into the kitchen looking for something to drink. Since she was alone, Zo and I thought it was a good time to talk to her."

"I was more than a little pissed that she brought him to the house," Zo continues. "And then he thought it was okay to make himself at home. I was afraid if I waited any longer to talk to her I might lose it and air blast Free to the next county. So I pulled her aside and told her we had something important to talk about. She was confused but she listened, at first. Looking back on it now, I think my approach was a little...abrupt." She sighs.

Rory nods. "You think? You kinda bum rushed her."

"I know. Ugh. I just wish she hadn't brought Free here. Seeing him made me remember the horrible way Rodolfo was beat up and everything we learned about Free's other life. Then here he was — acting like nothing happened — in my house. I don't exactly remember how I told her, but think I blurted out the whole story and used some colorful language when it came to Free and his family."

Rory shakes her head vigorously. "Pretty much. You sure didn't hold back on how you felt about Free and went back to when we first met him. You said something along the lines of his arrogant ass not getting bitch slapped that first night, AND that you knew he was no good. Val didn't like that very much." Rory crosses her arms and looks at Zo, who slaps her forehead with her palm and groans.

"Why do I have to be such a hot head..." She says into her hand. "This is all my fault."

"You *and* Val are hot heads," I say gently. "I agree that the way you told her probably wasn't great, and that you should have at least waited till we got here. But we can't change what happened. We need to move forward and see how we can fix this. We need Val back, and we need to get her away from Free. With that kind of violence in him, it's only a matter of time before he hurts her too."

Val and Rory look at each other, grave expressions on their faces.

"What should we do, Lina?" Rory asks.

"Let's give her some space for tonight. You guys know how she is. When she's angry enough, she won't listen to anything or anyone. I'll call her tomorrow and ask if I can meet her for lunch so we can talk, okay?" I put my hand on top of Zo's and give it a gentle squeeze.

"Okay," she says. "Space. That sounds good."

"Just try and get your mind off this. You go to work tomorrow. Rory, you go to class. Treat it like a normal day and I'm sure we'll have her back at the house before you know it."

Gabriel smiles kindly at my sisters. "*Hermanas,* Lina is a peacemaker," he says. "I'm sure she'll get through to Val and things will be back to normal." I see them visibly relax their shoulders. There's something so calming about the way he speaks.

When I wake up the next morning, I feel a sense of heaviness from the night before. My eyes, my heart, and my head all seem to weigh even more and I have a hard time getting out of the blankets to get ready for work. The nightmare about Val with the black eyes came back. I woke up shaking and my stomach was so upset that I couldn't get myself to fully commit to going back to sleep. After what feels like several minutes, I finally find the willpower to pull myself out of bed and shuffle over to the bathroom. Gabriel is already there shaving. He smiles broadly when he sees me. I smile back sleepily, heading to my sink.

"*Hola, mi amor.* Were you able to get any sleep?" he asks. "You were tossing and turning a lot last night." His eyes are still looking into the mirror as he shaves carefully over his chin.

"I don't think so. I'm still tired." I say with one eye open, after splashing my face with cold water. He rinses off the shaving cream, patting his face clean with a towel. He wraps his arms around me from behind, looking at me in the mirror.

"I'll have coffee ready in a couple of minutes." He kisses the top of my head, then heads out into the hallway toward the kitchen. I grab my toothbrush and continue my morning routine.

The smell of fresh coffee wafts through the air, awakening my senses. As I emerge from the hallway, Gabriel hands me a steaming cup exactly how I like it, with hemp milk and a dash of maple syrup. Warming up my hands with the cup, I take a sip and allow the coffee to lift the fog from my brain.

Watching my expression with amusement, Gabriel asks, "Does that help?"

"Ohhh, yes. The world is better again." I take another sip, then set the cup down and put my arms around him, leaning in for a kiss. "Thanks for being so good to me," I say against his lips. When I pull away, I notice lipstick on his mouth. Giggling, I wipe his lips with my thumbs.

"Sorry, Professor. I seem to have rubbed off on you this morning."

"Is it my color?" he asks, pouting his lips playfully.

Cocking my head to the side, I regard him for a moment. "Hmm. A little too fuchsia. You might need something on the rosier side. You know, to match your cheeks." His eyebrow goes up and we both laugh.

He kisses my forehead then grabs his keys from the table. I watch him, mesmerized by how well his slacks hug his muscular backside.

He notices me and then covers his buttocks with his hands. "Hey! My eyes are up here!" he says sassily, pointing to his face. The sass sounds even cuter with his Spanish accent.

"Oh. Sorry. I got a little distracted." I say with mock embarrassment.

"Thank you, Miss Luna. I would appreciate it if you refrained from that type of inappropriate behavior. My fiancée might get upset." He winks.

"Oh, I wouldn't want to upset your fiancée. I hear she has quite the temper," I say in a hushed tone, enjoying the chance to play along.

He nods seriously then leans in, saying, "She's a monster. If you make her angry, she'll imprison you in a block of ice. Then? She'll send you down the river where you'll never be found again."

"Meanie!" I say, grabbing some drops from a glass of water and throwing little icicles at his face, which he waves away. We both laugh again.

He blows me a kiss before he heads out the door. "I love you, beautiful!"

Taking another sip of my coffee, I look down at my phone. No messages from Val. I didn't expect one but I secretly wished she would reach out and say something to me. Even a scathing message is better than complete silence. I hope she'll be open to talking after having a night to calm down.

I put my phone back into my purse and walk out the door to go to work.

CHAPTER TEN

I'M DROWNING IN MY QUARTERLY expense spreadsheet when I hear a knock on my door. I've left at least three voicemails and several text messages for Val, but she still hasn't contacted me, so I took on a project that would keep me occupied. Relieved for the mental break, I say, "Come on in!"

"You've been holed up all morning and I've been waiting to hear about the concert!" Mama Joyce walks in, grabbing a rose-shaped Chehalis mint from my candy dish. I stand up, giving her a hug.

The concert. It seems like it was a lifetime ago, but it has only been a couple of days. I wish I could go back to when we were listening to Marc Anthony's angelic voice and dancing. "Sorry, Mama. I'm just working on this quarter's expenses. I wanted to get it done before lunch..." I look down at my watch and realize it's already late afternoon. I missed my lunch hour a while ago. "Uh. I guess that didn't go as planned." I fold my arms and shrug.

"Baby girl, you have months to get your sheets done. You have time. Ooh these are so good." She sits down in the chair in front of my desk, grabbing another mint.

"I know. Today I just needed a distraction." Joyce's eyebrow raises. "The girls had a huge blowout this weekend. Val actually hit Zo." She sits forward with wide eyes.

"Has she lost her damn mind? What would make her do a thing like that?" she asks, her voice etched with tough mama love.

"This guy Free has a hold on her like I've never seen before." I say, staring ahead. I explain what happened the night of the concert with Rodolfo's attack, then what we found out later about Free and his family. She pounds the table a few times at different parts of the story in disbelief and outrage.

"And now she isn't returning my calls or messages," I continue. "She seemed so hurt and angry, like we betrayed her. She didn't believe a word. She said that we don't want her to be happy..." My throat clenches up. I take a deep breath to stave off the tears. I feel the warmth of Mama Joyce's hand over mine on the desk. I keep looking down because I know if I look into those caring eyes I'm going to lose control and start crying. I hear buzzing and realize it's my cell phone vibrating on my desk. Oh! Maybe it's Val!

I grab it and see that it's Zo. Since I'm in the middle of a conversation with Joyce, I decide to answer it and ask if I can call her back.

"Zo! Hey. Are you at work?" I ask and then I hear a panicked Zo begin a long string of sentences that are so fast I can't make sense of it all. "Zo!!! Zoë Iliana Luna! Slow down, take a breath. What happened?" Mama Joyce huddles close by.

I hear breathing on the other end of the line before she starts speaking again. "Okay. Okay. I'm sorry,

Lina. I'm at the house. I had a client cancel so I came home to grab something to eat and when I walked by her room, the door was open. I thought she might be home, but her room was emptied out. Like hangers are in the closet and the bed is there, but all of her clothes, her computer, everything... Val's gone."

I sink down in my chair and cover my face with my hand. She really did leave. She took his side over ours. It just doesn't make sense.

"Lina?" Zo says, jolting me from my thoughts.

"Oh! I'm here. Sorry." I sit up straighter. "Did she leave anything? A note? A message?"

"I didn't find anything, but I didn't really look. I called you right away. Oh man, Rory is going to be so upset," she sniffles.

Next to me, Joyce grabs the phone. "Baby girl, it's Mama. We'll be right there." She hangs up and puts her hand on my shoulder.

I look up at her and shake my head. "I don't understand," I say. "This feels like a nightmare. Why won't Val talk to me?"

"Let's go find out some answers, Lina. Come on, I'm driving." On the way out, Joyce tells Sydney at the front desk that we have a family emergency and we may not be back the rest of the day.

Zo isn't in the living room when we enter the house, so we head straight for Val's room where we find Zo sitting on Val's bed. Her face is streaked with tears, her mascara partially down her cheeks in a blur of black. She croaks out a small greeting and a wave. "Hey."

Mama and I sit next to her. I interlace my fingers with hers and snuggle in next to her. "Hey."

"I did this, Lina," she says in a strained voice. "I pushed her away." Her body shakes as she starts crying, burying her head in my shoulder. Mama Joyce strokes her hair and looks at me sadly.

I wipe the tears away from Zo's cheek. "No, you didn't. Don't take the blame for this. Val made this decision all by herself."

"I don't know, Lina. She acted like a completely different person, and I feel like I'm the one who made her snap."

We hear the front door open and shut, then Gabriel's voice call out, "Hello!"

"We're back here!" I yell. He must have talked to Sydney at work and figured I was here. Within seconds, Gabriel appears in the doorway.

"I stopped by your office and Sydney said you had a family emergency. I came as fast as I could." Mama Joyce stands up and embraces him. He kisses her on the cheek, then kneels down in front of Zo and me.

"Thanks for coming, babe. I'm sorry I didn't text you. Mama and I came over as soon as I got Zo's call."

"It's okay. I know. It had to be something important for you to leave right away." He regards Zo, who's still sniffing. She gives him a sad smile. "*Hermana,* you were the lucky one who discovered this?" he asks. She nods silently. "I'm sorry. This must have been a shock for you." He bends to look at her eyes. Her mouth twists as she tries not to cry again. He hands her a pack of tissues from his pocket.

"Oh. My. God..." We look up and see Rory. Her face is ghost white. Walking in slowly, she looks at the remnants Val left behind: a closet full of hangers, drawers open and empty, bare vanity mirror. "When did this happen?" she asks quietly.

"Some time after you both left this morning," I explain. "Zo came home and found her room like this about an hour ago."

"It's so...clean," Rory says. "She didn't just take her things. It's as if she was never here. It's spotless. Did she have a team of cleaning fairies or something?" Rory looks at the vanity that once housed a wide variety of makeup palettes, tubes, and organizers. I hadn't had a chance to look around the room before now. Rory is right. Even the bed is made. She didn't leave anything behind. In general, Val isn't what you'd call tidy so it makes me wonder if she had help. With Free's financial resources, he probably had professional cleaners come in and take care of the room. It truly is as if she were never here, which makes it even more painful.

I catch Rory's reflection in the vanity mirror. Tears are silently falling down her cheeks. She peers into the open drawers, looking for clues or mementos. After several minutes, she holds up a photo. "Look," she says. It's an old photo of the four of us and our parents. I was probably five or six years old.

"I haven't seen this in a really long time..." I say, gazing at the bent, fragile photo in her hand. It looks like Christmas time. There are presents on the floor and a flocked tree in the background. My dad is so handsome, with his turquoise blue eyes and jet black hair. He always reminded me of Superman. His chiseled chin had a dimple right in the middle. I remember what it felt like to put my little finger in that dimple. Rory is about two years old in the photo. She's laughing as my dad holds her up. She's wearing a ruffled red dress; her ringlets are in pigtails. Zo is on Mom's lap, snuggling a bright pink My Little Pony. Looking at my mom's face I realize how Val is the spitting image of her when she was younger. My mom's eyes are a darker brown, but she has the same facial structure as my sister. She looks carefree and happy — not the shell of the person who left us during our teens.

I focus on Val and me in the foreground. We're on the floor with our new presents. She is proudly holding her Rainbow Bright doll, still in the box, and I'm holding up a coloring book with markers. I bet we played for hours with those presents. I wish I could go back and relive those memories because I have so few of our family like that.

I look up in the mirror and see something in black written on the other side of the photo. "What is that?" I ask Rory, reaching for the photo. I turn it around and see Val's distinctive handwriting in black marker.

LOST FOREVER

Rory, Zo and I look at each other, perplexed. "What do you think it means?" Rory asks.

"I don't know," I say. Mama Joyce and Gabriel look at the photo and inspect the back. Getting up from the bed, I look inside the drawer to see if I can find anything else. Nothing. I look under the bed, inside the closet, and on top of the drawers. Everything is clean, except for what looks like a black smudge on the bottom inch of the wall.

"Huh." I say, bending down to get a closer look. There is black residue in the crease of the wall, next to the bed. Looking around I see that the residue is in several places in the room — like a shiny soot with glimmering specks. It's different than remnants left behind from a fire. It reminds me of something I saw after my mom left and we were cleaning her room. I found shiny black soot similar to this, and broken pieces of a gem or crystal...

I shake my head. Something's gnawing at me, telling me there's more to all of this, a connection. I just don't have all the pieces yet.

"Rory? Can you take a look at this?" I ask. She puts the photo down on the bed and kneels down beside me. Gabriel, Joyce, and Zo look on curiously. I point out the spots all over the room where the black dust is. "What do you think it is?"

She narrows her eyes and peers in closer. Touching her fingertip to some of the soot, she recoils, rubbing her finger against her pants. She grimaces as she continues to wipe her finger clean. I look at her then at the wall, startled by her reaction.

"What is it, Rory?" Zo asks, also alarmed.

"I don't know, but it's awful. It's making me feel sick to my stomach, like I just touched something poisonous. But it isn't charcoal, or dirt, or anything I've ever felt before. This feels..." She stops, putting her hand on her stomach and searching for the right word. "This feels...angry. I know that doesn't make sense but that's what I feel. Like it wants to hurt me." My heart drops and I look at Gabriel. His eyes are wide. This whole situation just took a different turn.

"I think I've seen this before..." I say. Everyone turns to look at me. Rory is still trying to rub her finger clean, a look of disgust on her face. "It was after mom left. I was cleaning her room and I saw little pockets of this shiny black dust on the floor, along with broken pieces of a dark stone. Kind of like the stone Val was wearing last night…"

"Lord Jesus." Mama Joyce says quietly, looking around the room. "What in the good Father's name got ahold of our girl?"

Did something get a hold of Val besides her blind love for Free? What exactly are we dealing with?

"We should leave," Gabriel says, getting up from the bed swiftly and extending his hand for me to take. "I don't know what this stuff is and what effect it will have on all of you — especially with your sensitivities and powers. Until we figure out what it is, don't come in here." We hurry out of the room, Mama Joyce swiftly ushering us out.

We spend the next few hours inspecting the rest of the house, including our mother's old room, which has been Rory's art studio for several years. Nothing out of the ordinary. No black dust. No messages from Val. Spurred on by Rory's visceral reaction to it, we decide to get the black dust out of the house. Mama Joyce grabs a mason jar with a lid from the kitchen while Gabriel opens the door. Working quickly and methodically, Zo does a sweep of the room. Blowing air back and forth, left to right, and over her head, she collects all of the dust in a baseball sized black cloud. When every speck is removed from the walls, she lifts it over Mama Joyce's open jar, placing it inside carefully before sealing it shut. As soon as the jar is sealed, the ball loses its shape, settling into the bottom of the glass in a quarter inch of shiny black particles.

Holding the jar up, the rest of us regard it cautiously. Rory peers over our shoulders into the room. "I have some sage and crystals, I'll clear the space and get rid of the bad juju. Whatever that stuff is, I can still feel it. Gross." She runs to her room swiftly to find ingredients.

"What do we do with this?" Mama Joyce says, still holding the jar with both hands as if it were going to explode.

"I'll take it." Gabriel reaches out so she can hand it to him. "I'll bring it to the lab on campus and ask my colleague to take a look. He may be able to give us some insight."

My fingertips graze over the pale purple sterling roses alongside the rooftop garden wall. Peering over the side of the building, I see the Percival Falls skyline as it kisses the downtown horizon and nearby marina.

"I remember these were always your favorite," I hear a familiar voice say behind me. When I turn around, I see my father with a rose in his hand.

I can't believe my eyes. "Daddy? Is that you?"

He smiles, his aqua blue eyes crinkling up at the sides exactly as I remember. He opens his arms and I run to embrace him. I squeeze tight when I hug him, not wanting to let him go. In my mind, I know he's been dead and this can't be real. Even if it isn't, I have the chance to hug him one more time.

"I've missed you everyday..." I say, my head against

his chest. He strokes my hair and continues to hold me. There's just too much I want to say to him. I don't know where to start.

"*Mi hija*, I have missed you too..." I keep holding him, afraid he will disappear when I move. "I don't have much time, Lina. I have something important to tell you." When I look up at him, his face is sincere and worried. "Look," he says, pointing toward the skyline.

When I turn my head, we're in the forest. Black branches are everywhere; sharp and pointy edges cutting me as I try to clear a path. Beneath me, my feet are bare and covered in mud that feels like quicksand, pulling me down. Crying out, I look around for help and see a faint shadow starts to materialize. As it moves toward me, the shape's outline forms into a woman. The woman begins to laugh, a menacing and frightening sound. Inches from my face, the figure becomes Val. Her eyes are black and hateful.

"No! Val!" I scream, reaching out to touch her, but I keep sinking deeper as Val smiles and watches. Her hands go up in flames and she throws fire streams at the surrounding branches, igniting them.

"We're going to die! Val, please. Help me!" I scream, desperately trying to pull myself out of the mud, which is now up to my stomach. Val laughs again, then hunches down to look at me.

"Lost forever," she hisses before disintegrating into black dust. Screaming, I reach out for her and all of the ashes fly away. All of the sounds of the forest stop. I'm left kneeling on the ground.

"Lina?" My father's voice cuts through the void. I look around and see nothing but the rose stem he was holding on the ground next to me.

"Daddy?" I pick up the rose slowly, looking around for any sign of him.

"Fiona has the answers you need."

"What?" Looking at my hand, I see that the rose is gone and I'm now holding a piece of paper with a name: Fiona Zolas. Where do I know that name from?

"I don't understand. Daddy? Where are you?"

"I am always with you." I hear his voice surrounding me, like a blanket of comfort.

"Don't leave me, please don't leave again!" I cry, reaching out and feeling nothing.

"Lina! Wake up, baby. Wake up!" My eyes flutter open and I'm disoriented. Gabriel is looking down at me, his eyes wide and frightened. I'm covered in sweat and shaking, tears streaming down the sides of my cheeks. He moves my hair from my damp, sticky forehead. "Breathe, baby. Breathe. It's okay. I'm here," he coos as he strokes my hair, his touch calming me down.

As I try to slow my heartbeat and breathing, I look around the room. It's dark except for our night light illuminating Gabriel's face. I grab his hands. They are real. They don't disintegrate. I sit up quickly, wanting to feel his warmth. Throwing my arms around his neck I bury my face into his shoulder. I don't want to let him go. I just want to feel safe again, and forget what I saw.

My stomach starts doing flip flops. Tasting saltiness in my mouth, I get up and run to the bathroom just in time to throw up. While I heave into the toilet, I feel his gentle touch as he holds my hair back. At some point Gabriel puts a cold wet washcloth on my neck to help keep my nausea at bay. When I finally stop vomiting, I lean back against him and he wraps his arms around me. Holding on to him, I wonder why I've been getting sick from these nightmares. I don't usually have such a sensitive stomach.

Snuggling up against him, I say sleepily, "Can you take my nightmares away?"

He tucks a stray hair behind my ear. He murmurs, "*Mi amor,* if I could, I would take every bad dream away. That is what I wish my special power could be. I'll tell you what. Bring me into your dream and I'll fight off whatever it is that's hurting you, okay?" His words make me smile and I turn around to hug him.

"I'm so tired...but I'm afraid," I say as a tear runs down my left cheek.

"I know, *mi vida.* I know. Let's go to bed. Just remember that this time, I'll be in your dreams too so you don't have to be alone." He gets up, pulling me to my feet. We walk over to the bed together and he lays me down, pulling the comforter over me. He disappears for a minute, then comes back with some water. Propping me up, he says, "Here. Drink." The water feels restorative, strengthening me. He lays me back down, putting the glass on the nightstand.

Snuggling in, he puts his arms around me and I lean up against his chest. "Remember what I said. Bring me into your dream and we'll fight it together," he whispers. I smile then close my eyes.

Before I doze off, I hear Gabriel humming "*Sana, Sana,*" a comforting Latin lullaby I remember my mom sing whenever we were hurt as children. I bury my head in the crook of his arm, falling asleep within minutes.

When I wake up the next morning, Gabriel's still holding me. I peek at the alarm clock and decide to let him sleep a few minutes longer. He looks so serene.

Carefully, I lift his muscular arm so I can sneak out of bed. He moans and hugs the pillow, which is too adorable. Even in his sleep, he's trying to protect me.

After going into the kitchen to start a pot of coffee, I spot the jar of black dust and pick it up to examine it. Rory's words echo in my head: it felt angry — as if it wanted to hurt her.

"Good morning, beautiful." Gabriel is leaning against the wall near the hallway, watching me. His voice startles me and I jump. "Sorry. I didn't mean to scare you," he says with a chuckle. His curly black hair is tousled and he is barefoot, wearing only his pajama bottoms which hang down around his hips exposing every inch of his abdominal muscles. Even freshly awake, he is so handsome that my knees feel weak.

I clear my throat, regaining my composure. "It's okay. I was just in my head for a minute. Looking at this mysterious stuff," I say, putting the jar back down on the counter. He walks toward me and holds his hands out to pull me in for an embrace. I lay my head against his bare chest, feeling his strong heartbeat bumping against my ear.

"Are you feeling better?" he asks, his deep voice vibrating against my ear.

I nod and squeeze him a little tighter. "Yes, I got a few hours of sleep thanks to my protective ninja warrior." I look up and smile at him. He leans in and kisses my lips.

"Thanks for making coffee," he says and kisses me again.

"It's the least I can do. It probably isn't as good as yours, but I think it's drinkable." I say, backing out of his arms so I can pour him a cup. He laughs and goes to the refrigerator to get the hemp milk out for me.

We both stare at the jar over our coffees. I think about what my father said in my dream last night. What was that name again? Fiona Zolas. He said she'd give me answers. My dreams have been so vivid and prophetic lately that I wonder if it could truly be a message from him.

Watching me lost in thought, Gabriel cocks his head. "Want to talk about it?"

"Hmm? Oh, I'm just remembering something that happened in my dream." I say. "You know how I've been having nightmares about Val? I had another one last night, but in this one I actually saw my father. He said he needed to give me a message."

Gabriel sets his mug down on the table, listening intently. "Your dad? I couldn't imagine what that must have been like for you. Was he the way you remembered him?"

I nod. "Exactly. It felt like he was with me again." I start tearing up at the memory of hugging him and I close my eyes. I don't want to forget him.

Then I remember the piece of paper he showed me. "He gave me a name and told me this person is supposed to help me. Fiona Zolas." I say.

He retrieves my laptop from across the table, opens it and starts typing. He finds a website for Fiona Zolas, Psychic, in Centralia. I recognize her immediately when he shows me, even though I was very young the last time I saw her. Fifi! Zo found her picture the other day out of the blue and we talked about her. My mom used to say that she *knew* things, but I didn't know what that meant. I didn't know she was a psychic, or that she was still around.

"Gabriel...I knew her!" I exclaim. "We all did. She was my mom's closest friend. She came to my house all the time when we were kids. We used to call her Fifi..." Memories start flooding back: her contagious laugh, her broad smile, the baked goods she would bring. That message had to be from my dad.

"That's incredible, Lina," Gabriel says. "She has to be important if your father told you to see her." His eyes are hopeful as he lays his hand on mine.

"I know. She's only about 20 minutes away. I'll call and see if I can make an appointment with her today. Maybe I can see her on my lunch break. I'll take the container with the black powder and see what she can tell me."

CHAPTER ELEVEN

WHEN I GOT TO THE office and told Mama Joyce what I planned to do, she practically pushed me out the door and told me to take all the time I needed. I didn't have time to call Fiona to make an appointment, I just headed to the interstate.

About 10 minutes into the drive I glance over at the glass jar of dust in the passenger seat. I hope she can give me insight into what is happening with Val. My GPS directs me to a turquoise and white cottage with a wooden sign on the porch that reads:

FIONA G. ZOLAS | PSYCHIC MEDIUM
APPOINTMENTS AVAILABLE

I park out front, open my purse, and shove the jar inside. Walking up the steps to her door, a lazy gray and white calico opens one eye in greeting from its bed near the door. It apparently doesn't see me as a threat and closes its eye to resume sleeping. "Hi kitty, kitty," I say gently while reaching for the metal door knocker. It may look docile but I don't want to take any chances.

I've been attacked by my share of seemingly cute cats that suddenly turned into ferocious beasts.

"Come in!" A throaty female voice calls from inside. I turn the knob and push the heavy wooden door open, which creaks from the movement. The smell of freshly baked cookies hits my nostrils, reawakening childhood memories. When I peer in, I see a warm, inviting waiting room. The carpet is a cream and blue ornamental. There's a navy couch and loveseat, and a small table with a ceramic midnight blue lamp. I'm surprised this place isn't a bed and breakfast. The surroundings are cozy and homey, as if you will be taken care of the minute you walk inside.

"Have a seat, I'll be right with you," the voice calls out from somewhere else.

"Ms. Zolas, my name is Lina. I don't have an appointment but I was hoping I could talk to you. I'm happy to wait if this is a bad time." I walk further into the room, looking at the artwork on the wall — abstract mixtures of blues, greens, and purples. I hear footsteps and I turn around. Fiona's hair is silver now and she has gotten a little curvier, but she's still the woman I remember. Our Fifi. Same dark blue eyes, same high cheekbones, same expressive eyebrows. She's holding a tray of cookies in front of her and smiling as if she knew I were coming.

"Oh my Goddess. So, it's *you*! You grew into a brilliantly beautiful woman, didn't you?" she exclaims, looking me over. "Here dear, take a cookie. Just made them fresh. They're my special chocolate hazelnut recipe." She motions for me to sit down, and puts the tray on the table in front of me.

Stunned, I just stare at her.

"I know, it's always a bit of a shock to hear you were expected, but please, try to relax." As I sit carefully down on the couch, she claims the chair closest to it.

"I'm...I'm sorry...but you knew I was coming?" I say in a squeaky high-pitched voice. I wonder if she can read my mind, too. I make a mental note not to think about Gabriel in a way that would make him blush if he were to meet her.

"Well, I was told that I would be visited by someone special from the past — so my sources weren't *that* specific. But I am glad it's you. I miss my sweet Luna girls. I never forgot about your family. You girls used to call me Fifi, which I always adored. I've been waiting for you for a long time." She leans forward, patting my knee as if the gesture was the most natural thing in the world.

So many questions flood my mind. I lean back in the couch and put my hands to my sides to steady myself. Fiona regards me and folds her hands in front of her. "You came here because you were seeking answers."

I nod, nervously playing with my engagement ring. Part of me is relieved that she says she can help me. Another part of me is afraid of what I'll find out.

"Yes. I came to ask you some questions and I hope you can help. My sister is in trouble." I reach into my purse and pull out the jar. I almost drop it when I hear a shrill sound come from down the hall.

Laughing, she holds her hand up. "Hold that thought. My kettle is telling me our hot water is ready for tea. Follow me inside, Lina. Bring the jar." She walks down the hall with quick steps as I follow. The hallway leads to a bright white kitchen where the whistling kettle is furiously blowing steam. Fiona takes the kettle off the burner and moves it to another side of the stove. She grabs two multi-colored ceramic mugs from an overhead cabinet and sets them on the white tile countertop.

"Black tea or herbal? I have a drawer full of flavors so whatever you are craving, I'm sure I'll have it." She turns around and looks at me, pointing to the drawer at her side.

"Black tea is just fine," I say. "Thank you." She opens the drawer, which does indeed hold an impressive collection of teas. She pulls out two sachets for the mugs, then pours the steaming water over them.

"How about we sit here in the breakfast nook? I like the dazzling energy on this side of the kitchen today." She motions to a sitting area surrounded by windows, overlooking a lush garden in the backyard. A weeping willow has several colorful glass ornaments hanging from the limbs.

"You've grown into such a beautiful young woman. By the looks of it, you're going to get married. Who's the lucky fella?" she asks.

Looking down at my ring with a smile, I say, "His name is Gabriel. And I feel like the lucky one. He's perfect in every way."

She tilts her head and smiles. "I'm picking up on some intensely adoring vibes from the man who gave you this ring. He thinks he's the luckiest man on earth. He's willing to do anything for you, including anything it takes to protect you and your sisters."

"Thank you for saying that," I say. "I feel the same about him. I'd protect him with my life." I look over at the glass jar then put it on the table in front of us. "Fiona, is there anything you can tell me about the substance that's in this jar? I think it has something to do with my sister, Val."

Fiona slides it closer so she can see it. A look of disdain clouds her face. She takes a big sip from her mug, still looking at the jar. Under her breath, she says, "Still trying to take what you can't have, aren't you? Persistent bastard."

My spoon clunks loudly against my mug as it drops from my hand. I look at the jar, then at her. "You know what this is?" She nods, then takes another drink.

"What you have in that glass is a shadow left behind by something dark and sinister. And honey, you were right about your sister being in trouble. But it's even worse than you know."

My heart starts beating faster. The mood just turned deadly serious. I can feel in my bones that what she's saying is true. Without intending to, my hand freezes the contents of my mug and it begins to form tiny icicles on the outside. Fiona smiles and reaches her hand out to touch mine. I look down, alarmed that I allowed myself to be so careless about using my power in front of her.

"It's okay, dear. I know all about your abilities. And so does he. That's why he wants all of you so much. Just take a deep breath. I need you to get through what I'm about to tell you without turning my kitchen into an igloo." Slightly embarrassed, I take a few breaths to calm myself down.

"You've seen this before, haven't you?" she asks, motioning to the jar.

"I think so," I say quietly. "It was a long time ago, in my mother's room — a few weeks after she left. I was cleaning the floors and found the same black dust and some broken pieces of a gem or stone."

"That was him. He got ahold of your mother." I can feel the blood drain from my face.

She folds her hands in front of her, staring intently into my eyes. "This thing is a demon. An ancient, evil succubus that feeds off of souls. He targets the ones that have been broken by a recent trauma or event. In your mom's case, he felt her pain after your father died. Her devastation called to him, like meat to a hungry wolf. He's always slithering beneath the surface of our world, watching. That dust is what he leaves behind when he crawls in from the walls. Watching you sleep, listening to your thoughts and dreams."

As she talks, I think back to the weeks after we got the news of our father's death. My heart felt like a shell. Everyone and everything around me collapsed. I would sob when I was alone in the shower with the music turned up so no one could hear me. I never wanted to let on that I was broken too, so I put on a brave face for my family. My mom could barely get out of bed when she came home from work. She stayed in her room with the blinds closed. She didn't eat. She barely talked. So I took on the role of caretaker. I made sure the girls and I got to school on time, and kept the house clean. I did whatever I could to take any additional stress away from my mom.

Now that I understand what that kind of love is like, the full weight of her loss hits me. I don't want to imagine what my life would be without Gabriel. Tears burn my eyes as I am flooded with empathy for my mom, losing her other half while trying to find the strength to go on and take care of four girls and a home.

Fiona's eyes are full of tears, too. "You may not remember this, but your mother and I were very close," she says. "Sylvia was my best friend. When you have a gift like mine, it's lonely and scary. There aren't many others on this planet that understand what that feels like. She used to be haunted by her abilities too, so we connected instantly."

I look at her, not quite understanding. My mom didn't have special abilities, did she? She was scared about anyone finding out about what my sisters and I could do. I always felt she was ashamed of us.

Seeing my confusion, Fiona smiles sadly and continues. "Yes, she also had a gift. It terrified her. She struggled with it since she was a little girl. She had premonitions, which to her, came in the form of vivid nightmares. After waking up screaming so many times, she finally told her mother about the dreams. Since your grandmother was a very religious woman, she told your mom to pray for God to take the visions away — that her dreams were nothing more than dreams.

"But when her dreams starting coming true, your grandmother was convinced your mother's gift was unholy and that she needed divine help," Fiona continues. "Afraid that she caused these things to happen, your mom believed her. They went to her church and tried several 'therapies' to get her to stop having visions. Lina, these therapies used tactics that were brutalizing and inhumane. She almost died."

"Sylvia came up with a plan to run away. She reached out to the only family she trusted, an aunt who lived in Oregon. Sylvia hadn't seen since her she was a child, because the family disowned her for loving another woman."

My mother rarely talked about my grandmother or her childhood. Now I understand why — and why she was so afraid about people learning about our powers.

"By the time Sylvia was eighteen, she'd saved enough money to buy a bus ticket from Texas to Oregon. Since she was of age, and her family expected her to leave the house, they never came looking for her. She reinvented herself, left her past behind. Her aunt and her aunt's partner ran a small café where Sylvia worked. Those two women helped make up for the trauma your mother grew up with and she blossomed. They helped her enroll in nursing school, and she eventually met and fell in love with your father."

I have a vague memory of a backyard swing and laughing with two older women. They were the only family we had on my mother's side: *Tías* Blanca and Rosie. Even though Rosie wasn't her aunt by blood (or even Mexican), Mom still called Rosie *tía* out of respect. When I was about three, Blanca died from cancer; Rosie died of cancer too, less than a year later. Every fall for *Dia de Los Muertos*, Mom had photos of Blanca and Rosie on our altar, along with two plates of chicken tamales and Modelo beers.

Fiona sips her tea and continues. "It'd been a long time since she had one of her dreams, but one night, shortly after your father got his last assignment, your mother dreamed about his death. She wanted to ignore it, but she knew better. She pleaded with him not to go but she couldn't tell him why. He was such a responsible, committed man, your father. He was proud to serve his country and took his role as a soldier seriously. He told her he was going to be just fine, that he'd be back before she knew it. I told her she couldn't have stopped him, but she never believed that. She blamed herself.

"The demon grabbed hold of that guilt and that heartbreak. He twisted it and used it, convincing her that your father never really died and that he could reunite them. There was a token. A ring. The demon told her that all she had to do was put it on and he'd bring your father back. The ring is the last step before he takes over. When the wearer puts it on, he crawls inside and alters your sense of reality. People who love you suddenly become your enemy. Things that once brought you joy now repulse you. He takes away all the things that make you yourself."

"Oh my God..." I cover my mouth and rise from the table, walking to the window. I look out at the serene, beautiful garden; a stark contrast to my inner turmoil.

"Val...wasn't herself when we saw her the other day," I say after a few seconds. "She acted like we were all her enemies. And then she hit Zo. Are you saying this same thing happened to my mom?"

She nods somberly. "Yes, dear. This is the same thing."

I shake my head, trying to make sense of it all. "How did you find all of this out? Mama left suddenly. Did she come and see you and tell you all of this?"

Fiona gets up, heading to the cupboard to get another mug for tea to replace the one I froze. Dipping the black tea bag in and out of the steaming water, she gets a faraway look in her eye. "I hadn't seen or heard from Sylvia for a little over a week. After the funeral, I checked in on her every couple of days. I'd stop by or call. After a while, she stopped taking my calls, stopped answering the door. I went to the hospital where she worked; they told me she'd quit. I finally decided to come during an evening when you girls were there. Do you remember that night?" She walks over and hands me the mug.

"Yes, I remember you coming over and bringing cookies," I say. I think back to a weeknight when I was making dinner. Val answered the door and let Fiona in. The girls were excited about the cookies. Fiona asked to see my mom. I don't remember exactly what happened, but I remember her leaving in a hurry. She looked upset.

"Yes, I brought you girls some chocolate macadamia nut cookies. Little Zoë used to ask for them all the time. When I went in to talk to your mom, she wasn't herself. She was laying in bed and staring at the wall. Her voice was cold when she asked me why I was there, said she'd made it clear she didn't want to see me. At first I thought it was her depression. I told her I was there for her and that I loved her. That made her even angrier. She looked at me with so much hatred, it startled me. She lashed out, yelling at me to leave her alone and never come back. Then she got up from the bed and pushed me out the door with such force... I almost fell. I wish I'd known then what was going on. But at the time it stung. I thought somehow that I'd hurt my friend and lost her friendship.

"I could barely sleep that night. I was wracking my brain trying to figure out how I'd hurt Sylvia, and wondering what I could do to fix it. It was about midnight when I got a visit. From your father."

I think back to the dream I had of him last night.

A lump burns in my throat and clenches my vocal chords. "My...father?"

"He was standing next to my bed, just as plain as you're standing here. He looked so worried. He reached out his hands. When I held them, he showed me how the demon made his way into your mother's life. Before he let go, I saw a glimpse of the demon using your mother's body. I wish I could erase it from my memory. Evil incarnate. Black tar seeping out of her eyes and mouth."

I gasp, holding my ribs a little tighter. "That's the same vision I had of Val."

"Then he told me the worst part," Fiona continues. "The victim will kill everyone they truly love, to destroy the pieces of their heart belonging to their loved ones. With each kill, their soul blackens and becomes his. He said I had to destroy the ring to save you all."

My blood runs cold. Death. Kill. Not words I want to hear when all I wanted to do today was figure out how to save my sister. I suddenly realize I'm holding my breath. Inhaling and swallowing hard, I ask, "What happened to her, Fiona? I found the broken pieces of the stone, so did something go wrong?"

She puts her head in her hands for a moment, then looks up, wiping tears from her eyes. "I really thought I had fixed it. I went to the house during the day, when you girls were at school. I used the spare key and came into her room, armed with a hammer to break the ring. I found her sleeping. I tried to get the ring off her finger. When she woke up... she was so vicious. She fought and fought, but I managed to take it off. She started crying and hugging me, telling me she was trapped inside her body and she was afraid she'd never get out. I had the ring in my hand and I told her we had to destroy it. And we did. We smashed it to pieces. We believed it was over."

"What happened?" I ask.

Fiona furrows her brow and shakes her head. "When I left that morning, she was in good spirits and determined to make a better life for all of you. She felt like she had a second chance. But that night, a little after 1 am, I got a phone call from her.

"She said she had a dream — a premonition. It was very clear. We hadn't stopped him and eventually, she was going to kill all of you girls. Even though we took away the ring, somehow the demon still had ahold of your mom. She was on my doorstep soon after. I'll never forget the look on Sylvia's face — a sad look of resolve. Sometime between the phone call and her drive over, she'd made up her mind. She said the only way to make it stop was for her to die before she could hurt any of you."

"Oh...no...oh my God. Are you saying she killed herself?" I ask, my hands over my mouth. This can't be happening right now.

"I wouldn't let her," Fiona replies. "I told her there had to be another way. I begged her to allow me to reach out to the other side for answers. So that's what we did. I went into a trance and asked for guidance on a way to protect you girls and not let my friend die. Your great, great, great aunt Melina came forward with the answer.

"She was one of the first in your bloodline to have an otherworldly gift. She was a witch in her time. Besides her control of all of the elements she practiced ancient spells, ones that have long since been forgotten. Melina knew more about the demon than we did. She said it wanted you girls because of your powers and even though he only left a trace inside your mother's finger, his resolve to possess all of you was so powerful that he was fighting his way back with a vengeance. The only way everyone was to survive was for Sylvia to break her connection with you girls. She would have to leave you…and forget you."

My mom didn't want to leave us. She had to.

"It wasn't the answer we wanted, but your mother was willing to do whatever it took to keep you safe," Fiona continues with a sigh. "That was almost more heartbreaking than dying: to know she wouldn't be able to watch all of you grow into the women you were meant to be. But she didn't hesitate. She asked Melina to show us what to do.

"As a medium, I can be a physical conduit and allow spirits to take over my body. Melina used my body to work a spell. She created a potion that would wipe your mother's memories and break her ties to everyone she loved, so the demon couldn't get to you. When your mother was far enough away from you girls, she'd have to drink it. The spell would remain as long as you girls were safe.

"After it was done, your mother and I said our goodbyes. I think I cried more that night than I ever have in my life. Her plan was to make preparations for you girls. When you left for school she would leave, taking only cash for the bus, the potion, and the clothes on her back. I wasn't allowed to know where she was going to ensure all ties were severed."

"I think I'm going to be sick." I say, holding my stomach and running over to the sink. Angry bubbles burn inside my belly. I turn on the faucet, pouring it over my cupped hands and gulping to keep the bubbles at bay. The water's effect is quick; I feel restored within minutes.

"Are you okay, hon?" Fiona is behind me, her warm hand patting my back. "I know. It's so much to take in. I feel like I've been talking for an hour and we haven't even brought out the tarot cards." I have my hands on either side of the sink, taking steadying breaths. When I start feeling normal again, I stand up straighter and turn to look at Fiona's concerned face.

"I'm okay. I just needed some water." I say. Looking over Fiona's shoulder, I spot a framed photo on the wall I hadn't noticed before. It's a picture of Fiona and my mother. I walk toward it to get a closer look. "I've never seen that photo." My mom's arm is around Fiona's neck and her head is thrown back in laughter. The background looks like our house. They're sitting on our living room couch with the front window behind them.

Fiona takes the photo off the wall for a closer look. She smiles, then passes it to me. "Your father took that photo of us," she says. "I don't remember what we were laughing about. I just remember we used to laugh like that all the time. She had a great belly laugh. God, I wish we hadn't lost her that day, and that you girls would've grown up with a mother. It's my biggest regret in my life. Melina assured your mom and I that you girls would be okay. There was already someone in your life who was ready to care for all of you."

Mama Joyce. They knew she was going to be there for us. Mama Joyce didn't know it then, but even she was part of this greater plan to keep the Luna girls safe from harm.

It's hard to remember my mother being as happy as she looks in the picture, or what her laughter sounded like. Deep down I think those memories are still there somewhere. I hand the frame back to Fiona.

"Fiona? Do you think she...died?"

She shakes her head vehemently. "No. Absolutely not. I have spies on the other side, you know. She is hard to keep track of. I can't tell exactly where she is, but I know she's alive."

I try to imagine what my mother's life was like after she left, no longer knowing who she was. She made the biggest sacrifice that a mother could make that day, and I'll never get the chance to thank her and tell her I forgive her. Now I need to make sure the same thing doesn't happen to my sister.

It's all starting to make sense. The ring that I spotted on Val's hand must've been the demon's ring, which means he already has a hold on her.

I take Fiona's hand. "Thank you for all of this," I tell her. " You've given me so many answers today that I didn't have before. If I had time, I'd stay longer." Her eyes twinkle as she places her hand on top of mine.

A faint buzzing catches my attention. Looking over to the table, I see a light flashing from my phone inside my purse. I have a few text messages: one from Gabriel, one from Rory, and one from Val.

Val! Skipping over the others, I quickly open her message. My heart stops.

"LINA, CAN YOU COME GET ME? FREE HURT

ME AND I LEFT. I AM HIDING AT THE WATER-
FALL."

"It's Val. She said she's hurt!" I show the message to Fiona, who puts her glasses on and holds the phone closer to her. She looks up at me gravely.

"Lina, did you say she already has the ring?"

"Yes, she was wearing it the last time I saw her..."

"It took weeks for the demon to take over your mother, but with the powers you girls have, I can't predict how quickly it will happen. This could be a trap."

"Even if it is, I have to go. My sister needs me. I know I can get through to her." I grab my purse and start fishing out my keys, walking into the hallway with Fiona close behind.

"Lina, wait." She grabs my arm, halting me midstep. She searches inside an apothecary cabinet, finally pulling out a small cobalt blue bottle with a dark liquid inside. She blows off some dust then rubs it against her shirt sleeve before handing it to me.

"This is the last of the forgetting spell that Melina made. I know how powerful you are, and I know you'll do everything you can to save Val. But if the demon is too strong, this is your final defense to save your sister and the rest of your family." She puts the bottle in my hand and closes my fingers around it. Looking down at the bottle, I consider the possibility of telling my sister to forget us. I hope to God it doesn't come to that. I don't know if I'll have the strength.

I hug Fiona tightly. "Thank you," I say as I hold her close. "For everything. I'll be back after all of this. Not just to hear more about what happened with my mom, but because you're part of our family. We've lost way too much time."

She puts her hand over her heart, then kisses my forehead. "Nothing would make me happier than to be in your lives again. Bless you, sweet child — and be careful. I'll be sending protective light your way."

As I head outside, the sun is starting to set. I'm noticing the pinks and oranges coloring the sky but instead of my usual admiration, all I feel is a chill that goes straight to my bones. I have to succeed where Mama and Fiona failed.

CHAPTER TWELVE

B EFORE I START THE CAR, I text Val to let her know I'm on my way. I get an immediate response back:

"PLEASE HURRY."

With that, I rush to the freeway without a moment to spare. I didn't get a chance to read the messages from Gabriel or Rory. I'll have to ask forgiveness later. I'm sure they'll understand. I am focused on my singular mission: Save Val. Everything inside of me is telling me I can help her. If I can get close enough, I'll take the ring and completely extract the demon's essence from her body. When Fiona tried to save my mom, I think this is the piece that was missing. It was me — or more accurately, my abilities.

While I'm driving, I start mentally preparing for the state I'm going to find Val in. She could be injured just as badly as Rodolfo was. She must be scared. My mind is so preoccupied that I almost miss my exit and have to turn at the last second to get off. I hear a barrage of furious honking behind me. Sorry, guy. I have more important stuff to deal with than you right now.

My heart catches in my throat as I approach my

destination. This place brings back memories. The waterfall isn't really a waterfall at all. It's a large clearing in the middle of the forest close to our childhood home. It looks like it could've once been a waterfall, but it dried up years ago. There's a little creek nearby and several willowy trees that made my sisters and I feel as if we were in a magical fairy land when we played there together as kids. It was a hidden spot we discovered via a long pathway behind our house. My sisters and I would come out here to cry and scream, to dream of better lives, and to test out our powers. It was our secret hideaway. Our safe place. It makes sense to me that Val would run out here to escape from Free.

The pathway to the waterfall is accessible only by foot, so I park at a dead end next to a fence leading to the forest. Free's car is here. Did Val take it to get away from him, or did he follow her here?

There's a fence that wasn't here before; I suspect wayward teens are the culprits. They probably caused the housing association to make the pathway off limits. The opening is covered by overgrown bushes and weeds. When I walk up, I see charred black leaves off to the side. A fresh streak of bloody fingerprints paints the top of one of the metal pillars. Val!

I frantically move the leaves out of my way and head toward the waterfall, led only by my rusty memory. The pathway is overgrown and invisible to an outsider trying to use it. The trees begin curving into themselves in twisted shapes. I hear the soft babbling of the creek. I know by that sound that I'm going in the right direction, even if everything looks different. Sure enough, I see the creek appear. It looks so much smaller now. As

I follow it down, I hear what sounds like a male voice. Like Free. My blood freezes. He's here.

I start running. I'm not going to let him hurt my sister. Trees are lining the pathway, making it difficult to see ahead of me, but soon the waterfall clearing emerges.

I rub my eyes to make sure I'm not hallucinating. I see a set of bloody hands tied behind a tree with rope. Dear God! What did he do to her?

"Val! I'm here, sweetheart. I'm here!" I scream, rushing to the front of the tree.

But it isn't Val.

It's Free.

"Jesus." I whisper in shock and step back, horrified. He's slumped over with his arms tied behind him, his legs bent at odd, unnatural angles. His face is barely recognizable with all of the bloody wounds and bruises. His shirt looks like it's been burned; black welts cover a large portion of his chest.

"Please. Please. Make it stop. I'm sorry. I'm so sorry," he mumbles to no one in particular. He looks disoriented, delirious.

"Free. Hey. It's Lina," I say, lightly slapping his cheek to get his attention. "What happened to you? Where's Val?"

One of his eyes opens at the sound of my voice. He strains to lift his head, breathing hard through trembling lips. "Lina... Make her stop. Tell her I didn't mean it." His voice trails off and he starts sobbing. "She's crazy. She's going to kill me."

"What do you mean, Free?" I ask incredulously, looking over his injuries. "*Val did this to you?*" My sister has a temper but I could never imagine her inflicting this kind of violence on anyone.

"Thanks for coming, sis. You're right on time."

Val's voice startles me, piercing through the air like a gust of wind. She sounds cold, devoid of her usual warmth and spunk. I see movement from between the trees. A dark silhouette emerges from the shadows, making its way toward me and Free. He starts squirming and weeping.

"Val? What happened? You said you were hurt...?"

Val moves in closer and I see the face from my nightmares. Her eyes are black, her lips curled into a snarl.

I swallow my fear and ground my feet, desperate for some type of stability. Voice quivering, I proclaim, "I know what you are, and you can't have her. I won't let you." My fists close, attempting to hide my shaking fingers.

Val's eyebrow cocks up. Her hands tent in front of her, the dark ring glistening.

"Oh, but I already do have her," I hear her say, in a voice so low and scary that it makes my knees buckle. "She is the most delicious soul I have ever tasted. So potent. I almost feel at home with these powers."

She opens her hands to reveal a dark red fireball, flickering angrily. She passes it between her hands. Free cowers and cries as she does, trying in vain to undo the knotted rope his hands are in.

"Nooo! Nooo! No more fire!" He sobs. Without thinking, I position myself between Val and Free.

"That's enough," I say. "Stop using my sister's body to do your dirty work, you sick bastard." Val smiles again, holding up the ball of fire with her right hand.

"You might not feel so protective of him after you learned what he did. After all, if it weren't for him, I would've never found Val."

"Wh-What do you mean?" I stammer, then look at Free's mutilated face.

Val sneers. "Such a typical weakling... taking out his insecurities on your sister. Oh, he started out nice and sweet. Showered her with gifts and flowers, made her feel so special," she says in a sing-song voice, rolling her eyes, revealing a sliver of white beneath them.

"But his dark side reared its head," Val continues. "One minute so affectionate, the next a monster. The reason why he loved her fiery spirit is because he wanted to break her and possess her. He believed she was his property. The minute she did something he thought was disrespectful, he punished her. The first time was a hard slap across the face." She reaches up to touch her cheek, eyes focused on Free.

"And of course, Val left him... at first. But he knew how to win her back. And then it would happen again. I could feel her pain, taste her isolation. Such delectable despair that called to me. She was so deeply ashamed, she refused to let any of you know what was happening. What was it you always said to her? Ah, that she was the strongest of you all. And yet, here she was, running back to a man who beat her. That ugly secret started a magnificent hole of anguish, one that just grew and grew."

My eyes sting with emerging tears. Anger and guilt sear through my body.

I am partially to blame for this. If I hadn't put that expectation of strength on her shoulders... If I'd been there for her... If I'd been more insistent about checking in and telling her my concerns about Free... none of this would've happened.

I failed in protecting my sister.

"I used to visit Val in her dreams," she goes on. "I told her I was an angel and that I felt her pain. I gained her trust and she confided in me. She told me how much she loved Free, about the pain he caused her, and about her fear of disappointing you, Lina. Her oldest sister who believed in her so much."

The words hit me like a ton of bricks, reinforcing my shame. My lips tremble and remorseful tears make their way down my cheeks.

"I knew that when the time was right, Val would accept my offer to relieve her from her pain. And Free? His soul is weak and corrupt. He's so easy to manipulate, I didn't even need to enter his body. I just whispered into his ears at night then put the ring in his path. The trip was his opportunity to give it to her along with an empty promise to change. When she put this ring on her finger, that was all I needed.

"And after that? Well, things played out just beautifully on their own. She pushed all of you away and isolated herself further. Then Free here did something that sped up my arrival even more..."

Val dissipates the fireball, moves her face to the side and opens up the collar of her shirt. I cover my mouth in shock. The far right side of her face is deep purple and her neck is covered in bright red choke marks.

"Oh...Val..." I cry out. "I'm so, so sorry."

Val scoffs and keeps going. "She overheard a conversation she wasn't meant to hear between Free and his little brother," she says. "It confirmed everything you told her, everything you'd accused him of doing. When she confronted him, he became enraged. He beat her and choked her. Almost to the point of death. Before she lost consciousness she saw me standing over her body. When I asked her if she wanted me to make it stop, she was ready. Really, you should thank me for saving her.

"And the revenge? It was very, very sweet. I savored every blow I gave him after all of the pain he put her through. I made him sorry he ever laid a hand on her." Free is still crying and shaking his head back and forth.

"I was wrong, alright?" he pleads. "I was wrong. Please don't kill me. I'll do anything you want. *Please... please...*"

Before I can block her, Val moves around me to Free's side. Pointing a finger at his collar, her fingertip transforms into a sharp, black point. She drags it over him, leaving a thin trail of blood from her touch. He sucks in air through his teeth in pain, then moans weakly.

She leans down close to his ear and cradles his head with her other hand. "Kill you?" she hisses. "Oh no. You're not going to die, Jeffrey Simon. You made all of this possible. I'm going to give you a front row seat to enjoy the fruits of your labor. You will live out your eternity as my slave, dear boy." She smiles again, bringing the fireball back and holding it steady in her right hand while he cowers.

I begin stepping back with my hand behind me, drawing energy from the creek. "I've heard about you," I say. "You're going to get rid of all the people that Val loves — that is your M.O., isn't it? Maybe you don't understand something. You picked the wrong family to mess with."

Val smiles, then cocks her head toward the fireball. "A fight, eh? Well that sounds like a lot of fun. Let's see what you got." She flings the fireball at me. I bring the water into my hand, shaping it into a sheet of ice in front of me to block the fire, then dissipate it to stand ready for her next attack.

She gives me a slow patronizing clap then says, "Bravo. The Luna sisters are such sublime creatures. I have grand plans for your souls and your powers. Yield to me, child. Join me and I will no longer fight you. I can make your wildest dreams come true." She puts her hands down, palms up, walking toward me.

I hold both hands out in front of me. With a large swoop, I create a lasso of water and throw it around her, pinning her arms to her sides. "Not in a million years, bitch," I say.

She struggles momentarily but laughs and easily shakes loose before her entire body becomes engulfed in flames. I watch, awestruck. Val's power never manifested that way.

"That is so cute," she says with a smirk. "Foolish, but cute. You think you *actually* have a chance fighting against me. You can't win, child. Make it easy on yourself and your sisters. Don't you want to be with Val? How about riches to build a lavish life with that handsome man of yours? Or perhaps you want to be invincible? Powerful? I can make it happen for you. Just say yes." She advances toward me smiling as I back away, moving closer to the creek and a nearby cluster of drooping trees.

"Run, Lina! Get out of here!" Free yells. Looking at

me with his one good eye, he nods his head in the opposite direction to show me which way to go.

In a split second, Val shoves me forcefully and I smash my head against the tree behind me. Pinning me against it with her hands on my shoulders, Val towers over me, looking bigger and intimidating.

With her face inches from mine, she whispers, "Last chance. Yield to me. Let me in so I can enjoy those sumptuous powers of yours. Just. Let. Me. In." The demon's voice is hypnotic. My mind starts feeling cloudy and confused. I shake my head.

Holding up my hand, I stroke the bruises on her cheek. Concentrating on the pool of blood vessels beneath the surface, my hand glows bright blue as I begin to heal her.

"Val..." I look into her black eyes. "I love you, Val. I know you're in there. Do you hear me? I love you and I'm not giving up on you. Come back to me."

For a moment, I see Val's expression soften. A look of uncertainty flits across her face. But then her lips curl inward and she steps back, igniting her hands into flames.

"Wrong answer," she snarls, grabbing for my hand. I ball up my fist and hit her hard with a stream of ice, encasing her. She growls as her flames rise higher, exploding the ice into pieces.

I run back and jump into the creek, gaining the full strength of the water. As soon as my feet feel the water through my shoes, I can feel its power coursing through me. Breathing deep into my belly, I become one with the energy, feeling it penetrate my bones and muscles. Raising both arms, I grab cascades from either side of me and begin shooting Val with jets. She maneuvers around them, throwing fireballs at me. I absorb the blows with waterfalls in front of me, then start launching ice spears toward her. She dodges all of them, moving unnaturally as she runs toward me at full speed.

Tackling me, we both fall to the ground behind the creek. I try to focus, but all I see are stars. The wind has been knocked out of me and I gasp, trying to catch my breath. Val grabs both of my hands, dragging me over poking twigs and rocks. I try to break free of her hold but it feels like a vice. Stopping, she grabs me by the shirt jerking me up with such force that my feet fly up from under me. She holds me above her head, staring at me before throwing me several feet away. My head smacks hard against a tree trunk, making me cry out in pain. I wince and instinctively touch the sore spot. The back of my head feels wet. I see blood on my fingertips.

"Val?" I look at her eyes, desperate for her to recognize me.

Expressionless, she gazes at me and the blood on my fingers. She puts her hands together in front of her. I see black sparks inside her palm as she forges a fireball. The flame begins to take the shape of a black rippled dagger. Cocking one eyebrow, she proudly holds her creation out in front of her.

I inhale, trying to quell the paralyzing fear coursing through me. "Sweetheart, I love you," I wail. "Fight it, Val. You have to fight it. Please!" I reach out, hoping my touch can cut through the hold the demon has on her.

Still looking at the dagger, she turns it around and admires it, then turns back to me. Seeing my hands outstretched, her eyebrows pinch in confusion. Reaching her hand out to mine, she turns my hand over to touch the blood on my fingertips. The hand holding the dagger slowly drops down to her side. A glimmer of hope.

"Oh Val..." I whisper. "Let me save you."

Crack! The bones in my hand snap as Val forces it back. I scream in agony as my hand dangles limply. It feels like a million needles are piercing me all at once, the pain radiating up through my arm. She grabs me under the chin and forces me to look at her.

"Val. Isn't. Here." Her voice sounds like multiple voices at once, nightmarish and chilling.

"Don't listen to it, Val," I cry. "You are not weak. You never were weak! You *have to fight*! Please!" I'm screaming, determined to make her hear me from wherever she is. She has to be able to hear me. I know it.

Shaking her head, she says, "What a waste." Pulling the dagger up from her side, she places her other hand behind the handle, then drives it through my heart with one swift blow.

It feels like a hard punch to the chest. I gasp, straining to breathe. At first my brain doesn't comprehend. I look down at the dripping blood in such a detached way that I don't realize what happened. I reach my good hand up to feel the dagger, cold and sharp. Then my fingertips move to the warm blood seeping from the wound, snapping me back to reality.

How could I have been so wrong?

CHAPTER THIRTEEN

I REALIZE I DON'T FEEL THE searing pain anymore, or any shortness of breath. I'm not even sure I am breathing. There's an absence of sensation altogether. I feel...lighter, like I'm floating or rising. I am above my body, looking at myself lying on the ground. Val is walking away, toward the tree where Free is tied up, but I can see a golden energy moving inside of her, as if trapped and trying to escape. It has to be Val.

I want to reach out and tell her that I see her, but I can't. I'm floating further and further away. I feel less and less connected to what is going on as it gets smaller in my line of sight. No more sounds. No more feeling.

A voice I don't recognize says, "You are going to be okay." It sounds like a young woman, her soft voice calming, a welcome change from the demon's.

"Hello?... Who are you? Where am I?" All I see is white nothingness.

"I'm Bella. I've been with you for some time now. You thought I felt like butterflies."

A memory floods my mind. The flutter I felt the night I had that first nightmare about Val... it wasn't just stress-induced nausea. The white glow in my belly when my sisters and I connected our powers the night Gabriel proposed... that was our baby.

Gabriel and I have a baby.

"Bella.... I've always loved that name."

I see her gentle eyes — bright blue-gray. The rest of her is blurry, but I can see curly light brown hair flowing around her, like she's floating in water. She has Gabriel's hair. "Oh! You are so beautiful! I can't believe you're here!"

Then I remember... I'm here because Val killed me.

No! I can't die. Gabriel. My sisters. I can't leave them yet. And now Bella. I was going to be her mother; now I won't have the chance.

"Bella... Am I dead? Is this heaven?"

"No. You are in between," she says. "You have work to do with the living. You are not going to die today, Lina. This is not your time."

"I'm...not...? But the stab wound... I could feel myself dying."

"It's true that you have left your body, but you haven't crossed over yet," Bella explains. "We both have the power to heal. Here you have the powers of our ancestors with you. Together, we will send you back."

Behind her, images start appearing. One by one, faces start coming into focus — relatives I've never met but feel familiar. Then one appears next to me, the most familiar of all.

"Daddy!" I cry. My father's kind aqua eyes are unmistakable. He smiles down at me and I feel enveloped by love in its purest sense, a cosmic embrace.

"My brilliant, strong Angelina."

"Daddy, was that really you the other night in my dream?"

He smiles and nods. "You needed me. My girls are in trouble and I had to help."

"We've always needed you, Daddy." I say, thinking back to the terrible hole his death left in all of us.

"*Mi Angelina,* we don't have a choice when it's our time to leave, but I've been with you every day. I've sent you messages to let you know you weren't alone. I'm so proud of you and your sisters."

Memories start popping into my head — songs he used to sing us coming on the radio when I'd be thinking of him, finding photos or things of his in unexpected places. Then there was the time I was sitting on a park bench overlooking Puget Sound. It was my first year of college and I felt so lonely and unsure that I had what it took to be a college student. A stranger came over and handed me a single white rose. Smiling, she told me that I was never alone. Even though it was odd at the time, it did bring me comfort.

"Thank you for the messages, Daddy," I say. "I wish I knew at the time they were from you."

"Remember how much love you carry," he insists. "That love will save you and your sisters." As he says this, both of our chests begin to glow with a warm bright light.

"And another thing. When you go back, I want you and your sisters to be true to your hearts. Live your lives fully. Follow your passions. Do that for me - for us." I look around at the rest of my family members. Rays of light are beaming down to me from their hearts, filling me up with the most powerful energy I've ever felt.

In the midst of the golden light, my heart starts glowing deep blue and clenches unexpectedly. "Lina!" I hear Gabriel's voice from afar.

"What's happening? Did I just hear Gabriel's voice?" I ask Bella.

"This is what happens when our living loved ones call out to us. They are with you now. Look." Bella motions beneath us. I see Gabriel, Rory, and Zo on the ground next to my body. The girls are holding my hands as Gabriel clutches my lifeless body close to his chest. My blood is covering his shirt and hands. He must have tried to revive me. Their cries are primal and deafening, the sounds of complete devastation. Hearing them hurts even worse than being killed.

"How did they find me?" I ask.

"Rory sensed it as soon as you were stabbed. She was leaving class when she felt your pain. She called Zo and told her to get Gabriel and meet her in the forest. She was the first one to find you."

I look at Rory again. She looks traumatized, her eyes staring ahead and her lips trembling. My poor baby sister. I can't stand it. I have to help them.

"Where's the demon? Is it going to hurt them?" I ask, looking around them for signs of Val.

"The demon took Free back to his house and is resting. Using Val's power took a lot of energy."

"Bella, I need to go to them," I insist. I feel my father's hand on my shoulder and look up at him. "I'm sorry I can't spend more time with you up here. But they need me."

"Yes, they need you now more than ever," he says. "You can save them, Lina."

A woman with deep brown eyes and high, proud

cheekbones steps forward. Without saying a word, I know it's my Great Aunt Melina, the one who helped my mother and Fiona from the other side. She smiles and holds her hands out to mine.

"Angelina, *eres tan poderosa,*" she says. "You have such greatness and purity inside of you. They make you more powerful than you know. When you go back, you will carry all of us with you. Remember that. Your heart is your greatest power."

"*Gracias, tia.*" I say, squeezing her hands. She kisses my forehead.

I step back to give my father a big hug, wanting to savor that embrace so I can remember it every time I miss him.

"I love you so much. I'll be looking for your messages," I say to him with a smile.

"And, *mi hija*? I could not have chosen someone more perfect for you than Gabriel." He kisses the ring on my finger. "I know he'll make you very happy, sweetheart. Take care of each other." I hold him again. Oh, how I wish Gabriel could meet him in person.

"I would've been so proud to be your mother." I say to Bella, touching her cheek.

"Our hearts are bonded," she says reassuringly. "I'll be with you again soon. It won't be in the same way, but I'll find you."

My heart begins to glow so bright that it is blinding; as it does, Bella's facial features fade and become part of the light. When it dims, I see her body take shape, so she looks like the rest of my non-living family. Laughing, she puts her arms around me and hugs me tight. I stroke her curly hair, feeling the silky strands between my fingers. I hope I never forget what it feels like to hug my daughter.

Before I know it, I feel myself falling. I look up. Bella, my father, and all of our loved ones are watching me with affection.

"Love is with you, always," I hear my father say.

My hand goes over my heart and I feel it begin to thump.

"I'm coming home," I say to myself.

My eyes are closed and my entire body screams with pain. I feel Gabriel's embrace, heaving as he cries into my ear. He kisses me between cries, saying my name over and over. Tears well up in my eyes and I feel drops fall out of the corners. I still can't open them. They feel too heavy. My sisters' warm hands are on mine, gripping them tightly. I try to wiggle my fingers but every inch of me feels like cold lead. I can't move anything.

"I'm here! I'm here!" I try to say, but the words are just thoughts in my head. I want to give them a sign so they don't have to hurt anymore.

Rory! I think I can get through to her. Focusing on the cold soil and rocks beneath me, I send my thoughts through to her, telling her I'm not dead. I'm here. I came back.

I feel Rory's hand tremble over my left hand. "Lina? Oh my God! She's alive, you guys! She's here! We have to move her."

"You felt her? But how?" Gabriel asks hoarsely,

stroking the back of my hair with his hand and still holding me close to his chest.

"Her energy. I felt it through the ground. She's trying to communicate with us. We have to move her to the creek. She has to heal!" Yes, Rory. I knew I could count on you. I feel Gabriel's strong arms lift me up, his lips kissing my cheek in desperation.

"Come back to me, *mi vida*," he pleads. "Come back to me. *Diosito por favor, ayudame.*" He places me into the creek. I can feel his legs beneath me as he continues to hold me and cradle my head. I hear splashes as my sisters get into the water next to us.

As the water rushes over me, feeling returns to my toes, my fingertips, then the rest of my limbs. I wiggle my fingers and feel my chest go up and down with each breath.

"*¡Gracias a Dios, gracias a Dios!* It's working!" Gabriel exclaims. "Lina baby, that's it! Come back to us." He covers my face with kisses, and I feel warm droplets on my skin — his tears. I hear my sisters crying next to me. My eyelids flutter open. I struggle to focus. Rory, Zo and Gabriel are above me, faces stained with tears. Zo's trembling hand is covering her mouth in shock.

Spreading my fingers out next to me, I take a deep breath and absorb the power from the creek. The water around us bubbles ups and glows with bright blue healing energy. My open wounds start closing and healing. Power pulsates through me, restoring me.

I sit up and am immediately engulfed in a bear hug from my family. I hold onto them, my heart so full, it feels like it might burst. The water slowly returns to normal as the creek ebbs and flows around us.

When they finally let me go, I look at Zo and Rory

and say, "One moment." They look at each other in confusion. "First things first." I turn to look at Gabriel, his eyes red and fatigued from his tears. I touch his cheek, then pull him in for as passionate a kiss as I can summon. When I let him go, he looks like he might pass out.

"Normally I'd tell you to get a room, but I think I'll let that one pass," Rory says, smiling through her tear soaked lashes. I hold my arms out and grab her and Zo so that our heads rest against each other.

"I'm so sorry." I let them go and look at them.

"You're sorry for dying? Um, yeah. Don't ever do that shit again or I'll have to kill you myself," Zo says, still sniffing.

"I'm sorry to put all of you through that," I say, then look at the creek. Red streaks of my blood flow downstream. Touching my belly, I close my eyes and think of Bella. When I open them, I feel tears pricking the sides of my eyes.

"Lina?" Gabriel says, putting his hand on my shoulder.

"I was with our family on the other side," I tell him. "And I met... someone very special. Her name was Bella. She was our daughter, Gabriel. She sacrificed herself so I could come back."

His face is confused, and I can see the wheels turning in his head as he considers the possibility of my pregnancy. Realization sets in and his eyes well up with fresh tears.

"She had your hair." I say, touching his curls.

"Oh my God, Lina." Zo hugs me, followed by Rory. They're each shaking, both from the freezing creek and the trauma we've all just been through.

"How did this happen?" Gabriel asks, his voice clouded with anger. "Who did this to you?"

"It was Val, wasn't it?" Rory whispers. Gabriel and Zo turn to look at her in disbelief.

"Yes," I tell them. "Val has been taken over by a demon," I say.

"What?! A demon -- like the things scary movies are based on? How do you know that?" Zo asks.

"I could feel the hatred inside her." Rory stares forward, visibly distressed. "Sometimes having this power really sucks."

"Hey now, sweet girl. That power of yours brought all of you here to find me," I tell her. "And it was how I was able to tell you that I came back." I turn her cheek to look at me. "Thank you." She smiles sadly.

"I'll tell you the whole story on the way home. Let's get you guys dry first," I say. Holding out my hands, palms up, I lift us out of the water with gusts of air and place us back on the embankment. They stare at me open-mouthed as I push all of the water out of their clothes.

"Huh." I say. "The air thing is new."

They look at each other, then at me.

"Lina, I think you brought back new powers!" Rory says in awe.

I look down at my hands. I just wanted everyone to be dry, I didn't even think about making us fly. Maybe I did bring back new powers. Kneeling down to touch the ground, I close my eyes. I feel something I've never felt before — a deep connection that's beyond roots, animals, and water sources. Picking up a piece of bark, I stand and throw it into a clearing several feet away. Holding my arms out and planting my feet into the ground, I concentrate on making it grow. Before our eyes, it begins to sprout limbs and leaves, weaving itself into a dark green bush with little yellow flowers.

"Whoa, Lina!" Zo exclaims.

Holding my hands together, I create a small fireball. The warm sensation feels strange, but familiar at the same time. I dissipate it and look at them. "I feel different now. But it's...okay. It's amazing, actually."

Gabriel comes up and holds my hand, kissing it. "All I care about is that you're back, my love. Powers or not, you're all that I need." I lean over to kiss him, feeling the stubble of his cheek beneath my fingers.

"What are we going to do about Val?" Zo asks, looking down at the blood on the ground from our fight. "She killed you, for God's sake!"

I sigh. "Yes, she was very powerful when she attacked me. But — Val is not gone. I saw her. She's trapped inside her body. I know we can get her back. Come on, let's go back to the house. I'll tell you everything I know and we will figure out how to get her back...as a family this time."

I tell them the whole story on the walk to the car and the drive home: my meeting with Fiona, what happened with Mom and Melina's spell, Free's abuse and Val's possession, and the messages I received from our family on the other side. We're back at Zo and Rory's kitchen table by the time I'm done. Gabriel, Zo, and Rory sit stunned and speechless.

Finally, Zo walks over to the cabinet and brings back a bottle of tequila. Taking a big swig then coughing, she hands the bottle to Gabriel, who also takes a few gulps. He tips the bottle and cocks an eyebrow at Rory, who shakes her head. He shrugs his shoulders then hands the bottle back to Zo. Rory gets up from the table and heads over to the freezer to grab some ice cream. After gobbling a big spoonful, she closes her eyes dreamily.

"Woooo. I needed that," she says as we all laugh. I notice Zo and Rory's eyes are full of tears and I take their hands in mine.

"Did Daddy really say he was proud of us?" Zo asks quietly.

"He really did," I say. "He told me he wants us to be true to our hearts. And that he's always with us." Zo wipes away a tear, then takes another swig from the bottle.

"So how do we get Val back?" Gabriel finally asks.

"The demon doesn't know I'm alive, or that you guys know what happened. We can use that to lure it into a trap. It wants both of you, and your powers. It will do anything to get you. But I know now that the best way to defeat it is together."

"Care Bear stare?" Rory says through a mouthful of ice cream.

"Exactly," I tell them. "We'll combine our powers and hit it with everything we have."

Gabriel puts his arm around me and pulls me close. "Lina, I'm going too," he says with quiet resolve. "Powers or not. I'm not losing you again." I snuggle into the crook of his neck.

"I know, my love. You won't lose me again. I need you — you're the other half of my heart." He kisses me.

"Lina, what if it isn't enough? If we can't bring her

back?" Zo asks, a grave undertone in her voice. All of their eyes fix on me, hoping for an answer that doesn't involve killing our sister.

"Then we have this," I say. Without intending to, I use my mind to open my purse and take out the glass vial that Fiona gave me. My family stares at me, surprised by my newfound telekinesis. "Melina's spell."

"Lina! You just did that with your mind!" Zo exclaims, slamming her hand on the table. "That isn't like any of our powers."

I frown, confused. I'm not sure how I did that.

When I was in the "in between", our family members shined their light on me and it was such an incredible feeling. Like the euphoria of falling in love; so pure and powerful. Maybe when they did that, they also shared their powers with me? I know nothing about what abilities our family had, or the legacy of our gifts. This is completely unknown territory.

Shaking my head, I say, "I guess I have a lot to sort through later. My mind just doesn't have the capacity to figure it out right now..."

Rory looks at the potion in my hand. "Is that the same spell that took Mom away from us?" she asks. Zo and Gabriel shift their gaze back to the dusty glass bottle I'm holding.

I nod. "Fiona saved the remainder that Mom didn't take," I say as I put it down on the table. "This was the only way Mom could defeat the demon. I hope to God we won't have to use it. Val would live, but we'd lose her forever..." I can see the weight of my words sink in as their faces turn grave and white, making me sorry for forcing them to face this possibility.

"Get some rest, you guys, I say as I rise from the

table. "We've all been through a lot — and we're going to need every bit of strength we have tomorrow."

"Oh, wait... you're leaving?" Rory asks with big puppy dog eyes.

"No way. Gabriel and I are staying here tonight. I need to be around family."

Rory and Zo smile, then get up and hold their arms open for a tight embrace. My chest stings from the pressure, a reminder that I still have internal bruising. "Ooh, careful. Still healing, here." I say, holding my breath a little to keep the pain at bay.

They both stop hugging me abruptly and apologize. I exhale with gratitude and put my arms around their necks. "I love you both so much."

Gabriel and I head back to Val's room, collapsing on the bed in exhaustion. Facing him, I kiss his nose and trace my finger down his jawline. He pulls me in to him, his body melding with mine.

"*Mi vida,* I really thought I lost you," he whispers. There's so much emotion in his voice that it hurts my heart.

"For a moment there, you did," I say. "I wish to God you didn't. My father's death broke my mother. I would never want to hurt you like that, not in a million years. I heard you when I was...gone." I hug him close and press my head against his chest, tears welling up at the memory of his cries.

He holds me tighter. "You are my everything... you know that? I didn't know how I was going to live without you." His voice is strained and hoarse. I kiss his chest, wrapping my legs around his.

"You're my everything too, Gabriel." I let him go and look up at him. His eyes are red and full of tears, still puffy and somber. "You're stuck with me now," I try to lighten the mood and make him smile. The side of his mouth curves a little, but he still looks forlorn. His hand makes its way down to my belly, his thumb stroking it.

"Tell me about Bella," he says quietly. I see a tear make its way down the side of his face. I wipe it away and tell him about the adoring, brave young woman with the blue gray eyes. When I'm done, we hold each other and drift off to sleep, thanking our sweet girl for bringing us back together.

CHAPTER FOURTEEN

A RAY OF SUNSHINE PEEKS THROUGH the window shades in Val's room, waking me up. I'm still in Gabriel's arms with my ear against his chest, which moves up and down gently as he breathes. I turn slowly so that I'm on my back, staring at the ceiling.

This is where the demon started watching her. Right in this bed. My thoughts stray back to our fight and the way it taunted me. It's going to use my guilt against me. I can't let it get to me this time. Zo and Rory are not going to experience what Val and I went through. *Focus on the love,* I remind myself. *My father and Aunt Melina told me to remember the love we carry.*

"Hey, beautiful," Gabriel says with a smile. He looks at me sleepily with one eye open. In the light of day, I can see the toll from the stress he went through last night. His eyes look a little more sunken in, framed by a shadow of dark circles. I lean over to kiss him.

"Hey, handsome." I interlace my fingers with his, kissing his knuckles. He smiles and pulls me on top of him, making my hair cascade over his face.

Moving my hair out of the way, he looks up at me in a way that makes my heart stop. It has so much intensity and reverence. I nuzzle his hand, closing my eyes and feeling the warmth of his palm on my face.

"Are you ready to face her again?" he asks, his tone serious. I sit up, facing away from him. He sits up and kisses my shoulder.

I nod. "More than anything. I know we'll get her back."

"What is it, then?" he asks, turning me so I can face him.

"Val is trapped inside her body," I say. "I think she's experienced everything that happened. I'm worried about how she will heal when we get her back. She's going to blame herself. I can't let her." He hugs me tightly.

"I can't imagine what it must be like for her..." he says quietly. "But we'll help her heal, Lina. First we have to chase the demon away."

After Gabriel and I get dressed and ready, we head to the kitchen. Rory is up and making breakfast — hash browns and what smells like sausage, though since she's a vegetarian, I assume it's vegetable-based. Still, the tantalizing sizzle and savory smells dance into my nose.

I walk in and kiss Rory's cheek. "Good morning, sis. This looks amazing! Meatless sausage, I presume?"

She grins and nods. "Yes! My new favorite. I made some fresh *pico de gallo* too."

"I can't wait," I tell her. "Smells delicious."

Gabriel starts the coffee pot while Zo shuffles in, still wearing her pajamas. Her eyes are droopy and smudged with back makeup she must have slept in.

I wonder if she polished off a little more of the tequila after I went to bed.

"Hey, sunshine," I say to her brightly. She smiles sleepily then throws her arms around me. I give her a tight squeeze. It's so nice to feel normal again.

After breakfast, Gabriel gets up for more coffee. He refills everyone's cups except for Rory, who's nursing a mug of green tea. She's lost in thought, staring out into the living room. I grab her free hand from across the table. She blinks and smiles, coming back to reality.

"*Chiquitita,* are you ok?" I ask, peering into her face. Her downcast gray eyes close momentarily then flutter up to look at me. They're devoid of her normal playfulness, serious and glistening with emotion. She turns my hand palm side up, runs her finger along the lines.

"Yesterday, these palms were cold, covered in blood," she says. Her words stop my heart. My poor baby sister. "I held your hand the whole time. You... felt like ice."

She continues, shaking her head. "I knew something was wrong all day. I couldn't figure out what it was, until it was too late. You were dying by the time I found you. I wish to Mother Goddess I'd found you earlier..."

"Oh sweetheart..." I say, my voice a hoarse whisper. I move my chair closer so she's within arm's reach and pull her in for an embrace, holding her for several breaths. "No. If you'd been there earlier, she would've hurt you, too." I stroke her hair, caressing the soft brown ringlets with my fingertips. She nods, sniffling and holding on to my neck as if she doesn't want to let me go. Her emotion is so raw that I find myself crying, too. "I'm so sorry you found me like that. I am so sorry...." I say over and over, trying to soothe us both.

When we finally let go, Zo is behind Rory and Gabriel is behind me, their hands on our shoulders.

Rubbing her eyes, Rory finally says, "I don't know, it feels unreal. One sister is possessed by an evil demon, then she killed my other sister, who miraculously came back to life thanks to powers from our dead *familia.*" Hearing her say it out loud sounds so ridiculous that we just stare at each other, both at a loss for words.

"Man," Zo says, "after all the impossible things we just experienced in the last 24 hours, I wouldn't bat an eye if *La Llorona* herself walked through the front door right now with flowers in one hand and a latte in the other!" She waves her arms around her face to illustrate her vision of the ghostly urban legend. *La Llorona* terrified Zo as a child. It was a long time before she could say her name because she was afraid that she'd be stolen in the middle of the night. I start giggling through my tears. Rory giggles, too.

A sharp pain pierces the inside of my belly. I double over and grab Rory's arm for support. Gabriel is down on his knees next to my chair in a flash.

"Lina!" he yells. I feel his hands on my face, but my eyes are shut tight as I struggle to breathe. Zo is at my other side, her arm around my shoulder, kneading my neck. When I open my eyes, I see blood pooling underneath me. I shift my legs so they can't see it.

"Baby? Speak to me. Are you okay?" Gabriel's face is close to mine, his eyes wide and urgent. I nod and plant a small kiss in his palm.

The pain slowly subsides. I feel myself breathing normally again. I lean over to kiss Gabriel's cheek and whisper that I need a towel. He hesitates, then dutifully gets up to retrieve one. Rory and Zo exchange worried glances.

I take both of their hands. "I'm okay, really," I say, putting on a brave smile. "This body still has some healing to do. That's all it is." Gabriel hands me the towel. I tilt forward so I don't cause myself more pain, gently tucking it underneath me.

Zo brings me a glass of water, which I gratefully accept. Each sip feels restorative, permeating my insides slowly. My stomach still throbs with a dull ache. Pouring the rest of the water into my hand, it surrounds it like a glove. I bring it close to my core, allowing the blue healing energy to seep in and find the spots that need repair. Rory puts her hand over mine, followed by Zo. I feel the energy change and my hand begins to glow a different, deeper shade of blue, then purple.

Gabriel gasps, then points at my chest and says, "Look!" My heart is glowing. The pain in my belly is replaced by a warm, peaceful feeling. Rory and Zo's hearts are glowing the same way, their hands enveloped by the bright purple glow. I think about Bella and what it felt like to hold her before I returned.

"Oh! I see her," Rory exclaims, tears in her eyes.

Zo is crying, too. "I see her too, Lina! Oh my God."

Gabriel looks on in wonder, eyes wide. With my free hand, I put my palm over his forehead so that the glow can envelop him. His lips start trembling and his eyes close, tears falling down his cheeks.

"She..is...so beautiful..." he says softly. "She looks so much like you."

I think about Bella's words, "I'll be with you again soon." Her voice feels like a calming wave and her face is so clear. Her blue-gray eyes look directly into mine, adoring and reassuring.

Just as I'm about to reach up to try and touch her face, her image fades, replaced by my father. Behind him are the rest of our ancestors on the other side. Their smiling faces feel like sunshine rays, warming our hearts and changing the color of our collected glow from a purple to a light pink, nearly white. The energy expands and takes shape into a small orb, encompassing the hands on my belly, before it fades and shrinks into a tiny spark and floats away. I smile through bittersweet tears at Gabriel, who looks shaken. Rory and Zo are still recovering too, wiping tears from their faces with their shirt sleeves.

"Are you okay?" I ask Gabriel.

"I can't even describe it," he says, bringing his hand down to my belly. "I never knew what it was like for you. For all of you. It was the most incredible thing I've ever felt." He shakes his head in awe, then he looks back down at his hand on my stomach.

"Those nights you were sick..." he says quietly.

Zo's eyebrows raise in surprise. "You knew you were pregnant?"

"No... I didn't. I thought I was just upset because of the nightmares." I look past my sisters at the living room where only a week ago I was meeting Free for the first time. I had the first glimpse of the demon that night. Could those dreams have been a warning... from Bella?

Warm fingertips touch my arm, bringing my attention back to the concerned family right in front of me. Rory's gray eyes are puffy and pink, her face solemn. "Lina, you need more time to heal. You've been through too much."

I look at Zo, standing next to Rory with her arms crossed in front of her, and Gabriel, kneeling down and caressing my abdomen. None of us have come out unscathed by this. Placing my hand over Rory's, I shake my head.

"I'm going to be okay, *Chiquitita*. Being here with you is making me stronger. We aren't going to lose anyone else. Bella and the rest of our family gave us a gift and we can't let it be in vain. We have to save Val - and we are running out of time."

There is still an air of sadness hanging over us, a silent acknowledgement of the damage done.

Looking up at the ceiling, Zo breaks the silence and says, "Thank you, beautiful, sweet Bella." The rest of us smile and look up too. "Thank you Daddy. Thank you *familia*. Thank you for bringing Lina back to us."

After getting cleaned up, I join my family on the back porch. They are looking out at the forest behind the house, quiet and preoccupied. There's a comfortable foot cushion in front of Gabriel's chair so I sit, leaning back into him. He puts his arms around me, nuzzling me closer.

The plan is already in place. Rory texted Val, saying she was worried about her and now I was missing too. As we hoped, Val responded and said I was with her, asking Rory to meet us at the waterfall. Rory sits cross-legged on the grass, with Zo in a chair across from us.

"I can feel her," Rory says, hands at her sides on the ground. "Val's back in the forest. I feel Free too. He's wounded. Val's energy is still there but she's fading. That thing is so strong. Val isn't going to be able to fight it for much longer."

"I know," I reply. "Every time the demon hurts one of us, it makes Val weaker. This demon is pure evil. It's strong. It's smart. It will use our weaknesses against us and try to separate us. We have to stay together—no matter what."

"And if we fail...we use the spell?" Rory says quietly.

"Only as a last resort." I reassure her. I don't want to give too much weight to that option when the ultimate goal is to bring her home with us.

Gabriel stands up, arms at his sides. "I'm ready. Let's go." His jaw is clenched and his eyes have a steely resolve.

I stand, facing him. "Gabriel..."

His eyes soften but his jaw remains hardened. "There is no way I'm leaving your side this time." I grab him around the neck and kiss him, catching him off guard. When I let him go, he exhales and cocks his head at me.

"Even your amazing kisses aren't going to make me change my mind, Angelina," he says, holding my face.

I know that the demon will automatically target Gabriel. I stroke the side of his cheek, wishing there was a way to ensure his safety.

Then I get an idea.

Glancing over my shoulder at Rory, I ask, "Rory, can

you help me make Gabriel fireproof and bulletproof?" Gabriel's eyebrows shoot up.

She perks up. "We still have Daddy's old tactical gear," she says. "That would be easy for me to work fireproof elements into it."

"I know where it is!" Zo says. "I'll find it. Rory, start gathering what you need." She runs into the house while Rory kneels on the ground and closes her eyes. Her hands begin sinking into the earth and it starts shaking beneath us like a tiny quake. Gabriel and I hold on to each other to keep steady.

"Gotcha." Rory's eyes open as she slowly pulls her hands out of the ground. She has handfuls of jagged stones that she piles up next to her. "Limestone," she says, slapping her hands together to get the dirt off them. "It's used to fireproof buildings — but I can fuse it with the fabric in the bulletproof vest."

Zo comes out of the house holding a dusty, bulky black vest with straps. On the front is an embroidered name badge that reads LUNA. It's been years since I've seen it. Zo puts it on the ground next to the pile of stones. In her other hand, she holds our father's dog tags: SGT. LEONARDO LUNA.

"I know he would want you to have this," Zo says, holding the necklace out to Gabriel. "This is so perfect — it's like he's going to be with us." She puts her arm around my waist and squeezes me. Gabriel kisses the tags, holding them respectfully between his hands before he puts the chain around his neck.

Looking up at us Rory says, "You guys ready? I'm going to need both of you to do this right." Zo and I kneel down next to her. "I'll crush the stone. Zo, you keep the dust particles contained so we don't breathe them. Lina, I'll need you to liquify the broken-down rock so we can integrate it into the fabric. Ready?"

"Look at you, taking charge!" Zo nudges Rory with her elbow.

"Shut up. That's an order," Rory says authoritatively, following it up with a wink and mischievous smile. She places her hands over the pile of rocks. Zo creates a ball of wind that she moves over Rory's hands so that they, and the rocks, are safely enclosed. The rocks vibrate violently until breaking down and a dust cloud turns the inside of the ball white. Putting my hands inside next to Rory's, I gather the rock and dust, transforming it into a paste before it liquifies. Zo dissipates the sphere so I can spread the liquid onto the vest. While the mixture settles, Rory holds up the fabric, stretching and moving it so that the vest transforms into a full body suit with sleeves, legs, and a mask. When she's done, she holds it up proudly. The once bulky vest is now lightweight and the integrated stone makes it shiny, like iridescent fish scales.

"I was going for a ninja vibe," Rory says. "Since you are a kung fu master, you need to look the part." She holds out the suit and mask to Gabriel for an inspection.

He whistles, regarding the the suit with admiration. "This is the most marvelous warrior suit I've ever laid eyes on." He feels the fabric between his fingers, running his hand along the side of it. The "LUNA" name badge is still on the front. "It will be an honor to wear this."

"Lina, try to melt it with some fire," Rory commands, her hands inside the suit pulling it taught so I can give it my best shot. I turn my palm up, closing my eyes and imagining fire flickering within it. Sparks prick the inside of my hand before igniting into an orange ball of flame. I turn my palm, shooting a stream of fire directly at the suit. After several minutes, I dissipate the flame.

"Totally cool from the inside," Rory says, impressed by her handiwork. "I didn't feel any heat whatsoever."

I run my fingertips over the shiny material. "Rory, this is perfect. Thank you." I hand Melina's spell bottle to Gabriel. "I need you to keep this safe. If things go south, you know what to do." He nods, quiet reserve in his face.

Looking back at Zo and Rory, I say, "I think we're ready."

Rory gets a head start walking through the forest. Rather than driving a few blocks to the other entrance, she's taking the old pathway behind the house. It's overgrown with weeds and bushes, but as Rory walks, the pathway clears in front of her then closes again when she's through. After she disappears into the thickness of leaves, weeds, and branches, Zo takes Gabriel to fly overhead and keep an eye on her, careful to stay hidden in the trees. The element of surprise will be important, especially since the demon believes that I'm dead. The girls will keep it occupied so it doesn't discover that I'm alive until the time is right.

I'm going to travel underwater so I can sense everything that's happening, while also staying completely out of sight. I've never done it before, but I have an idea that might work.

As I wait for Rory to be far enough away so that

she's out of my line of sight, I walk down the path with my heartbeat pounding in my ears. I'm still terrified to face the demon, but this time I feel stronger, going in with open eyes and my family by my side. Hearing the gentle lapping of water, I know I'm close.

As I get close to the creek, I pause to take a deep breath and calm down. Closing my eyes, I think about my family on the other side and ask them to watch over and protect us. A warm breeze grazes my face like a soft kiss, and I open my eyes. The wind encircles me, carrying pink and white flower petals like a whirl-wind. They spiral around me for a few moments before settling on the creek below me.

I look at the ripples and see my father's smiling face in the reflection. It fades away so quickly that I wonder if I imagined it, but I trust what I feel. I know he's watching over me.

"I love you too, Daddy." I whisper.

Taking my shoes off, I step into the creek and sit down into the freezing water. The rocks underneath me are sharp and a little slippery. Stretching my legs out in front of me, I close my eyes and imagine myself breathing underwater. My feet start to tingle, followed by prickling sensations over the rest of my body.

I open my eyes, rubbing them to make sure what I'm seeing is real. My feet and legs are morphing into one emerald green and blue fish tail. I reach up to my neck, feeling gills form out of flaps of skin.

"Okay, this is definitely badass," I think. I've always wanted to be a mermaid.

I lay back into the water smiling with my hands above my head, then speed through the creek almost like I'm flying. It feels effortless and natural.

Through the vibrations in the water, I can feel Rory's footsteps, as well as Val's. Rory is closer to the clearing where Val is waiting for her. I stop swimming to get a better sense of what's happening. My senses are heightened, as if I can see everything.

Free is laying on the ground, gagged and shaking. His clothes are soaked with sweat and blood. He has several burns on his arms now, in addition to the ones he had from before on his chest. I resume swimming then stop a little further down the creek, hidden by branches and leaves.

Rory's steps slow down then come to a full stop a few feet away from where she found me yesterday. She calls out Val's name. She sounds so grown up — and angry. The energy in the ground changes, pulsating in response to the emotions exuding from Rory's body.

"Hello, little flower," Val says coldly. I feel Rory's heart rate quicken. Opening my eyes, I crawl out of the water, careful to remain hidden. Looking up, I see the top branches of a tree moving and catch a glimpse of Zo and Gabriel, waiting for their moment.

"You killed her," Rory says, staring her dead in the eye. Val cocks her head and puts her hand on her chest in mock offense. Her eyes are black, but now black veins course through her skin, including her face. Just like in my nightmare.

"What? Oh, so you did find Lina," Val says. "How'd you know it was me? It could've been anyone. She could've had an accident, playing with sharp objects." She smiles menacingly.

"I have the ability to see more than you can imagine," Rory says, unwavering.

"Ahh, I can taste your delicious power, little one."

Val closes her eyes and breathes in deep. "Mmm. Well, you should know that I gave Angelina a choice — a choice I will also offer to you." Walking toward her, Val smiles and toys with her ring. "I don't want to hurt you. Oh no. What I want is so much more. I want you to join me. Together we will do the most spectacular things."

Rory steps back and I grip onto the branches around me.

Come on sis. Hold your ground.

"Not interested," Rory says. She tries to sound fierce, but there's a quiver to her voice.

Val's laughs. "No? You don't sound so sure. What if I told you I could get you any girl you wanted and you didn't have to live in fear anymore of people knowing *what* you are?"

Rory steps back again. Her hands and knees start to shake. "I may not be out and proud yet, but that doesn't mean I'll let some psycho demon take over my body just for a little confidence," she replies. My eyes well up with pride.

"You are a fraud," Val snarls at her, taunting her. "A liar. You've been a complete fake around your family this entire time. Every time you weren't your real self, it poked holes into your heart. I can see them all."

"Hey, bitch. No means no." Zo snaps. She and Gabriel land directly behind Val, who jumps in shock. Zo pushes her hands out in front of her and knocks Val down hard with a blast of air before joining Rory's side.

"Sorry, did we come at a bad time?" Zo asks Rory, who's still visibly shaken.

"Watch out!" Rory screams, then stomps her foot

hard. A sheet of rock shoots up in front of them to block a blast of fire Val launches in their direction.

The wall goes down and Val laughs. "This is precious, and very convenient," she says. "Now that all of you are here, it makes my job even easier. Even the brokenhearted fiancé showed up. I needed a new boy toy. The last one is almost broken." Val purrs and smiles, blowing a kiss toward Gabriel. I can see him gritting his teeth.

"Oh, now don't be like that," she coos at him. "I won't be as rough with you as I was with Free." She gestures to Free, passed out on the ground. "In fact, you'll probably love it."

"You're going to pay for what you did to her," Gabriel says, his voice low and resentful. Val smiles, conjuring a bright red fireball in her hand.

"Heads up!" Zo yells, throwing an air blast at Val, which she successfully avoids by moving to the side. Val launches the fireball at Gabriel, who blocks it quickly with his arms. The fire dissipates when it touches Gabriel's suit. Good craftsmanship, Rory. It worked.

Standing and dusting herself off, Val pouts and saunters over to Free's unconscious body. She burns through the ropes binding him with her fingertips.

Looking down at Free, she says, "Normal humans are really just shells. Their essence isn't that much use to me; not like you extraordinary Luna sisters. But every now and then, they make excellent dolls." Turning Free's face up toward her, she rubs her fingers together, creating a smoldering black powder, which falls into his mouth. His body writhes and convulses. He jumps to his feet, staring at them with black eyes.

"Holy. Zombie. Shit." Zo exclaims.

Rory kneels down to grab a stick from the ground. Holding it with both hands, she stretches it into a thick staff.

"Here!" She throws it to Gabriel, who catches it and twirls it skillfully in preparation for battle.

"Now, let's not get any scratches on that pretty face of his, okay darling?" Val says to Free, who stares impassively at Gabriel. As he walks toward Gabriel, his broken bones crack and slip, making his movements jerky and unsettling.

Without warning, Free charges at Gabriel and they begin fighting. Gabriel punches him in the face, making his head swing back; then knocks him off his feet using the staff. Free gets up and attacks again as if nothing happened. If he can't register pain, Gabriel won't be able to wear him down. Val successfully took Gabriel out of the equation by keeping him busy.

"Ahh, now where were we, girls?" Val creates another dark red fireball. Zo and Rory take defensive stances.

It's time. I spray cascades of ice at Val, knocking her down and encasing her hands. She yells out, completely caught off guard. Soaring in on a bed of ice, I land in front of Zo and Rory. She stares at me in disbelief, her eyes wide.

"Silly demon. Don't you know it's dangerous to play with fire?" I say.

CHAPTER FIFTEEN

VAL SCREAMS IN FURY, HER body lighting up in crimson flame. The ice melts away into a puddle around her feet.

"I killed you," the demon says in its real voice, multiple gritty and hallowed noises. She stares me down, black liquid seeping from her eyes.

"Go give Gabriel a hand," I tell Rory and Zo. "I have some unfinished business to deal with." My eyes are still zeroed in on Val. My sisters look unsure, but nod and head off in Gabriel's direction. I face Val squarely, waiting for her next move.

With a nefarious smile, she brings her fists above her head, then pulls them apart to reveal a shiny black sword. She shrieks and breaks into a run, swinging the sword in my direction. With an outstretched arm, I focus on the sword with my mind, forcing it to fly out of her hand into mine. She stops running, confused. I smile back at her, then melt the sword into black liquid and throw it on the ground.

"Got anything else?" I ask sweetly, eyebrow raised.

"What? How did you..?" She looks at her hand and back at me. "Picked up some new tricks, I see?" She sneers. "I'll just have to keep on killing you, then." She lets out a guttural scream, igniting herself again.

"Lina!" Gabriel yells.

I turn and see Free on the ground, immobilized by the ropes that Rory tied him in. When I turn back to Val, she has a crooked smile on her face, staring in Gabriel's direction. She has created what looks like a machete, and is ready to throw it.

"Leave him alone!" I scream. I blast her arm with a stream of ice, throwing her off balance. The machete drops from her hands and onto the forest floor. Pointing my fingertips in her direction, I lift her off the ground, carrying her several feet before I pin her against a tree. She writhes and bellows like a captured animal.

I approach her, steps away but still within arm's reach. Seeing her angrily spit and curse at me, my fury disappears and is replaced by compassion. Keeping her restrained and unable to move, I take the ring from her finger and throw it on the ground behind me.

"Now!" I yell. Zo and Rory race up to join us. I grab Val's right hand while Zo grabs her left. "We're coming to get you, Val," I say.

In unison, Rory, Zo, and I meld our abilities, creating a bright golden orb that encompasses all of us except Gabriel and Free. Their voices are muted, but I can hear Free speaking. It's working. We've weakened the demon and it is no longer controlling Free.

Val looks around, alarmed. "What are you doing? Stop it!" She shrieks, struggling to get free from our hold. A golden ray beams out from Rory's heart to Val's; she winces in pain. Zo's beam is next, followed by mine. Val screeches and howls, begging for us to stop. Releasing her hand, I place both of mine on Val's heart, trying to connect with her spirit.

"You have to fight, Val," I plead. "We need you to fight." She continues to wail and struggle. As she does, a small golden glimmer appears on her heart.

"Val!" I exclaim. "I see you! Keep fighting!"

She looks up, snarling and throwing herself against the orb wall.

"Let our sister go!" Rory yells, her voice resonating like a bell. The orb walls tremor each time Val hits them. She's going to break free if I don't do something.

Closing my eyes, I focus inward and call on the power of my ancestors. All of the noises around me disappear. In my mind's eye I am transported to the white void of the "in between" and the faces of all of the loved ones who met me there. Bella and my father stand in front, smiling warmly.

"You'll never get her back!" the demon bellows, bursting through the void.

When I open my eyes, everything is different. I feel like I am stretched outside of myself, sensing the life force of all that is around us. I don't see the golden walls of the orb anymore. All of us are cloaked in white light. Zo and Rory's eyes and hearts are glowing brightly. Their skeletons sparkle, making them look like ethereal *calaveras*. I blink and the walls of the orb become golden again, revealing a kaleidoscope of dragonflies around us.

Before I see them, I sense them. The souls of our family members are with us.

"I told you before. You messed with the wrong family." I say to Val, who looks around nervously at the dragonflies.

"We are one, and we are stronger than anything you can imagine." Rory, Zo, and I say in unison.

Beams of white light begin surrounding the orb, the sensation reminding me of what I felt with my family on the other side. When I look closer, the light is coming from each of the dragonflies.

One ray pointed directly at me is coming from somewhere else. Gabriel!

He's a few feet away, standing next to Free. His mask is off and his heart is lit up brightly like ours. We make eye contact and I hear his voice in my head, "You are my heart, Angelina."

Val covers her eyes, pained from the intensity of the light. "Aaaaaaaaaaah!" she screams. She starts coughing violently, spewing thick black liquid from her eyes, nose, and mouth. With my hands still over her heart, I focus on finding every bit of toxin inside her, compiling it and forcing it out of her.

"Fight it, Val! You can do this!" Rory shouts.

Val shrieks, shaking and writhing. Her body expunges the last of the demon in one final heave of pulsating tar. Her eyes turn white, then back to their normal light amber.

"Val!" Zo cries, grabbing her hand. Breathing heavily, Val blinks and looks around at us, then at the large, moving mass next to her.

The expelled tar morphs, shaping itself into a looming figure with menacing red eyes and a guttural growl. It looks at each of us with raw hatred, the face of evil incarnate.

"Whoa. I guess that's why you steal other people's bodies, huh? You are one ugly mofo," Zo remarks. The demon roars angrily.

Val puts her hand over her heart and closes her eyes. When she opens them, her heart glows, bright and powerful along with her bones. The orb pulsates and vibrates, humming with omnipotence.

Using my newfound telekinetic power, I bring the ring to me from where I threw it on the ground. The demon screeches, looking at it in my hand.

"You are going to hell where you belong and you will never come back," Val declares, her voice quivering but forceful. "Because if you do, we will find you."

With hands outstretched, we focus on the demon and hit it full blast with our light. It howls and recoils, melting into the ground below. It tries to fight its way up, clawing frantically at the ground, but to no avail. We push it deeper into the earth until we can no longer push.

I hold the ring up between us, allowing it to float on its own so I can disassemble it and allow us full access to the gem inside. Targeting it with our light, the color transforms from black to crystal clear. Closing my fist around the gem, it crumbles into fine powder. I throw it into the air above us where the myriad of dragonflies await. The wind carries the powder high up to the sky, along with the dragonflies. I watch as they disappear into the clouds.

"Thank you," I say, with my hands held over my heart.

The orb dissolves, and we're back on the forest ground. My sisters and I look at each other for a few moments, then, we tackle Val with hugs and kisses.

Gabriel joins us, throwing his arms around my sisters before pulling me off to the side. Holding my face between his hands, he kisses me with so much passion that I grab his shoulders to keep from falling over. I'm almost panting when he lets me go. His eyes are glistening with so much emotion I swallow hard, forcing the knot in my throat down to find my voice again.

"I love you, Angelina Luna," he says softly. "Thank you for not dying on me again."

"Anytime, Gabriel Santos," I say, smiling and touching his lips with my fingertips. I look down at his heart and place my hand over it. "This heart helped save the day." He puts his hand on top of mine, then closes his eyes and leans his forehead against mine. I look back at Zo and Rory. They look worn out but never happier, rehashing the events leading up to our victory.

Val, meanwhile, sits off to the side by herself, looking down at her hands with an unreadable expression. I leave Gabriel and make my way over to join her.

"It's so good to see this sweet face again," I tell her, offering a hand up from the ground. When she looks up at me, her eyes are wide and red with unshed tears. I can feel her shaking as she grabs my hand. She throws her arms around me and breaks down, weeping uncontrollably.

"I don't know how you'll ever forgive me," she says between sobs. "I saw everything that I did. I saw you die... and the things I did to Free..."

"Shhh. There is nothing to forgive," I tell her as I stroke her hair. "Do you hear me? That was not you, Val." I hold her at arm's length so I can look into her face, still contorted with her inner pain. "I was the one who failed as your big sister. I should've protected you. Not just from the demon, but from Free. I always told you that you were the strongest of all of us. You felt like you had to put on a brave face instead of telling me what was going on." My voice cracks as tears make their way down my chin, the guilt in my heart exposed.

She wipes the tears from my face and shakes her head. "You never failed me as a big sis," Val says. "Even when you were gone, you were still fighting for me." She inhales sharply. Her lips tremble and she closes her eyes in pain, tears seeping from them. She turns away, covering her face with her hand.

I grab her hand and turn her to face me again. "Val, you and I have a lot of healing to do, and we'll do it together, okay? No one is going anywhere again."

"Hey! Hello? Can someone come and get me out of this?" Free whines. Rory rolls her eyes and walks toward him.

"What are we going to do with jackass over here?" She asks. "After everything he did, he deserves to rot in jail. If we let him go, he's just going to ruin someone else's life."

Glancing at Free's wounded body, I think back to when he tried to save me. That one act of goodness doesn't make up for the trauma he caused Val. Not by a long shot. We could leave him here in the forest, prone to the elements and the wildlife; and there would be some satisfaction in that.

Rory's right, he is going to keep abusing. Leaving him doesn't stop the cycle.

But maybe the key to our healing isn't in punishing him. Maybe the key is in changing his path and breaking the cycle.

"Gabriel, do you still have that bottle I gave you?" I ask. He walks towards me, pulling out the cobalt blue bottle from a side pocket.

Reaching out to touch Val on the shoulder, I say, "Val, I know what he did to you." She looks away, holding herself tightly as if her arms were a security blanket. I continue, "Believe me, I want to beat the hell out of him right now for everything he put you through... But..." I look over at Free, broken and maimed. "You saw what the demon did to him. Now all I care about is you. I don't think hurting him anymore is going to help you. Your soul has been through enough." Val turns to face me, her lips trembling and tears flowing down her cheeks.

"What...What did you have in mind?" She asks, her voice hoarse.

I smile, and whisper into Val's ear. She looks at him, then nods in agreement.

"Zo, can you bring him to the creek for me?" I ask. Zo shrugs, then picks him up with a whirlwind and throws him into the creek with a hard splash.

"Ah, shit! It's cold!" Free yells out, drenched in the creek. He looks like a wet cat, tattered and cranky.

I wade into the water next to him. He jumps backwards instinctively.

"It's okay, I only want to heal you," I tell him. He looks at me suspiciously. I hold my hands up so he can see them. As they start glowing with the water's healing energy, his eyes widen and his mouth drops open. I take his hand, looking at the burn marks covering them. Holding my palm close to his skin, I scan over it slowly and carefully to make each wound disappear.

"Whoa! How did you do that? What are you?" he blurts out.

"I'm the sister of the woman you beat and nearly killed," I say coldly, looking him squarely in his eyes.

He holds my gaze for a second, unsure of what to say. Guilt registers in his eyes as he looks back at Val.

"I wish to God I could take it all back, Val," he says. "I am so, so, sorry." Gabriel, Zo and Rory stand by Val's side, their arms around her shoulders.

With hands over his chest, I continue healing the rest of his body; bruises fading, bones gently moving back into place, cuts closing. Just as I finish, I pull Melina's spell bottle from my pocket. I open and pull the contents from it with my mind, the liquid floating in the air between Free and me.

"Somewhere in there is a decent human being," I say. "He's the person who tried to save me when the demon attacked. You may not deserve it, but you are getting a second chance so you can be that person. Today, you get to start over." I start dropping the liquid into his mouth. He gasps and his expression goes blank.

"Your connection to Valencia Luna ends now. As far as you remember, she left you the minute you hit her. You will forget me, Gabriel, Rory, and Zo. You will forget Rodolfo and that night at the concert. You will forget about being Free Bird, about breaking the law, about hurting others. When you wake up, the only person you will remember is your little brother Steven. He looks up to you and he needs you to be a good brother. Teach him and yourself to be better."

The last drop falls into his mouth and I bring the bottle back to my hand. His eyes gloss over and he starts rubbing them and yawning. He shifts his weight so he can lay down in the water. I create a small wave to move him safely to the embankment.

Val is at my side, looking down at Free's sleeping body. He is smiling in his sleep, oblivious to the events leading up to his current predicament. Gazing upon her abuser, Val's eyes look conflicted. I hold her around the shoulders and pull her close, letting her lean on me for strength.

"Are you sure that's going to work?" she asks with uncertainty. "I thought the spell was supposed to make him forget the people closest to him. You're trying to change him into someone new."

"I'm not 100% sure, but I hope it will. With Melina's powers, I think I can alter the the spell so that maybe Free can redeem himself and change his choices." I look down at him again, his skin completely healed. "Come on, let's drop him off, pick up your things, and bring you back home." I say to Val, squeezing her hand.

"Are you ready to do this?" Val asks, her expression deadpan and serious.

"More than anything in the world." I say.

"Thought you'd say that," she giggles. "I guess we'd better get out there then." Linking her arm in mine, Val and I push open the metal green door. As we step out onto the center rooftop, the sunlight catches on the crystal embellished gown that my sisters and I made together. The reflection creates a cascade of rainbows on the fitted bodice, resembling mermaid scales. Looking out at the sea of happy faces, I am overcome with emotion and cover my mouth.

The rooftop is even more spectacular than before, a botanical paradise of floral bouquets in every color imaginable, various sized ferns, and water features.

It seems Rory found some inspiration from all those hours watching the Home and Garden Channel. To the side, a quartet of our center students play an orchestral version of Marc Anthony's "I Need You" while Jamal plays acoustic guitar and sings. I blow all of them a kiss. Jamal smiles and nods his head in acknowledgement.

Then I see him. The most magnificently handsome man I've ever met, the other half of my heart, waiting to marry me. Gabriel is dressed in a black tailored suit, complete with an aqua blue tie, which he said would match my eyes, and a sterling rose in his top right pocket. The look of love and adoration in his eyes takes my breath away.

Rory walks up, handing me my bouquet of sterling roses, lilacs, purple proteas, and smaller Pacific Northwest wildflowers. "You outdid yourself this time," I whisper. She winks at me then links arms with Zo.

My sisters look exquisite in their off-the-shoulder ombre aqua gowns, reminding me of sea sirens with how the material flows around them. We begin our walk up the aisle toward Gabriel and our officiant, Vernon, who are both waiting in a handcrafted gazebo that Vernon made just for the occasion.

I smile through blurry tears at each row of guests, all of the important people in our lives. Fiona beams from the back row, blowing bubbles at us and dabbing her eyes. My center staff family is all here, including many of our students. Joyce and Vernon's daughter Sadie, and their grandchildren. Rodolfo and his new girlfriend, Selina. Gabriel's brother Ramón and sister-in-law Cecile and their children.

Past the crowd, in a black dress shirt and pants is a very handsome and smiling Paulo. Zo stumbles when she notices him watching her. Val laughs and whispers, "You're welcome." Since Val's new catering business handled the banquet arrangements, she made sure to hire Paulo to bartend. From what she shared with me earlier, Paulo was more than excited to make the drive down from Seattle — not even caring how much Val paid him — as long as Zo would be here. I giggle and nudge Val conspiratorially.

When we get to the front row, Mama Joyce and Jade are holding each other and crying so much that my sisters and I almost break down. Taking a single rose out of my bouquet, I step forward and hand it to Mama, kissing her cheek. She smiles and holds it to her chest, too choked up to say a word. She and Jade join us, walking up to the gazebo.

When we reach Gabriel, our eyes meet. The rest of the world falls out of focus except for his face.

"Hi." He says quietly. He takes a deep breath, looking at me in awe.

"Hi." I smile back, unable to say anything else.

Val grabs Gabriel's hand, then places my hand in his. "I could never have asked for a better brother," she whispers to him. He smiles and hugs her before she joins Rory and Zo behind me.

As I stand across from him, a white and blue dragonfly lands on the floral arch above us. I smile and motion to Gabriel to see it. He gasps. "He's here," I tell him. I had a feeling my father would want to be part of today's festivities.

He covers his heart and closes his eyes, mouthing a silent, "Thank you."

Looking at Vernon, I say, "We're ready."

With my hand on his cheek, I kiss Gabriel for probably the 100th time tonight. "I love you, my handsome husband," I whisper.

He puts his hand up to mine and whispers back, "I love you, my beautiful wife." We're enjoying a quiet moment at our seats as our guests enjoy the delectable meal that Val and her team served: coconut rice, grilled salmon topped with mango salsa, green papaya and citrus salad, and crispy fried plantains. She designed the menu to integrate flavors of Gabriel's homeland with a bit of the Pacific Northwest. I can't wait to try the guava cake with raspberry lime curd. It's such a masterpiece that it looks too pretty to eat, adorned with Rory's flowers and her own hand painted designs. Her newly acquired art degree is already coming in handy.

As the wedding planner, Jaime did an amazing job transforming the center's gym into a magical reception hall. She wanted people to feel like they were under the sea, so along with white twinkle lights, she projected revolving blue and green images on the walls, designed to mimic ocean waves. Terrariums with glass pebbles and seashells are on each table. Fountains are scattered throughout, with an impressively sized champagne fountain next to the cake table. Rory contributed sprays of tropical plants and coral to hide the gym walls and add to the ocean fantasy.

Our table also has five lit white candles, honoring each family member who could not physically be here — Gabriel's mother and sister Selina, my father, my mother, and Bella. My sisters and I have already begun our search for our mother, now that we know she is out there. We'd hoped to find her before the wedding, but the research is proving to be challenging.

I hear a glass clink repeatedly, making the crowd quiet down in anticipation of a speech. Looking around, I spot Rory sitting with Mama Joyce and Vernon's family. She looks like she's leading the kids in a drawing activity. Behind them, in a quiet corner behind the bar, are Paulo and Zo. They've been inseparable since dinner started, when Zo made a beeline to order a drink so she could talk to him. I continue looking around at all the guests, trying to spot who is the brave soul willing to make the first toast.

Val is in front of the DJ table, clinking the side of a champagne glass. She changed out of her gown and is now wearing a white chef's coat. Her hair is pulled back in a ponytail, looking every bit the professional caterer. She clears her throat and grabs the wireless microphone out of the DJ's hand.

"Um. Hi everyone. I'm Valencia, one of the Maids of Honor, and sister to the bride. My team and I are the ones responsible for your meals tonight." As she pauses, the crowd breaks into applause at the mention of the food, which surprises her. She smiles, immediately relaxing. "Cool, thanks! I'm so glad you liked it. I want to thank our catering team for doing such a great job." She points toward the back of the room, where her team of three waves and smiles in response. She swallows, looking over at Gabriel and me.

"My sister Angelina married the love of her life tonight. I am so grateful that all of us are here to be a part of it. Lina is... well... she's my hero." My heart swells and a lump forms in my throat. Gabriel puts his hand over mine and gives it a gentle squeeze.

"And so is Gabriel," Val continues. "He's always treated my family like his own, accepting and protecting us like a big brother... The best brother I could have ever asked for... Lina and Gabriel have a love that is so powerful it can overcome the impossible. It can only be rivaled by the unconditional love between the crazy Luna sisters." I giggle through my tears. Looking around, I see Zo and Rory crying too. Vernon is giving a hankie to Mama Joyce, who wipes tears from her cheeks.

"Lina and Gabriel, I don't think I can ever repay you for everything you've done for me," Val says. "I love you both more than I can express. If anyone deserves a 'happily ever after', it's the two of you." Her voice trails off. Her eyes glisten with tears as she looks at me and smiles. I hold my hand over my heart, smiling back proudly. Today is a celebration not only of my marriage, but also of the life our family fought so hard to protect.

"On behalf of our sisters Zoë and Aurora, and our extended family, I'd like you to join us in blessing this partnership. Let's bring our glasses up to celebrate two people who were truly made to love each other. May you both always be completed, honored, and protected by the love in each other's hearts. *Salud!*" Everyone lifts their glasses and cheers. Gabriel and I get up to hug Val, joined by Zo and Rory.

"One, two, three!" I yell, throwing the bouquet over my shoulder at the group of women huddled on the sidewalk in front of the center. A tangle of arms fly up in anxious anticipation of being the lucky one. When the crowd parts, I see that Val has caught it. She holds it out in front of her with a baffled look on her face. Everyone starts clapping. Gabriel and I give her the thumbs up.

I run up to hug my sisters one last time before we head to the airport on our way to a Carribean cruise.

"Love, love, love you guys," I say, kissing each one on the forehead. When I pull away, I see that our hearts are each glowing softly under our clothes. We don't have to say anything else. With smiling faces, each of them cover their hearts then head inside. First Rory, Zo, then Val, who looks at me for a few moments before she turns to walk back. I cover my heart too, feeling the combined love from my sisters and thanking them for their role in pulling off the best night of my life.

After such an incredible but exhausting evening, my entire body feels sore. Even my cheeks are sore from smiling. My sisters promised an epic celebration and they delivered. I can't wait to see the video footage and relive it all again: the dancing, speeches, even the most mundane little moments with our friends and family.

I look inside the center from my spot on the sidewalk, seeing shadows of people dancing to "YMCA" and hearing them sing above the music. It makes me happy to know the party is going on without us. As much as I'd love to be inside dancing with our loved ones, I'm ready for some alone time with my new husband.

Turning around, I find him watching me intently, his honey brown eyes shining brightly. Leaning up against the shiny black limousine with his jacket over his shoulder, he looks devilishly smoldering.

"So, Mrs. Luna de Santos, are you ready for our next adventure?" He murmurs, stepping forward to close the distance between us.

"More than ready," I say, reaching around his neck to pull him close.

A familiar face jumps out of the front seat of the limo. Sam! Gabriel turns, patting him on the back and shaking his hand in greeting. "Congratulations, Mr. and Mrs. Santos!" he says, putting his hat over his heart and bowing his head.

Before I step inside, a feeling in the pit of my stomach stops me in my tracks. Startled, I look around for signs of anything out of the ordinary.

Nothing. Maybe I'm just imagining things.

Noticing my expression, Gabriel looks around too. "Is something wrong?" he asks.

Shaking the feeling off, I smile and grab Gabriel's waiting hand. "No. It's nothing." Turning to Sam, I say, "To SeaTac Airport, please, Sam." After crawling in, I pull Gabriel in behind me, ready to have him all to myself before we head to our honeymoon.

If there's something unusual going on, it's just going to have to wait.

For information about the other titles
in the Luna Family Chronicles series,
visit www.osalazardebreaux.com.

ABOUT THE AUTHOR

Photo credit: One Beautiful Life Photography

O. Salazar de Breaux grew up in Olympia, Washington with five younger sisters. An entrepreneur and community leader with a long career in public service, Salazar de Breaux is also an incurable creative who's inspired by her Mexican-American heritage. Her work incorporates her love of family, food, music, and culture.

She stayed in Olympia to study, earning a B.A. in English from The Evergreen State College, and still lives there with her husband – her sweetheart of more than 20 years – and their two sons, whom she considers her greatest achievements. *Sisters of Element* is her debut novel.